He was gone, pushing through the crowd...

"Did you check the label with your name on it?"

"What?"

"Did you check it?" The elevator doors opened and Gus led the way out through a crowd of people gathered in the elevator lobby.

"No, I didn't. It had my name on it so..."

He stopped. "Stay here. Let me check."

"What—why?" I peered past him. People were gathered in a group near the cafeteria, talking loudly. "What's happening?"

He was gone, pushing through the crowd into the cafeteria only to come back almost immediately. "Come on."

"Where?"

"They're calling an ambulance." He led the way into the elevator and punched the button for our floor.

"I didn't do anything wrong," I said. "I just put the label on my plate and—"

"I know." He tapped a staccato rhythm on the rail at the back of the elevator car.

"But I didn't—how did—why—"

"Don't worry about it. Just stay with me. We need to check and see if—"

The doors opened and we stepped out. "Check what?"

"Come on." He jerked my arm.

"Hey. Watch it." I tried to pull my arm away but he had me in a viselike grip.

"Come on. We've got to find Charlie." He tugged me through the entry foyer, past the receptionist desk and toward the kitchen/lunchroom.

"Charlie? Why do we have to find Charlie?"

Colcannon stopped so fast I ran into him. I smelled a tangy, woodsy aftershave and felt the hard planes of his body, rigid and solid. I peeked around his shoulder.

Charlie was lying on his back on the gray and white linoleum floor in the fifth floor lunchroom, the plate of brownies scattered nearby.

Brownies, Bodies, And Breaking The Code

by

JL Wilson

Brownies, Bodies, And Breaking The Code

Contact Information: info@thewildrosepress.com

Cover Art by *Kim Mendoza*

The Wild Rose Press
PO Box 706
Adams Basin, NY 14410-0706
Visit us at www.thewildrosepress.com

Publishing History
First Crimson Rose Edition, June 2007
Print ISBN 1-60154-078-7

Published in the United States of America

Dedication

To the Ladies Who Lunch and the potlucks
we have shared.

Chapter One

Winter can be murder in Minnesota. If the cold doesn't get you, the slick roads will. I managed to negotiate the icy parking lot and get into the building without dropping my tray of brownies, my laptop, or briefcase. Our office was on the north edge of Chaska, a north suburb of Minneapolis. There were days when it felt like someone had opened a door into the Arctic.

On the fifth floor, I dropped a curtsy to wave my dangling security badge against the door locks to the CodeBusters office suite. I punched the Handicapped button with my knee and voila, the door swung open like the portal to Oz, the Great and Terrible.

I got to my cube and shucked off my boots, coat and gloves by the light shining in from the atrium. My desk faced into seven stories of what would soon be sunlit space. I jammed my feet into my hand-painted Dr. Scholl's sandals when I heard the distinctive *whirr-clunk* of the security door leading to the stairwell in the room behind me. In the hushed space two male voices echoed.

"I can get it for you but I need time," someone said. "I'm sure I'm right."

"If you're caught, it could be bad."

Ooh. This was interesting. It sounded like insider stuff. The empty cube behind mine was on the aisle. The voices got louder as they neared. "I'm close. I just need another day or so."

"I can't be responsible." That voice had a distinctive rasp to it.

"I'm not asking you to be responsible."

"Keep your voice down."

I recognized Mr. "I can't be responsible." We shared a cube wall and the atrium window. Gus Colcannon had appeared out of nowhere last Friday and taken up residence next to me in CubeLand.

"Nobody's here," the first voice said. "There weren't any cars in the garage."

They must have walked up the stairwell as I rode the elevator. I'd seen a pristinely clean Ford pickup truck and a mud-splattered SUV in the parking garage when I arrived.

A coat was shed in the cube next to mine. I was just starting to ease my way out of my cube when Mr. Unknown said, "If anyone can find it, Jessie can. She's very good."

At the mention of my name, I screeched to a halt.

"She's also nosey," Colcannon said. I recognized his *I'm too busy to talk and please leave me alone* voice. I'd experienced it when I bopped over to introduce myself last week.

"That's what makes her a good tester," Mr. Unknown said. "She knows how to dig."

I crept to the wall of my cube. Since the walls are five feet tall and I'm only five-two, I was well hidden. This was very, *very* interesting. I longed to get closer but with my luck, I'd klutz it and knock something over. I held my breath and listened.

I heard a slamming noise. "This damn climate. I hate wearing all this crap."

Well, move, I thought. *It won't get any better until April. If then.*

He did move. The voices left his cube and went toward the kitchen. "We've only got another week to crack this so..." Then they faded out of my hearing.

I inched my way to the aisle and peeked around the cube, feeling like Inspector Clouseau. The coast was clear. I waited a few minutes then snatched up my Garfield mug and ambled toward the voices I heard in the kitchen/lunchroom, three cubes away. Gus Colcannon and Charlie Gordon were standing by the coffee machine, talking. I waved my mug. "Hey, guys. Any coffee yet?"

Colcannon turned, startled. He was about six-foot tall with a lean build. His thin, oval face and a close-clipped gray beard and mustache gave him a geeky look but his hair, steel gray, straight and thick, was somewhat long, making him look professorial. Beneath his wire-rim glasses were sharp hazel eyes.

Charlie Gordon was a St. Bernard to Colcannon's sleek Husky. He was big, burly, bearded, and blond, like Hagar the Horrible of comic book fame. Charlie was a programmer who'd moved into Marketing in TieLand, on the fourth floor. He and I had attended the same grief counseling class eight years ago when our spouses died. When a job opened at CodeBusters three years ago, he called me. Recently both Charlie and I had dipped our toes into the dating pool again and compared notes about the online services we'd each used.

"Just in time, Jessie," Charlie said with a smile. He filled my held-out mug.

"Why are you here so early, Charlie?" I asked. "I didn't think Suits came in before nine."

"I've got prep work to do for the conference." Our company's user conference was in Orlando in January. "Would you mind proofing my presentation for me?"

I often did 'skims' for people. "Sure, email it to me."

"I'll drop it in your mail slot," Charlie said, sipping his coffee. "It's on CD. Hey, speaking of mail—did you get any more emails from that guy?"

I busied myself adding creamer and sugar to my coffee. "Nope, he must have taken the hint." I hoped Charlie would do the same.

He didn't. "Jessie and I used the same online dating service. She got an almost perfect match but when the guy sent the introductory email he wasn't what he was cracked up to be." Charlie either didn't see or ignored my annoyed look. "She had to contact the service and have her email account changed and—"

"I'm sure Mr. Colcannon doesn't care about my romantic woes." I remembered the buxom Barbie blonde I'd seen Colcannon lunching with in the downstairs cafeteria. He obviously had no romantic woes. "Now, if you gents will excuse me, I have test programs to run."

To my surprise Colcannon fell into step with me as I left the kitchen. "Call me Gus. No need to be formal. What projects are you doing now?"

"I'm testing the Fairfield contract after I finish Nelson's stuff." Nelson Scott was a senior programmer who did database work for our government clients. Being a lowly tester, I wasn't privy to knowing who the actual clients were. "What about you?"

We got to his cube and I paused, assuming he'd go in and sit down. Instead he kept walking toward my cube. Given the maze-like configuration of our space, my area was three cubes down the aisle and one cube to the right, even though he and I shared a cube wall. Nothing was straight-arrow in CubeLand.

He stood in my entryway, watching as I unpacked my laptop then hooked it into my docking station. "I'm helping Marketing with some brochures for the conference," he said.

I busied myself with logging on to my computer then popped Barry, my Blackberry, into its synch cradle. Denise, a friend who worked in HR, had told me Colcannon was hired to work with John Slocum, head of R&D. What was the story? Was he lying?

"How's Nelson to work with?" he asked, sipping his coffee.

"He's fine." I pushed my potluck offering to one side. "He's a bit paranoid about his code, but his programs are solid." I sat down and brought up my email program on the screen.

"Paranoid?"

"Oh, you know." An email caught my eye. My online stockbroker had sent me an alert. It might be time to cash out some options. I realized Colcannon was still standing there. "What?"

"I asked, 'paranoid' how?'"

"Maybe not paranoid but protective." Another email caught my eye. *LABEL YOUR FOOD.* It was from the organizers of today's potluck, reminding us that they'd prepared labels for all our dishes based on the ingredient list we'd sent earlier. It was corporate policy now to label food in order to avoid any food allergy complications.

Colcannon was still watching me. I elaborated. "Nelson doesn't like it when I deviate from the test plans. I like to try out programs to see what they don't do as well as what they do. That peeves him sometimes."

"Sounds like thorough testing." His eyes flickered around my cube, taking in the Eric Clapton poster, map of the Boundary Waters Canoe Area Wilderness and photos, all pinned randomly to my cube walls. He peered closer at one photo. "Are you really on a dogsled?"

"Yep. I like to go up to Canada in January for a camping week."

His shoulders hunched. "How do you stand it?"

"What?"

"The cold."

I laughed. "Where are you from?"

"New Mexico."

"That explains it." I eyed his heavy turtleneck sweater, black jeans, and thick, clunky boots. His hands were red with the cold. Even his nose looked red.

"Explains what?"

I wiggled my socked feet in my sandals. Today I wore my festive Rudolph footwear with the Red-Nosed One peeking out from the bottom of my Levis. They matched my red Rudolph sweater. "You always seem cold."

He assessed my lightweight socks and sweater. "And you never seem cold."

"It's a state of mind." I turned back to my email, frowning when I saw one from Silver Harmony sent the night before. "It's cold here at least six months of the year. You may as well enjoy it." I gave him a questioning glance. "Why'd you move here? Surely there are programming jobs in New Mexico?"

"My wife got a job here so we moved."

"Hope it was a good job. That's a long move." I opened the email.

"I don't know. We got divorced."

"Ouch. When?"

He seemed surprised that I'd asked. "A while," he mumbled.

"So you're here temporarily?"

"Yep. I'll move back as soon as I can." His eyes went past me to my computer screen. "Have you used them? Are they good?"

I followed his gaze and saw the big red heart with *Silver Harmony* inside. "Not really." I scrolled past the lurid letterhead to the text. *Dear Jessie Patrokus: We value your privacy. At SilverHarmony.com we...*

Yeah, yeah, yeah. I skimmed past the BS and got to the heart of the matter. *As requested, we changed your email identity with Silver Harmony. As you know, we use stringent security to protect...* I wasn't reassured. This was the third time I'd changed my online identity. I scrolled through the subject lines in the rest of my email queue, freezing when I saw a subject line that I recognized.

Why don't you want to be my girl?

"Son of a bitch." I wanted to scream but settled for mild profanity instead. "Damn."

"Excuse me?"

I'd forgotten Colcannon was standing there. "Oh, nothing. It's just this email."

"Ah. The lovelorn admirer Charlie talked about?" His sharp eyes zeroed in on the screen.

I ran a hand through my hair. I was letting it grow and I wasn't used to having it all flyaway. "Not really. It's just—" I stopped, not wanting to share my dating trials with a stranger. "I can deal with it." I disconnected Barry from the cradle, moving my chair so I was blocking Colcannon's view of my screen.

He took the hint and started to edge away. "Good talking to you."

I waved a hand. "Any time. I'm always willing to be interrupted."

He smiled. I was surprised what a difference it made. Years fell away and he was warm, sly, and...sexy. His eyes took on a mischievous twinkle. "That's nice to know. I may take you up on that." He disappeared around the corner of my cube wall, leaving me staring after him.

My, my. Gus Colcannon as Dour Jekyll and Sexy Hyde? Interesting. I turned toward my monitor, glancing into the atrium. CodeBusters occupied the fourth and fifth floor of the seven-story building, with offices on each side of the atrium. Brian Bennington, my counterpart on the other side of the atrium, was just arriving. Brian and Bobby Morton had cubes opposite Gus and me. It was Bobby who'd told me that Brian had a crush on me and had hoped for more from our one 'coffee date', seven months previously. I wasn't about to get involved with a co-worker, and one who was ten years younger than me to boot. Besides, Brian was a bit...intense. I'd let Bobby know how I felt and Brian had backed off. It felt awkward, though, seeing him sitting there across the atrium, watching me sometimes.

I turned my attention to the latest email, sent just an hour ago.

I'll bet the people at Silver Harmony are getting tired of changing your identity. Why don't you just quit them? You've been with them for **131** *days and haven't found the man of your dreams yet. Or, wait—maybe you did and you decided he wasn't good enough. You know, you're not getting any younger. You really shouldn't look down on—*

"Psst."

I jumped, upending my keyboard. My CD player skittered across the desk, causing my cache of construction paper to slide toward the floor. I grabbed it just in time. I wheeled to the window and peeked around my wall. Colcannon was peering at me in the five-inch gap where the windowsill jutted out and the cube wall bisected the window.

"You scared me. Geez, why don't you knock or something?"

"Have you reported the email to the police?"

He was like a dog with a bone. "It's not threatening or anything."

"You never even met the guy?"

"No. He read my answers to the survey I filled out. I guess he figured I matched his criteria for Ms. Right." I shook my head. "When I started dating again I found out there's a lot of very interesting people out there."

Colcannon's eyes sparkled. "I'm finding that out, too. How long since your divorce?"

"I'm a widow. Bill died eight years ago. That's how Charlie and I met. His wife was in the same hospital where my husband was getting treatment."

"Oh. I'm sorry."

I suppose he'd had me pegged as another divorcee. People always got awkward when they found out I was a widow. "I decided it was time to get out and meet people." I made a face. "Look where it got me. Some hacker with a grudge."

"Hacker?"

I'd been thinking about this. "It has to be somebody who can hack into Silver Harmony's security system. It's not like it's a government database but the security must be—"

"What do you mean, a government database?"

Colcannon's sharp tone surprised me. "You know, nothing high security. Although some of those government databases are ridiculously easy to get into. I'll just cancel my account. That'll take care of it." I wheeled back to my desk, glancing out of the atrium window. Brian was watching us. The light reflected off his glasses as he turned away.

"Psst."

I wheeled back. "Yes?"

"If you need an escort to your car, let me know." Gus seemed so bookish, worried, and professorial. It was kind of cute.

I smiled. "Great. Thanks, Gus."

He smiled, too. Once again that mischievous twinkle came into his eyes. "Glad to help, Jessie." He disappeared back into his cube world.

I checked across the atrium. Brian was gone. I clamped my headphones on, slipped John Prine into the CD player then dug into my workload.

Two hours later I went to the fourth floor, hoping to quiz Charlie about that early morning conversation I'd heard. He was out so I dropped by Denise DelRey's desk. "Care to take a break?" I asked, twirling my mug.

She pushed away from her desk. Denise had been in my QA department until six months ago, when she transferred to Human Resources. She was my age and height but thin with strawberry-blonde curly hair, a loving husband, two kids, and killer fashion sense—a total contrast to me. We went to the fourth floor kitchen/lunchroom while I filled her in on the odd conversation I'd heard between Colcannon and Charlie.

Denise filled a mug with hot water and dunked in a Raspberry Rapture teabag. I settled for a second cup of coffee. We took seats at one of the seven tables in the quiet lunchroom. "What could anybody be working on that's dangerous? What are you testing right now?"

"Databases," I said. "Just insertion and deletion algorithms into databases—*big* databases, the kind that can take days to update. Nelson's designed a more efficient update method." I sipped my coffee. "So why would Colcannon say he's working with Marketing?"

"No idea. Maybe it wasn't work related. Isn't Charlie in some kind of bowling league?"

I made a noise. "For heaven's sake, they made it sound like the fate of the world hinged on this. And Gus was downright nice to me after he and Charlie talked."

"Gus? You're on a first name basis?" Denise raised one eyebrow. "How nice was he?"

"Not that nice. Besides, he's got the Blonde Bombshell and a recent ex-wife." Denise had been with me when we'd seen Colcannon with the blonde in the building's cafeteria. "So he's off the List of Possible Dates." I nodded toward the little flags set into Styrofoam blocks, lined up on one table. "What did you bring for the potluck?"

"Pasta salad. I suppose Paul is coming?"

I sighed. "I suppose so. The whole building is invited and he's on the first floor."

She laughed. "You're such a man magnet."

"In Paul's case I wish I was a man repellent." I finished my coffee. "Cripes, I go out for lunch with the guy and I can't shake him."

"Between him, Brian, and Mr. Email, you're a busy girl." Denise shot me a coy look. "And don't forget Gus."

"I'm not letting Gus Colcannon get within a foot of me. He's freshly divorced and on the rebound. And Brian was a mistake." I lowered my voice. "He's ten years younger than me—who'd have thought he wanted more than just coffee?"

Denise strangled on her last swallow of tea. I had to thump her on the back. "I'll say this for you, when you get back in the gene pool, you jump in with both feet," she managed to croak.

"I am not in the gene pool," I whispered. "I'm not even in the shallow end."

"Well, if you date Paul you are." She tossed her paper cup in the wastebasket, inspected the flags and plucked up the one that matched her pasta offering. "See you at lunch. Save some brownies for me, your recipe is to die for."

I went upstairs, passing the fifth floor lunchroom where our labels for the potluck were lined up in little soldierly rows. I took mine back to my cube and set it next to my brownies.

CodeBuster guests started to arrive for the potluck at eleven and the office party got underway. I renewed acquaintance with several wives and husbands then at noon we all started to gravitate toward the downstairs lobby. The CodeBusters Holiday buffet was an annual event we sponsored for the tenants in our building as well as our families. The other building occupants reciprocated in the summer with a barbeque. I joined the CodeBuster potluck providers in the atrium and put my brownies on the dessert table with their identifying label then joined Denise and her husband David in one of the lines. Paul was across the lobby/atrium, standing with his co-workers.

"He's a good looking guy," Denise said in a low voice.

I had to admit he was. Paul Henderson was big and broad-shouldered with an anchorman's clean-cut profile. He worked in the insurance office on the first floor. I'd met him in the building's gym when he and I were both working out. We'd chatted then we'd had a couple of lunches. I watched him examine the various food labels. Paul had an allergy to nuts, more annoying than life-threatening.

"Yeah, he is." I took a plate from the stack at the end of the buffet table. Gus Colcannon was in a line on the other side of the room, talking with Charlie Gordon and John Slocum, the head of R&D.

"He's a good looking guy, too," Denise commented.

Since Charlie was plain and John was plainer, I knew who she meant. "He's taken."

"You could give that blonde a run for her money."

Denise was a loyal friend and a bad liar. "That chick I saw him with the other day was a size two," I said as I took a dollop of mashed potatoes. "I haven't seen size two since I was ten years old. Nah. He's taken." I stifled a surge of disappointment at the thought. Gus Colcannon was cute in a bookish, nerdy sort of way. What a pity some babe had snared him.

Even though I'd vowed to take just a smidgen of food my plate soon filled up. We started for the cafeteria, turned over to us for this event. I glimpsed Paul inside.

He gestured to a seat next to him but I shook my head. "Going up," I said and pointed to the elevators.

"Coward," Denise called after me with a laugh. She and David went into the cafeteria, joining other co-workers who were already seated.

I laughed, too, and scooted into the elevator behind Charlie, Gus, Nelson, and some strangers. Charlie made room for me. "I made sure to grab a couple of your brownies." He nodded toward the extra plate in his right hand.

I glanced down. "Those aren't mine, Charlie."

"Huh?" He hefted the plate, which held two brownies nestled next to brightly decorated Christmas cookies. "They had your sign on 'em."

I shook my head. "Mine had powdered sugar on top, not frosting."

"What?"

I turned. Gus Colcannon was behind me. I nodded towards Charlie's plate. "Those aren't my brownies. Somebody must have mixed up the signs."

"There was another plate of brownies," Nelson said. He was tall and lanky with a Jimmy Stewart face that was almost handsome. I'd heard via the Rumor Mill that his brother or sister was sick, causing him to be absent a lot lately. "Somebody must have mixed up the signs." The woman standing next to him nodded. She was a small, wiry person with sun-roughened skin. I didn't recognize her but that wasn't surprising. A lot of family members came to this event and I didn't know everyone's spouse.

"Damn," Charlie said. "I wanted one of yours, Jessie. I hate brownies that have those nut chunks in 'em. Yours are chopped up just right."

The elevator door dinged open and we all stepped out. That's when it hit me.

It must have hit Gus at the same moment. "Allergies," he said. He set his plate down on the small credenza near the elevator and punched the 'down' button.

I set my plate next to his. "How did the signs get mixed up?" I muttered.

"You guys coming?" Charlie called out.

"No, go ahead." I waved him off as the elevator doors

opened. Gus and I stepped in.

"Somebody else brought brownies?" he asked as the elevator glided downward.

"I guess so." I chewed impatiently on a fingernail. "How did the signs get mixed up?"

"Did you check the label with your name on it?"

"What?"

"Did you check it?" The elevator doors opened and Gus led the way out through a crowd of people gathered in the elevator lobby.

"No, I didn't. It had my name on it so..."

He stopped. "Stay here. Let me check."

"What—why?" I peered past him. People were gathered in a group near the cafeteria, talking loudly. "What's happening?"

He was gone, pushing through the crowd into the cafeteria only to come back almost immediately. "Come on."

"Where?"

"They're calling an ambulance." He led the way into the elevator and punched the button for our floor.

"I didn't do anything wrong," I said. "I just put the label on my plate and—"

"I know." He tapped a staccato rhythm on the rail at the back of the elevator car.

"But I didn't—how did—why—"

"Don't worry about it. Just stay with me. We need to check and see if—"

The doors opened and we stepped out. "Check what?"

"Come on." He jerked my arm.

"Hey. Watch it." I tried to pull my arm away but he had me in a viselike grip.

"Come on. We've got to find Charlie." He tugged me through the entry foyer, past the receptionist desk and toward the kitchen/lunchroom.

"Charlie? Why do we have to find Charlie?"

Colcannon stopped so fast I ran into him. I smelled a tangy, woodsy aftershave and felt the hard planes of his body, rigid and solid. I peeked around his shoulder.

Charlie was lying on his back on the gray and white linoleum floor in the fifth floor lunchroom, the plate of brownies scattered nearby.

Chapter Two

"Charlie!" I tried to push past Gus but he held firm. "Holy shit!"

"Stay back."

"What? He's hurt. Somebody should help him." Then I had a horrible thought. "Oh my God, is he allergic to something? Charlie, are you—" I peered around Gus's arm. Charlie was pale and limp. He didn't look big any more. "Shouldn't we help him? Why are you just standing here? What if he needs help, we should—" I pushed again but it was like leaning against a brick wall. Colcannon turned and I was pressed against his chest. His smooth cheeks and the soft-looking hair of his beard were just inches away.

I jerked my eyes up and met his. He appeared calm but his eyes were angry. "Go to the front desk and have them call 911."

"But shouldn't we—"

"Go." He turned back to the lunchroom as I hesitated. He looked over his shoulder. His mouth was a thin, hard line in the softness of his beard. "Now."

I staggered to the front desk, nauseous with fear. What had happened to Charlie? Was I responsible? Did I mix up those stupid labels? Roberta, our placid middle-aged receptionist, smiled as I rounded the corner. "Can't wait to try those brownies. I hope they saved some for me, those are always the first treat to go."

I almost gagged. "Call 911. Charlie's sick or something." *Or something.* I was hot then cold with fear and panic.

"What?"

"Call 911." I almost lunged over the desk at her.

"Are you sure? What's wrong?"

"I'm sure, I'm sure." I wanted to shake her. "Just call

911." I raced back down the hall to the lunchroom. Nelson Scott was standing outside, the woman from the elevator next to him. She wore a bright red Christmas sweater and her tight curly brown hair reminded me of the father from the Brady Bunch, on TV.

"What's happening?" I craned my neck to look past them. Gus was in the lunchroom, bent on one knee next to Charlie, touching Charlie's neck. Bobby Morton was on the other side of Charlie, watching. "What's he doing?"

"Bobby and Gus know CPR," Nelson said. "They're doing what they can."

"We should stay out," the woman said. She looked unconcerned. Of course, she didn't know Charlie and thus had no reason to be upset. Still, it bugged me that she was so calm.

I leaned against the wall as the room started to spin around me. "I don't understand. I just talked to him. He was in the elevator with us. How could he be—" I didn't want to articulate it.

I heard voices in the hall behind me. Nelson tugged on my sweater. "Move aside." I was shuffled to the outskirts of the small crowd that was forming. My knees were wobbly and I had a sense of unreality, like things were happening around me but I wasn't really there. Shock, I decided. I went back to the lobby and sank down in one of the plush guest chairs, watching as people hurried past me.

I don't know how long I sat there, staring at the carpet. When the paramedics raced by me, carrying big cases and pushing a gurney, I shot to my feet, so claustrophobic I couldn't stand it any more. I went down the front staircase to the fourth floor, crossed the empty office space in TieLand then came up the stairwell to the fifth floor and the door near my desk. CubeLand was eerily quiet with only the sound of raised voices near the lunchroom to signal people were still there. I slipped into my cube, kicked off my sandals and sank into my chair.

I glanced out at the atrium where the bright sunlight was streaming into the lobby then downward at the buffet tables still there. When I looked across the open space I saw Brian, watching me. He waved and I waved back. I wondered if he'd even gone downstairs for the potluck or if he'd missed all the excitement. I turned away and buried my face in my hands, sure I'd be sick.

"Hey."

I jumped and my keyboard went flying into my stack of construction paper. Denise leapt into the cube, rescuing the pile before it could scatter.

"Whoa, calm down." She tidied the brightly colored paper that I'd harvested from the Odd Lot bin at the local craft shop. "What's happening? Somebody said Charlie's sick?"

"Oh, God, I think I poisoned him." I grabbed a piece of paper and folded it, snatched up my scissors and began cutting. I normally used a towel to catch my snips, but today little gnats of paper flew around me, some landing on the desk and others on the floor. The cleaning people had complained once about my untidiness. Well, the hell with them. I needed paper-cutting therapy. "The brownie signs were switched. Somebody put the wrong label somewhere and—"

"No, that just made a couple of people sick downstairs. Somebody said Paul had to go to the hospital. Is that what happened to Charlie?"

Red paper flew around me. I unfolded a twelve-point star. "I don't know. I just saw him lying on the floor. Colcannon was with me." I snatched up another square of paper, pleated it, and started cutting. "I rode up in the elevator with Charlie not more than a couple of minutes ago and he was fine—what could have happened?"

"Good question."

Both Denise and I jumped. Gus Colcannon was looking down at us over my cube wall. His gaze fastened on the paper in my hand. "What are you doing?"

"It calms me," I said, snipping like a madwoman. "It's called wycinanki."

"Vee-chee—what?"

"Vee-chee-non-key. It's the Polish art of paper cutting."

His glance flicked to the tiny shards of paper littering my hair, lap, desk, and floor. "Right. Listen, the police need to talk to you."

I almost stabbed myself with my embroidery scissors. Luckily these were practice scissors, not my pro models.

Otherwise I'd have opened a vein. "Why?"

"Because we were the last ones to be with Charlie." He said it with a dispassionate calmness that infuriated me. He must have seen something in my face because he held up a hand. "Don't shoot the messenger."

He was right but I hated to admit it. I took two more cuts at the paper and unfolded interlocked teddy bears holding candy canes, crafted from our old marketing brochures. "You're good," Colcannon said as I tossed the bears to one side. "Where'd you learn to do that?"

"Family hobby." I jammed my feet in my sandals and stood. "I'm ready."

He snorted. "It's not an execution. They just want to talk to you. It's a formality."

"Maybe you're accustomed to police procedure, but I'm not."

Denise followed me out of my cube. As we reached the main aisle, John Slocum, the VP in charge of Research and Development, came by. Veeps at CodeBusters had offices among the peons so I wasn't surprised to see John out walking among us worker bees. "Given what's happened, I think we'll call it a day," he said in a low voice. "Not much work will get done this afternoon."

Colcannon joined us. "Ready?"

"I have to see the cops," I told John as Colcannon led the way toward the lunchroom.

John nodded. "Makes sense. They'll want to try to figure out where Charlie was before—" He paused. "Before he got sick." He stopped at the cross-aisle that led to his office. "Why don't you leave after you're done here?"

"Thanks. I will." People were huddled outside the lunchroom. "Where are we going?" I asked as I hurried to catch up to Colcannon.

"Lake Superior," Colcannon said over his shoulder. He saw my blank look. "The boardroom, remember?"

My brain wasn't functioning if I couldn't even remember that our conference rooms were named after Minnesota lakes. "The cops got here fast." I wished I'd brought some paper to cut. Then I reconsidered. It probably wouldn't look too good to be snipping designs while being interrogated.

"The paramedics called them. Standard procedure."

We continued through the lobby, crowded with people, and into the south wing. The boardroom was a corner space with a panoramic view of the suburb outside. Denise gave my arm a consoling pat as we approached the door. "David and I are going out tonight but I'll be back by ten if you want to talk. Give me a call if you need to."

I watched her disappear into the maze of CubeLand and wished I could go with her. Colcannon paused with his hand on the doorknob to the boardroom. "I've already talked to them. They just want confirmation."

"Of what?"

He gestured me ahead of him into the room. "Of what happened."

"I don't know what happened." I turned to him but he'd left, closing the door behind me.

"Miss Patrokus?"

I whirled, almost overbalancing. Three men were seated at the big conference table. One was interesting looking, with white hair in a Marine's buzz cut. Another was younger with long blond hair and the other was dark-haired and clean-cut. They were all large, muscular-looking and had impassive faces that revealed nothing.

"Have a seat, please."

"How come?"

The white-haired one slid three business cards across the table. "You may as well get comfortable." His voice was very deep, almost rumbling. I suppose if a person were guilty, it might even sound menacing.

I took the cards and shuffled through them. Names blurred in front of me. I jammed the squares into my jeans pocket and sank into one of the leather chairs. "I don't know anything about how Charlie got sick."

"Sick?"

I nodded. "Isn't he sick?"

The blond glanced at the white-haired man and some message was passed. "He's dead," the older one said.

"Dead?" My stomach lurched and I had a vision of me up-chucking in front of the cops. I fought the nausea. "How? What happened?"

"That's what we're hoping you can tell us." I started to speak again but the older one held up a hand. "Let's just go through it, okay?"

My fingers twitched. I longed for something to occupy them. Instead, I jammed my hands in my pockets and hunched my shoulders. The men took turns asking me questions, making notes on the pads of paper in front of them. I gave facts about myself and where I lived, described my brownies, the little labels, the potluck tables, the elevator. We went through everything, step by step, minute by minute.

"Where were the labels?" one of them asked.

"In the lunchroom. Each floor had its own lunchroom and set of labels."

"Who made the labels?"

"Everyone who brought something emailed their ingredient list to the potluck organizers. They'd created a form and we filled it in. They printed the labels and made the bases."

"Bases?"

"Styrofoam with little sticks, to hold the labels. We've done it that way since I started working here."

"When did you get your label?"

"I think they were set out in mid-morning. That's when I got mine."

On and on and on. Question, answer, question, answer. We finally got to the moment when Gus and I realized what had happened, went downstairs then rode back up in the elevator and hurried through the lobby to the lunchroom. I described how he'd blocked the doorway and told me to get help. "How come you're done with him so soon?" I asked, giving in to nervousness and chewing on a fingernail.

The dark-haired one started to speak but the white-haired one interrupted him. "We're not done with Mr. Colcannon yet." He shuffled the papers in front of him. "We'll be re-interviewing him soon."

That made me feel better. "I heard him and Charlie talking this morning, early. Did he tell you about that?"

The white-haired one's eyes shot to mine. "What?"

"I heard them talking. I was in my cube when they came in. They were talking about something that sounded dangerous."

"Dangerous how?"

"I don't know." Now that I'd articulated it I realized

how melodramatic it sounded. "Colcannon said how something Charlie was doing was dangerous." I struggled to remember but all intelligence seemed to have flown the coop that was my brain. "I went to talk to Charlie about it later but he wasn't around. They mentioned me, too."

"They did?" The skepticism in his voice was tangible.

"They said I would probably find something when I did testing."

"Find what? While testing what?"

I threw up my hands. "I don't know. Ask Gus Colcannon. He's the person Charlie was talking to."

"What kind of testing?"

"I told you. I test software here. I assumed they meant that. I don't know for sure. I just overheard a bit of their conversation. I don't think they knew I was there."

The blond made a note on the pad in front of him. "Mr. Colcannon mentioned that he and Mr. Gordon were working together on a project. Did Mr. Gordon talk to you about his project?"

"No, he didn't. Charlie just switched jobs a few weeks ago. He works in Tieland now. I hardly ever see him."

"Thailand?"

"Tieland—you know, the place where they all wear neckties. He just transferred to Marketing." I looked at the sheets of paper on the table, longing to pick some up and pleat it. The urge to snip was getting strong. "Can I go now?"

The older one tapped his pencil against the tabletop, regarding me with steady, pale blue eyes that revealed nothing. They were glacially cool, like the pond behind my house. "Sure. If we need to contact you, we've got your number."

I popped to my feet. "You didn't answer my question," I said as I went to the door.

"What one was that?"

"How did Charlie die?"

"We're working on that." The tall-dark-handsome one tapped the pad of paper on the table in front of him. "We haven't processed the scene completely yet."

I had to get out. The nausea was building. I longed to recapture that feeling of unreality I'd had earlier, but I was firmly grounded in the here and now. I put a hand on the door handle.

"Miss Patrokus?" I peeked back over my shoulder. The older one was watching me. "Please don't talk to the press or any of your co-workers about this."

I opened my mouth then shut it. "Sure." I jerked open the door so fast it bounced against the wall. I walked, unseeing, through the crowd in the lobby and got to my cube without remembering the trip. I tucked my papers into the accordion portfolio I used for wycinanki projects then stuffed the entire thing into my briefcase. I moved with zombie-like precision as I packed my laptop before bundling up in my winter duds.

Charlie was dead. Big, laughing, funny Charlie—he'd just started to get his life back on track and now he was gone. Lord, it made me sick to think of it. How could it happen so fast? Was it a heart attack? What had happened? I slung my laptop bag strap over one shoulder, nearly toppling from the weight.

I started toward the elevator but I knew I couldn't stand being confined inside. I changed course and was almost to the stairwell door when Gus Colcannon stepped in front of me. "I've been looking for you."

I was in no mood to deal with his high-handed behavior again. "I'm going home."

He looked at my bulging briefcase and Sak purse slung over one shoulder and my laptop case slung over the other one. "You need help with some of that? It looks heavy. If you'll hang on just a second, I'll buy you coffee." He peered closer at me, his hazel eyes concerned. "You don't look so good."

"Thanks for the compliment. I'm used to the weight." I shifted my laptop strap, redistributing my briefcase to my right hand. I was accustomed to people trying to help me since I was so short and small. "I can manage it." He looked doubtful. I glanced around but no one was in earshot. "Why didn't you tell me about Charlie—you know?"

"That he was..."

I nodded.

"Let's talk. Give me a minute, okay?"

He seemed anxious so I relented. "Okay. There's a coffee shop down the street, across from the library. I'll meet you there. It's in the little strip mall."

"I know where it is. My apartment is near there. Just wait and we'll walk down—"

He reached for my briefcase but I sidestepped him. "I want out. Now." I slammed open the stairwell door. "See you there." I bolted before he could stop me. I went down the stairs carefully, stopping on the third floor landing to adjust my laptop bag and re-arrange some papers that threatened to escape. When I got to the ground floor, I made a beeline for the doors to the attached outside parking garage. I could still hear people one floor above me in the lobby. I wondered what had happened to all the buffet food. Were my brownies being taken into custody? Were they evidence?

I dumped my laptop, briefcase, and purse into the back seat of my car and got behind the wheel. As I did Gus emerged from the building with the busty blonde I'd seen him with the other day. She was almost his height and wore a long leather coat, tight dark pants and high-heeled boots. They were deep in conversation as they strode across the parking area to the sparkling clean truck I'd noticed that morning. I jammed my key in the ignition and started my car. Gus jerked then wheeled around, looking for the source of the noise. I shot him a glare and sped out of the garage.

I don't know why I was pissed off but I was. Did she work in the building or had he called her? Was he going to meet me with some babe in tow? I suppose it was all of the accumulated shock and surprise that made me so grumpy. I considered bypassing the coffee shop then realized I hadn't eaten any lunch despite loading up a plate at the buffet. My stomach growled, confirming the fact. I decided to get a sandwich, pump Gus Colcannon for information then go home and try to relax.

I was standing in line for my tuna sandwich at the coffee shop when I remembered I had an afternoon meeting. Presumably people would know that I'd left, but I'd shot out of the building and hadn't told anyone I was going. I pulled out my Blackberry to email a message then I spotted the public computer terminals on the far side of the room. I was far better with a regular keyboard than I was thumbing Barry. I took the sandwich and went to a terminal to log on to the company mail servers through the protected website we used when offsite.

I'd just gotten into my email queue when Colcannon came in—minus the busty blonde. I gave him a disinterested wave as he wove his way through the tables to join me.

"Why'd you run out of there?" He peeled off his knit gloves and pulled over a chair to sit next to me. No wonder the guy looked cold. The gloves were thin and his coat, although long, didn't look heavy.

I studied the email screen. It was a different interface than the one we had in the office and I wasn't adept at using it. "I thought you had to talk to the cops."

He paused. "I do."

"So why are you here?"

"I'm going downtown later to talk to them. Why did you leave so fast?"

"You were busy." It came out sounding whinier than I wanted. I took a big bite of tuna salad and turned back to the screen.

"I had some business to take care of." He peered at my screen. "What are you doing?"

"Email," I mumbled around a mouthful of tuna. Business? Five-foot-ten, thirty-six C business. I sniffed in dismissal as I composed a message to Nelson, who would be running the meeting, explaining that I was out for the day. I'd just clicked 'send' when the subject line on another message caught my eye. I choked on the bite of stale tuna in my mouth.

If I can't have you, no one can have you.

Chapter Three

I gagged on the tuna. “Are you okay?” Gus followed my horrified gaze to the computer screen. “What's that?”

I wasn't quite fast enough. He put a hand over mine on the mouse as I tried to close the email screen. “What is it?”

“I've been getting weird emails, I told you.”

“Open it.”

I glared at him. “You're awfully bossy for a guy I barely know.”

“Just do it, Jessie.” He gave me a look of long-suffering patience.

I decided it wouldn't matter. I clicked on the email subject line and the text flowed onto the screen.

You should take me seriously, Jessie. I told you I wanted you to be my girl. Now see where your stubbornness got you—your boyfriend is sick and it's your fault. You're lucky they found out about the switched food labels in time, otherwise—who knows what might have happened? If you're smart, you'll tell that smarmy pretty boy to get lost...for his own good.

The tuna in my stomach grumbled as my guts boiled. He was using my name. How did he get my name? He shouldn't know my real name. I always used an alias when I logged on to Silver Harmony.

Then the content of the email soaked in. I looked from the email screen to Gus then back to the words. “This makes no sense. Is he talking about Charlie? Charlie isn't—he wasn't my pretty boy. I don't have a pretty boy. I don't have any kind of a boyfriend.”

Gus leaned close to me to peer at the screen. I saw snow melting on the dark blue fabric of his topcoat. He'd unbuttoned it but still had the collar pulled high to his face. It accented his high cheekbones and contrasted with the white and gray in his beard. He looked a bit like Johnny Depp in *The Ninth Gate*—a gray-haired Johnny Depp.

He turned his head. We were only inches apart. His breath was warm and minty as he whispered, “Who's in love with you, Jessie?”

I almost laughed out loud. “No one. I haven't even had a date in fifteen years, much less did anything that would make somebody fall in love with me.”

His eyes searched mine then returned to the screen. “Who's the sender?”

I expanded the email header, scanning through the arcane mix of numbers, symbols, and letters. “It came through an anonymous email portal.” I pointed to the various numbers. “Those are the same IP addresses as before.”

“What?”

“IP address—Internet provider. They all have a numeric designation. That's the same one. I memorized it when I tried to track the first message. I can't get any info out of them unless I have a search warrant.” I waggled my eyebrows at him. “You don't happen to have one on you, do you?”

His eyes widened and his face got red. “What? No, of course not.” He turned his attention back to the screen. “What time was it sent?”

Hmm. That was an interesting reaction—and a good question. I checked the top of the email message. “Twelve-thirty this afternoon.”

Gus leaned back. “It was sent after the potluck started but before Charlie was found. Or right about the time Charlie was found.”

I considered that. He was right.

“Tell me about that dating service you used.” He hunched his shoulders and stretched out his legs. I wasn't fooled by his casual pose. Gus Colcannon appeared about as relaxed as Kong, my cat, when he was getting ready to pounce.

“Why should I?” I polished off my tuna sandwich. Gus wrinkled his nose. “What? You don't like tuna salad?”

“It's not that.” He watched me wash down the tuna with a gulp of coffee. “How can you eat pre-packaged stuff? Who knows how old it is? Who knows who made it?"

I gave a ladylike belch. "Quit being a food snob. I haven't gotten sick yet and I eat this stuff all the time. Roller dogs from the gas station are the best food on earth."

"Roller dogs?"

I mimed a spinning motion. "You know, the hot dogs on those little roller grills."

"You eat that?"

"And thrived all these years." I rolled my eyes at his pained expression. "You didn't answer my question. Why should I tell you about Silver Harmony?"

He nodded toward the computer screen. His hair shone in the overhead lights. It looked very soft and baby-fine, lying in thick waves on his head. His beard, too, appeared soft where it framed his wide mouth. He turned to regard me and his cheeks reddened when he met my gaze. "I'm curious, that's all." He grinned wryly. "After all, I'm silver." His glance flickered to my head, where I know my own silver 'highlights' glinted in my once-black shaggy hairdo. He frowned. I knew that look of perplexed recognition. "Are you related to—"

I shook my head, accustomed to this question. I'd been getting it for decades. My resemblance to a famous Olympic skating star had plagued me all my life. "Nope."

He grinned. "Do you ice skate?"

"Sure, I can skate. I grew up in Minnesota. But I can't do a sit spin like Dorothy Hamill. So, how long have you been divorced?"

"What's that got to do with anything?" He jerked his eyes away from me and straightened up in the chair, his shoulders still hunched.

"You probably haven't been divorced for long if you haven't gotten around to online dating services yet. I mean, there's not a lot of options for people our age." I sipped my coffee. "Unless of course..." I had just realized that maybe he didn't need a dating service. He had the Busty Barbie Blonde. Perhaps she was the cause of his marital breakup. Maybe he'd jumped right from one bed into another. It wouldn't be the first time and certainly not the last.

"Now what did I do?" he demanded.

"Huh?"

"You're glaring at me again. You do that a lot." He pointed to the computer screen. "Silver Harmony?"

"Forget online dating services. I need to do something about that email." I gulped more coffee. "I should give it to the police. The cops said they don't know what killed him. They should have this just in case they're investigating who switched the labels."

"I'm going to see them as soon as I leave you," Gus said. "Print it and I'll take it. They can call you if they have questions."

I stalled, staring at the screen. It didn't feel right to give him the email but I couldn't think of a reason not to. And besides, I didn't want to hassle with going to the police station and finding the right cops and…I dug in my Levi pocket. "Which one was which?" I muttered, staring at the business cards.

"What?"

"One was blond, one was tall-dark-and-handsome, and one was my age."

Gus gave an exaggerated sigh and tugged the cards from my hands, sorting them. He handed them to me one by one. "Blond. Dark-haired. White-haired."

I opened an editing screen and typed a brief note, then appended the received email. "I'll give it to this guy." I brandished the card that said Detective Alex Raney. I put my quarter in the printer, clicked the print icon then grabbed the page when it finished. Before Gus could take it, I stapled it shut six times then addressed it to the white-haired Detective Raney.

"Why him?" Gus asked when I handed him the paper.

"He seemed sympathetic." What I didn't say was that interesting men of a certain age were hard to find. It didn't hurt to expand my possibilities.

"Sympathetic?" He grinned as he took the folded paper.

I regarded him with narrow-eyed suspicion. "Do you know something I don't?"

"No, no." He patted his coat pocket. "I'll deliver your missive in person. Now tell me why someone is sending you email like this."

"No offense, but you're nosey for somebody who—"

"John Slocum and Bob Madison hired me to check into things at the office. There have been some problems."

I almost choked on my coffee. "They did what?"

Gus pulled out a cell phone. "Here, I'll call John. He can tell you himself." He held up a finger when I tried to talk.

My brain was in overdrive. CodeBusters employed some of the best programmers in the Minneapolis/St. Paul area, as well as recruiting people from around the country. The kind of work we did—specialized programs for government and industry—was cutting edge. All workers signed confidentiality agreements and some had to sign exclusivity contracts as well. Bob Madison was the CEO and founder of the company. John Slocum, head of R&D, was responsible for working with security to make sure our government clearance stayed intact and we stayed within contract guidelines. If Gus was in cahoots with them, he was working high up on the food chain.

Gus handed me the phone.

"Jessie, are you okay? I meant to talk to you after you met with the police but I was busy. I hope you're okay. I know what a shock this must be for you."

I recognized John Slocum's New Jersey accent. I easily visualized his bland, easy-going features creased into concerned wrinkles. "I'm fine. I just wasn't sure if I—"

"You can trust Gus. We brought him in because—and this is strictly private, Jessie—there's been a leak. I really can't go into details but Gus is…"

I could almost see the words spinning in John's bald head as he sought the right phrase.

"He's affiliated with a group that helps track down this kind of thing. This is strictly private, you understand. Nobody else is to know about this."

"Does that mean I'm not under suspicion?" I wasn't sure if I was teasing or not, but I wanted an answer.

"Of course not."

His immediate response was reassuring. "But what does my email have to do—"

"Jessie, we don't know for sure how far this thing goes. But I've asked Gus to examine anything that's unusual. So help him out, okay?"

Poor John. He sounded harassed. Then I remembered—he'd just had an employee die on the premises. No wonder he sounded stressed. "Sure, John. I'll do what I can."

"Great. Put Gus on, okay?"

I handed the phone back to Colcannon. "John vouches for you."

"Good. Keep that thought." He spoke into the phone. "I'll call you when I get done at the police station." His eyes flickered from me to the computer screen and my email queue. I moved the mouse pointer to close the screen but he put his hand on mine and shook his head while listening on the phone. "Okay." He folded the phone.

I looked down at his hand, which still covered mine. "You can let go now."

"Promise to be good?" His hand tightened on mine.

"Define good."

He released my hand and regarded me over the tops of his wire-rim glasses. "You tempt me." Before I could respond to this enigmatic comment he said, "Tell me about the dating place. I thought you were changing your email identity. How does he keep finding you? Tell me how this service works—how did you find them? When did you sign up?"

An impatient college-age kid was waiting for the terminal. I tidied up my tuna leftovers and headed toward a table on the far side of the room after logging off the system. Colcannon followed me, tugging his coat around him even though the table was under the heating vent. I tossed my jacket onto a spare chair and sat down next to the window.

"Charlie told me about the dating service. Like I said, he and I met when our spouses were in the hospital. It was him who called me about a job at CodeBusters. I'd been sort of drifting after Bill died. I just did some temp work and a few contract jobs. I didn't want anything permanent. I didn't want to settle in any place and make friends."

"It's hard to recover from a loss like that." Colcannon's raspy voice was lower than usual and his eyes were sympathetic. For a guy who hid his facial expressions behind a mustache and beard, it seemed easy to tell what he was thinking.

"We knew Bill's illness was terminal." I stared at the slush melting at the entryway. "Bill and I talked about it. I loved him but a person is capable of many loves in a lifetime. He knew that, too. Before he died we talked about me finding someone else."

"It's still tough. It's hard to take a chance when you've been hurt that way."

I shot him an assessing glance. He was twisting a swizzle stick that had been discarded on the table. "There are a lot worse things in life than having a broken heart."

He hunched deeper in his coat. "Touché."

I sipped my coffee, wondering how we'd gotten so far off the track. "When I started working at CodeBusters, Charlie was just getting back in the dating game again. He'd joined a singles group at his church and he kept nagging me to try to get signed up with someone. I don't belong to any church, so he pointed me to the Silver Harmony web site. He'd signed up with them and had a few dates. I figured, why not? Give it a shot."

I slouched back in my seat and regarded the snow swirling outside. There was a feeble glimpse of sun trying to break through the clouds and it made the glare on the window seem that much brighter. I squinted at the parking lot, seeing my sludge-crusted Subaru and Gus's now-not-so-clean truck next to it. "How do you keep your truck so clean? Do you take it through a car wash? Why bother? It's just going to get dirty again."

"Would you stay on task?" He sounded exasperated.

"I was just curious."

He tapped the table with the swizzle stick in a rhythm I almost recognized. I think it might have been *Inagodadavida.*

"Okay, okay. You pay a fee and fill out a bunch of questionnaires. They were thorough. I had to answer seventy questions on a bunch of different subjects. Then your info is fed into a computer and they try to match you with someone. You pay a fee for a certain length of time. I paid for six months. As new people come online, they get matched against you." I slipped my feet out of my snow clogs and propped them up on an empty chair.

Colcannon looked at my wiggling toes in my Rudolf

socks and shivered theatrically. "And you matched somebody?"

"Yep. I matched four or five, right off the bat, with about a sixty percent match. The service said that was good. I exchanged email with a few of them. A couple of the guys were from town but after we emailed it just didn't quite click. And the others were all out of state. Heck, one of them was from New Zealand so I gave up on that." I shrugged. "I'm not much of one for long-distance romances. Then I got email from the other one."

"The weird one?" Colcannon lounged in his chair, the coat almost hiding his face. He was probably anxious to get back to New Mexico now that his marriage had fizzled. What a drag to move somewhere then find that your wife wanted a divorce. Jerked away from your home then jerked around by your spouse. I wondered how John had found him so fortuitously. What kind of 'group' did Gus work for that did investigative work at software companies?

"Hello?" He snapped his fingers in front of my face.

"I heard you." I wiggled my socked feet at him and was rewarded with seeing him wince. "Yeah, the weird one. It was odd. He'd matched me on just about everything—hobbies, interests, books, music. The service was excited. It was a ninety-five percent match. They said that was amazing. But when we started exchanging email, it was like it was a different person. He didn't recognize any of the movies I mentioned, he said he didn't like cats, and he talked about music that I know I said I disliked."

"And that is?"

"Anything without a good guitar lead. You know, rap and hip hop and junk like that. Then he started writing about how he came from a traditional 'American background'." I used my fingers to indicate the quote marks. "His mother stayed home and raised the kids while Dad went out and earned the money. That's when I knew something was goofy."

"Why?" Colcannon resumed his tapping. Now I wasn't sure about the song. Maybe it was *Smoke on the Water*. Or maybe I just had old metal songs on the brain.

"I hardly had a traditional American background. My

parents were in the Army. My father was in the diplomatic corps and my mother taught code-breaking. I spent most of my first ten years overseas. I played lead guitar in a girl group in college and was thrown in jail for environmental protesting in the Eighties."

"Seriously?" He peered at me from the confines of his coat like a turtle poking his head out to examine a potential threat.

"It was a brief stay in jail," I assured him. "I'm not a hardened criminal. Anyway, that's when I decided something was fishy and I broke contact." I picked at a ragged fingernail, wondering how much to tell him. I trusted John Slocum, so I decided to shoot the moon. "I thought at one time it might be Brian Bennington."

"Brian?"

"Yeah. He and I went out for coffee and he sort of came on to me."

"Brian Bennington?" Gus's voice was strangled, like he was trying not to laugh.

"Yeah. We went out for coffee—" I looked around the coffee shop then back at Gus, raising an eyebrow at him. "Anyway, we had coffee. Bobby told me that Brian was interested in me. I wasn't interested in him so..." I shrugged.

"Nerdy Brian?"

"Don't point fingers. He's not unattractive. He's just a bit...plain and perhaps his clothing choices could be a bit more stylish, but..." Why was I justifying going out for coffee with Brian? Heavens, I'd thought it was a simple get-together, just like this one with Colcannon. How was I to know Brian had other ideas in mind?

"The guy who sits across the atrium? The one who must be color blind, based on the way he matches his shirts to his socks?"

Gus's amused tone irritated me but I chose to ignore it. "Brian used to be a super hacker in his day. I thought he might have tried to hack into Silver Harmony's database and copy my responses. But that's too much trouble." I sipped my cooling coffee. "I had to answer their survey thing in four different parts and they ask that you do it on different days."

"So?" Gus tapped the table again with the plastic

stick. It sounded the bass lead for Led Zepplin's *Whole Lotta Love*.

"It's hard to hack a database when the data is split across tables like that." I saw his perplexed look. Then I remembered. He wasn't really a programmer. "Trust me. Having someone fill out the survey on different days, times, and in different segments adds a layer of complexity. I doubt Brian would go to the trouble. Besides, he hasn't acted like he cares one way or the other since we went out, so I doubt it mattered that much to him."

"So what happened next?"

"I kept getting email. The guy from Silver Harmony just wouldn't give up. So I asked Silver Harmony to change my screen identity."

"But he figured it out and continued sending email?"

I nodded. "The thing that was really spooky was..." My voice trailed off as I decided to voice my fear.

He rapped my knuckles lightly with the swizzle stick. "Yes?"

"How does he know my name?"

"The service—" He stopped when I shook my head. "They don't give out your name?"

"No. You use a screen identity. I never used my real name in any of the screen identities they set up for me. The identities are like nicknames."

"Really? What did you use?" He resumed tapping on the table.

"Oh, I just made things up. You know, 'FlowerGirl' and 'ColdBuns' and stuff like that." I saw his quick grin. "It's like any online site, you can make up all kinds of information about yourself." I frowned. Something was niggling at my brain. If I could make up stuff, presumably the guy who matched me could do the same. But how could he match me so precisely? His answers on the survey had been almost a ninety-five percent match. The others who'd matched me were seventy percent at the most. No one could make up anything that matched me so well. If he hadn't hacked into their database, and I doubted he had, how had he found out my answers? There had to be a clue there but I wasn't sure what it was.

"Hold on." I pulled out Barry and thumbed a quick

note, ignoring Colcannon's exasperated look. I tucked Barry back in my purse and refocused on the conversation. "I've got such an unusual last name that it's a dead giveaway. If anyone knew where I lived and my last name, they could find me. So I made sure my screen identity was nothing like my real name."

"So how do you get the email?" He resumed tapping my hand with the plastic stick, obviously deep in thought.

"People send email to the mail servers at Silver Harmony and they forward it on." I sipped my now-cool coffee. "His emails have all come to me via Silver Harmony, but—"

He looked back at the screen. "He used your name. He addressed it to Jessie."

I nodded. "Yeah." I decided to finally voice my fear. "The question is—how did he get my real name? And what else does he know about me?"

Chapter Four

"That's why you said it was a hacker." Gus stared at my knuckles where his swizzle stick rested.

I followed his gaze and saw my chewed nails, rough skin and the lone ring on my right index finger. I jerked my hands out of sight and made a mental note to get out the hand lotion that night.

"It has to be somebody who knows how to get into a database like that?" He resumed tapping the table with the stick. My foot automatically kept time with him.

I nodded. "Like I said, Silver Harmony isn't the Department of Defense but they have to have good security just for confidentiality reasons." I pried off the lid to my coffee and peered inside. The whipped cream had melted down. I considered getting another shot just to get the whipped cream but restrained myself. I'd already had enough nerve-jangling events for one day.

"Earth calling Jessica."

I jerked my head up. "It's not Jessica. And quit being so bossy."

"Stay on-task. If it's not Jessica, what is it?"

"None of your business. So what kind of stuff did John ask you to check on? I heard you and Charlie talking about something this morning—was that it?"

His hand stilled and I saw the shock in his eyes. "What?"

"I heard you and Charlie talking when you guys came in. I was in my cube. What am I supposed to look for when I test?"

His face changed. It was like watching all lights go out for just an instant. Then he resumed tapping the stick again. This time I was sure it was Eric Clapton's *Badge*. "I really can't go into details about that. Charlie and I were talking in confidence."

“Fine.” I straightened up and rammed my feet into my clogs. “Thanks for dropping that email off at the police station. I'll give them a call later to make sure it got delivered safely.”

“Hey, hey.” He held up a hand. “Come on, sit down. Don't get mad.”

“I'm not mad.” I grabbed for my jacket but he got it first.

“Tell me how you do the testing. What kind of things do you do?” He wrapped his arms across his chest, pinning my jacket.

I flopped back in the chair and plucked a flyer for a local band from the napkin holder. “I don't try to find anything in particular.” I pleated the flyer. “That's the point. If a client has given us specs on what they need—a certain kind of computer they use or the speed they need from the program—I recreate that and make sure the program does what we say it will.” I found my travel scissors in my purse and unfolded them. “Other than that, there are canned test programs we run and there are a few that I've set up to troll the code, checking on error messages and things.” I began snipping the fluorescent orange paper. I had a Peter Maxx design in mind for a Christmas gift for my niece, Andrea, and I needed to get the kinks worked out.

“Troll the code?” He tucked his hands under my jacket, watching as orange bits flew.

“It's not that cold,” I said, as he burrowed into the warmth. He gave me what I was coming to recognize as an exasperated expression. “Okay, okay. I set up little scripts that open up the different files in the programs. They go through and check for keywords that indicate comments or error messages.” I had a sudden thought. “Do you know anything about programming? Or are you undercover?”

He rolled his eyes. “Nothing that glamorous. Yeah, I know something about programming. I used to program in Fortran.”

“Really? Where? White Sands? That's in New Mexico, isn't it?” I unfolded the paper and examined my efforts. Not bad, but it needed work. I carefully refolded it. “There's a big government base there, isn't there? Or is it all radioactive or something? Didn't they test a bunch of nuclear bombs there?" I caught his annoyed look and got back on task, snipping as I talked. "I set up JavaScript that targets the code that looks unusual and pulls it out for me to examine later. If I think that part needs further testing, I do it." I eyed my jacket.

He avoided my look. "Are you the only tester?"

"No, there're four of us. We each handle specific kinds of programs. We all switch back and forth, of course, if needed but that's how it usually ends up." His fingers, long and blunt-tipped, tapped a rhythm on top of my jacket. I wondered what tune he was playing now. He didn't wear any rings and I didn't see a telltale dent where a wedding band had recently sat. I wondered how long it had been since he'd been dumped, if dumped he'd been.

"Who's your boss? Who approves all the test plans?"

"My old boss just took a job at the University so for now, Nelson Scott is our boss." I snipped some more, frowning at the design. I was aiming for a Yellow Submarine theme, but it was coming out more like a pregnant cigar.

"Isn't that tricky?"

"Hmm?" I glanced up. Colcannon was watching me, his eyes flickering from my hands to my face. "What's tricky?"

"You're testing the code that your boss writes. Isn't that tough? What if you find something in the design that he goofed up?"

I shook my head, abandoning my submarine. "Nelson usually doesn't write code, he just works on program design. Charlie was the primary government programmer and he just switched to Marketing." Then I remembered. "I mean, he used to be the primary..."

It suddenly hit me again. Poor Charlie was dead. My eyes filled with tears and my scissors clattered to the tabletop.

"Hey." Warmth enveloped me. I smelled aftershave, damp wool and warm man. Colcannon was leaning over me, one arm around my shoulders. "It's okay. It's a shock, I know."

"It's just that it was...Charlie," I whispered. "He was

just starting to get his life back on track after Janet died. I know how hard that is. I just hate to think that he's dead." I wiped at my eyes. "Did my brownies make him sick?"

"I'm sure it wasn't that." He gave my shoulder a squeeze then sat back down. "The cops will figure it out. You're not to blame."

I felt bereft without his solid comfort. The guy was annoying but it felt good to have somebody hold me like that, even for a minute. To cover my confusion I grabbed another flyer, this one a dark green, and pleated it.

"Don't you ever sit still?" he asked.

"I'm sitting still."

He looked at my foot, tapping out a rhythm then to my hands, cutting the paper. "Right." His eyes shifted to the window. I followed his gaze and saw light snow falling. "When does it get warmer here?"

"May, if we're lucky, although it has snowed in May. Why wasn't I fingerprinted?"

His head swung to me so fast I heard it creak. "What?"

"The police didn't fingerprint anybody. How come? I've watched those cop shows on TV and they're always dusting and fingerprinting and doing all that CSI crap." I snipped at the paper, pleased that my hands were steady again after my outburst about Charlie.

"I don't know. Are you going to be okay tonight?"

He was lying. I could hear it in his voice. I considered accusing him but decided to let it pass. Maybe I was wrong. Or maybe I just didn't want the hassle. "What do you mean?"

"I just thought—if you're upset—" He pulled over my discarded paper cutting and jotted a phone number on it. "If you need to talk, call me. I just live down the street." He gestured to the window. "I've got an apartment in West Wind, over there."

"I'm used to it." I unfolded the paper in my hands and considered my efforts. "Being alone, that is."

"Yeah. I know what you mean." He stood up, handing me my jacket. I refolded my paper cutting and watched as he buttoned his coat so high I could barely see his face. His alert hazel eyes peeked over the edge, framed by gray hair.

"You know, if you're going to be living here you really need to get used to the cold."

"I'm just here temporarily," he said, tugging on his gloves.

I tucked my paper cutting and the one with his phone number into my bag, folding each one so it wouldn't get crushed by the other effluvia I carried. "I suppose after the divorce there's no real reason to stay, is there? It must have just been luck to get this job with John, right?"

I almost missed the confusion in his eyes as he turned to lead the way out of the coffee shop. "Yeah, right." He held the door for me.

I pulled my coat on as we walked out. I've always enjoyed kicking through fresh powder and did so now, swinging my Sak handbag. He stomped beside me, the embodiment of grumpiness. I eyed his truck as we approached. The dark maroon finish was splattered with mud spots but otherwise it shone in the pale sunlight. "So how do you keep it so clean?"

"I bought a pass at the car wash."

I almost pointed out how futile it was to keep a car washed in Minnesota in the wintertime but one glance at his disgruntled expression and I shut up. He eyed my crusted gray Subaru disdainfully as I jerked open the door, which needed oiling. I paused before getting in. "Good luck doing whatever it is you're doing for John."

"Are you sure you'll be okay?" He stared down at me. I was surprised at the obvious concern in his eyes.

"Yeah, I'll be fine."

"If you need anything, call."

He sounded insistent. "Okay." I got into my car and watched him get into the truck then drive slowly away. Granted, the roads were slick with the latest snowfall but all in all it wasn't bad. He was obviously uncomfortable with winter driving conditions. I followed him with more speed, my mind in overdrive.

Why was he lying? I was almost sure he'd lied twice: once when we talked about the police and once when I mentioned his divorce. He'd looked surprised when I said that bit about being lucky to get a job with John so soon after his divorce. What was Gus Colcannon hiding?

I popped *Guitar Gods of the 70s* into the CD player and pondered the question as I drove west to Victoria, where I lived. Colcannon knew damn well why the police hadn't fingerprinted anybody but he wasn't saying—why? I hadn't gone back by the lunchroom, so maybe they had brought in all the CSI guys with their dusting powder and cameras. But surely they would have taken fingerprints from anybody who was near the lunchroom, including me?

I struggled to remember what questions the police had asked me as I drove on autopilot on the two-lane blacktop that wended through the countryside. We were having one of those white days so typical of Minnesota in the winter. The clouds were white, the air was white with powdery snow and the frozen ground was white out to the horizon, far in the distance. Only the occasional stubble of corn or angular shape of trees broke the monotony.

The whiteness reminded me of the cop—Raney—and his white hair. He was handsome in a rugged, outdoorsy way while Colcannon was handsome in a professorial, tweedy way. I drove through Victoria (population 1000 with two stop lights and one stop sign) and pulled into my quiet dead-end street a couple of minutes later. Tom, my retired neighbor, had cleared my drive. We had a deal: I mowed his lawn in the summer and he plowed for me in the winter. His wife, Norma, was my regular hair person at the Clip and Curl Salon of Beauty. She was standing at her kitchen window as I pulled into the drive. I waved as I goosed Sally the Subaru up the long driveway and into my garage.

I entered my kitchen, dropping my bags on the bench near the door. My two cats, Kong and Faye, ambled out to greet me. I appeased them with plates of food, docked my laptop and set up Barry to synchronize with my computer, then wandered into the living room to turn on my stereo. Eric Clapton's soothing voice started to sing.

I stood at the picture window that faced my deck, looking at the snowy woods behind my house. Bill and I had remodeled somewhat when we bought the house fifteen years ago, but it was still just a basic rambler with bedrooms upstairs and a walkout from the family room in the basement. The small back yard sloped down to a large pond forty yards below. Although it was only four in the afternoon, the woods were already darkening, reminding me that we were approaching the shortest day of the year. The monochromatic scenery was hypnotic—black ribbon of water, white snow on the banks, black tree silhouettes, white snow on the branches.

The phone on the end table rang. I glanced at the caller ID and saw "Chaska PD." I answered and a deep male voice said, "Miss Patrokus?"

"Yep." I carried the phone with me to the couch, where I flopped down.

"This is Alex Raney. Mr. Colcannon suggested I give you a call."

I heard a woman's voice in the background, saying 'It's not your fault. You did what you could and...' It sounded like people were near the phone, or maybe the phone was on a speaker. Then Raney said, "Miss Patrokus?"

"I'm here." I watched Faye, my petite Persian cat with the light brown hair, jump nimbly onto the hassock. She settled down with a contented sigh. I longed to emulate her.

"I just wanted to let you know that we got that email printout. Mr. Colcannon dropped it off. I'd like to discuss it with you, if you have time."

"Sure, let me get to my laptop." I went down the hall to my den, which overlooked the back yard. As I passed the window to my desk, I paused. There were dark shapes in the woods near a small clearing next to the pond. I grabbed my field glasses from the hook near the door and stepped closer to the window. My nearest neighbor at the back of my house was a mile away, across the pond and up the far slope, but the pond was linked to the trail system in town so I occasionally had visitors. I pulled the thin curtains aside and focused the binoculars, expecting to see the small herd of deer who'd been making forays into my yard, led by a male I'd dubbed Broke-Antler Buck.

What I saw was a man with a rifle.

"Well, shit," I muttered.

"Excuse me?"

Oops. I'd forgotten I was still holding the phone. "Sorry. There's a guy with a gun out here in my back yard."

"What?"

He'd shouted. I jerked the phone in surprise. "A hunter, out here in the woods, behind my house. Hold on a second." I put the phone down and peered outside. Raney's voice was loud behind me on the phone. The angle was wrong from this room. I picked up the phone. "I'm going back into the living room for a minute. Do you want me to call you back?"

"There's a man outside with a gun?"

He spoke fast and loud. Voices in the background behind him sounded excited.

"Yeah. They're not supposed to." My house was on the fringes of town and west of me was open land. Hunters often used the trail although they weren't supposed to be so close to the houses. I refocused the lenses, straining to see details, but all I could pick out was a camo jacket, brown pants, and a head in a dark ski mask as it turned to face up the hill, toward me.

"Well, that's stupid," I said.

"What?"

I recognized that distinctive raspy voice. "Gus?"

"Answer the damn question, Jessie."

"My, my, aren't we in a pissy mood? Why are you talking to me? Where's the cop?" I held the binoculars up again. I was right. The hunter wasn't wearing blaze orange, which was either stupid or illegal or both. I took a step back from the window and turned. That's when I saw Broke-Antler Buck standing down slope and twenty yards to the right of the hunter, who appeared to be oblivious to the presence of a large amount of deer meat on the hoof.

"Raney's right here. Answer the question—what's stupid?"

"The hunter isn't wearing orange. I thought that was a law. And there's a deer right there. He's sort of a tame deer. Well, not tame, but he's not spooky wild like some deer. Man, that bastard is going to kill that buck right on my land. That is so not right. Listen, I've got to deal with this, I'll call you back."

"Jessamine Katherine Patrokus, don't you dare hang up this phone!"

"What?" I almost dropped the phone in surprise. "How did you get my name?" I turned the binoculars back on the hunter, who still seemed ignorant of Buck standing nearby. I didn't want that deer killed on my land. The bastard hunter would probably demand to bring the carcass up the hill near my house, which was the closest point to any road. The smell and the blood would attract every critter for miles around. Not to mention the fact I'd grown attached to that stupid deer in the two years I'd watched him grow up. He wasn't the brightest bulb on the Christmas tree, but that didn't mean he deserved to be shot like a fish in a barrel.

"What's going on there?" Gus demanded.

"I have to deal with this. Just hold on for a second. I'm not hanging up so don't get excited." I set the phone on the coffee table and pulled my slingshot from the coffee table drawer. I kept a cache of rocks near the door to the deck and I paused to take a handful before stepping out on to the slick planking. I'd practiced for hours to keep the crows away from my bird feeders and the coons out of the compost heap so I was a good shot. I moved two steps forward and took aim for the trees above and behind the hunter.

Buck heard me and broke cover. The hunter, startled, turned at the sound. I fired five quick shots, which thunked into the trees around the human. As I moved back to the shelter of the house he twisted, lost his balance and tumbled backwards toward the pond. Despite days of below-zero temperatures, I knew it wasn't frozen solid. That hunter would get a cold, dirty bath if there were any justice in the world.

When I got into the house I heard squawking from the phone. "I'm back." I picked up the phone and hurried down the hall to the den. I peeked out and saw the dark shape of the hunter, getting to his feet. The deer was nowhere in sight. I smiled with satisfaction.

"What the hell are you doing?"

"I told you, there was this hunter out back. I wasn't going to let him shoot a deer down the hill from my house. Do you know how—"

"What did you do?"

"I used my slingshot to scare the deer away." I decided not to mention I'd aimed at the hunter. That *might* be against the law. "Honestly, aren't you overreacting? This kind of crap happens all the time."

"It doesn't happen on the day somebody dies in your office, does it?"

I paused as I walked back toward the living room. He had a point. "So what are you saying? I'm supposed to call the police?" Then I remembered. "Oh. Wait. I was talking to the police. Put him back on the phone—the sympathetic one."

"Jessie, I swear, you need to—"

"Wait." I heard a noise in the woods behind the house. I went to the window. The hunter was still out there. He had his arms raised.

That's when I heard the gunshot.

Chapter Five

"Holy shit, he's firing!" My gaze swept the woods, expecting to see a bloody corpse and twitching antlers. Nothing, thank God. "He's firing his gun—call the police. No, wait. This is the police. Call the police out here." I took a step back from the window.

"What do you mean he fired?"

"He shot his gun." I peeked out the window. "I think."

I heard Gus say to someone, "Shots fired."

The hunter was hurrying away, following the bank of the pond. As I watched, he jumped over a marshy spot of ground and disappeared behind a stand of trees. A public trail near there led to the small city park or, if the hunter kept walking, he'd loop around and emerge not far from Tom and Norma's house across the street from me. "He's gone. I hope he didn't kill that deer, if he did—" Somebody knocked on my kitchen door. "Hold on."

"Jessie, damn it, would you stay on the phone?"

I talked as I walked through the living room to the kitchen door. "It's not your problem, it's mine. We get hunters out here now and then. I'll file a complaint with the city and—" I pulled open the door. Tom was there, bundled up against the cold in his ancient brown Carthart jacket, his anxious expression speaking volumes.

"Jessie, I saw somebody walking along the—oh, I'm sorry, I didn't know you were on the phone." He was wiry and small, with wavy white hair, sparkling green eyes, and a bushy gray mustache stained yellow from years of pipe smoking.

"Come on in." I held the door wider.

"Who are you talking to?"

"Honestly, Gus, it's really none of your business." I held the phone aside. "It's just a guy from work," I said to Tom. "I'll be done in a minute." I put the phone back to my ear.

"John Slocum made it my business when he hired me." Now Gus sounded really peeved. "Jessie, if you don't answer my questions I'm going to come out there. Did someone fire a shot at your house? Who are you talking to?"

I sighed loudly enough so he could hear my exasperation. "I think I heard a shot but I don't know where he was firing at and it's my neighbor, Tom, standing here. Now put the other guy on the phone or I'll hang up."

There was a long, ominous silence. I gestured to Tom to come in but he shook his head, pointing down to his wet boots thawing on my welcome mat. "Is this about that hunter?" I whispered. Tom nodded. "I saw him, I'm on the phone with the cops and—"

"Miss Patrokus?" It was Alex Raney. I recognized the low, rumbling bass voice.

"Oh, good, it's you." I mouthed *the cops* to Tom. "Listen, there was a hunter out here. They're not supposed to be so close to the houses on this side of the pond and—"

"I contacted the Carver County Sheriff's office," Raney said. "They have jurisdiction in your town. They said they'd send someone over right away."

"Oh. Okay. Hang on a second." I pulled the phone away. "He called the Sheriff," I told Tom. "I've got to talk to this guy about something at work. Could you keep an eye out for the cops for me?"

"Sure, no problem. I'm just glad you're okay, those hunters have got a lot of nerve trespassing like that."

"Trespassing?" I put the phone to my ear.

Tom jammed his stocking cap back on his head. "Yeah, they cut right through your yard and down to the pond. I swear, I don't know what this world is coming to."

"That's weird."

"What's weird?"

Once again I'd forgotten I was on the phone. I held the kitchen door for Tom and watched as he made his way down my steps to the garage then out to the driveway. "My neighbor said the hunter cut right through my yard to get to the pond. There's a good trail not far from here so why would somebody trespass?" I turned down the volume on the stereo and went back to the window. The woods were quiet now with no evidence of the intruder. Behind me the timer clicked on for my Christmas bubbler lights that outlined my bookcase.

"How often has this happened?"

It was Gus talking. "What are you doing here again? Where's that cop? I was talking to that cop, how come you keep interrupting?"

"I'm here, Miss Patrokus." Raney's voice rumbled through the phone lines. "Mr. Colcannon is on the extension. Could you please answer the question?"

"Why is he being given such special treatment? I thought he was just a civilian or some kind of accountant John hired. How come—"

"Accountant?" It sounded like Gus was choking.

"You know, one of those auditors. They come to monitor what—"

"We've asked Mr. Colcannon to consult with us on this," Raney interrupted. "How often do you get hunters out there? Have any of them ever trespassed before?"

Consulting? I wondered what that meant. I went to the den and thumbed a note on Barry: *Gus, consult?* "I get hunters once or twice a season," I said into the phone. "Nobody's ever cut through my property, at least not that I know of." I sat down at my desk and brought up my email queue. Nelson had replied to my apologetic note about missing his meeting but other than that, there was just the usual SPAM and a note from John about Charlie's '*unfortunate accident*', asking us all '*to cooperate with the police as much as possible.*'

"That email I got must be about Paul Henderson." I stared at my computer screen. "Paul's so handsome and sort of a pretty boy. The note doesn't mention Charlie by name, but I thought it meant Charlie because of what happened."

"Who the hell is Paul?"

It was Gus Colcannon again. I kept my temper, determined to 'cooperate with the police as much as possible'. "He's just this guy I dated a couple of times. He works in the building. I know he has an allergy to nuts. If the labels were switched, maybe it was to hurt Paul. So that means—" My mind was once again in high gear, sorting and sifting possibilities.

"The emailer is here in town," Gus finished for me. "He saw what happened at the potluck lunch."

"Or he has a spy in the building," I pointed out. "There are four or five companies in CodeBusters' building. It's possible the emailer knows somebody who saw what happened. That person could have even switched the signs." I heard several voices in the background on the other end of the phone. I heard Gus say *in the lunchroom, so anybody could switch them*. Then a woman's voice said, *I'll check Henderson, maybe there's a lead there*. "I don't mean to sound paranoid, but you guys seem to be awfully worried about this." I looked at my large picture windows, overlooking the darkening woods.

There was silence on the other end of the phone. Then Gus said, "I told you, John asked me to check on anything unusual. I think this qualifies as unusual."

I thought about some of the contract work our company was doing and pieces started to click into place. Nelson was working on a hush-hush D.O.D. project, part of which I was testing. And some big scientific contracts were coming down the pike, programs that we'd designed for a pharmaceutical giant. This was probably just part of the heightened security we put in place for projects like that.

I heard a car pull into the driveway. I went into the kitchen and flicked open the curtain on the window that faced the front of the house. A squad car was parked in my drive and a young officer was getting out. Tom was bustling across the street. He'd probably kept watch from the warmth of his own kitchen. "I've got to go, that cop you called is here. Is there anything else you need from me? Do I have to stop in at your office?" I slipped my feet into my snow clogs before going to the kitchen door leading to the garage.

"We'll call you if we need to talk with you. And I'll report to the Sheriff's department about that hunter in your yard."

"I'll see you tomorrow, Jessie," Gus said. "Remember, if you need anything, you've got my phone number."

"We'll talk tomorrow, Gus. You can count on it." I heard someone laugh and say *You're in for it now, Colcannon*, then the connection was cut. I grabbed my jacket and hurried outside to talk to the Law for the third time that day.

I was reassured by the time Officer Quinn left a half-hour later. He examined the spot where the hunter stood, followed the tracks through the woods, and inspected the outside of my house and garage. By the time he finished it was full dark, but my exterior Christmas lights had come on, which added illumination. He told me it appeared the man had used the trail to the city park and was probably gone by now, but he'd double-check to be sure. "There's no sign of damage so I'm betting he was just startled and got a random shot off. We'll talk to the residents who live near the park and see if they remember anybody parking there earlier today."

"But Tom said he saw the guy cut through my lot earlier. Why would he go up the trail after firing his gun? Wouldn't his car be around here somewhere?"

"Maybe somebody dropped him off. We'll check on it. And just to be on the safe side, we'll keep an eye on things for the next few days."

Quinn looked big, solid, and competent. My earlier paranoia started to vanish. I thought of my five other neighbors on the street. Three were retirees, like Tom and Norma, and the other two had school-age kids who often played outside. I hated the thought of some hunter's accident causing serious problems in our little corner of Minnesota heaven.

Tom and I watched the young officer drive away then Tom went back to his house to report to Norma, who would undoubtedly call everyone on the street to reassure them about the presence of the squad car at my house.

After a quick dinner of microwave popcorn I got a beer then dragged over my pile of scrap paper and started cutting, letting my hands choose the design as thoughts bounced around my brain. Nothing seemed to fit together. The emails I'd gotten had to be unrelated to what happened to Charlie, but who was sending them? I thought of the hunter in the woods—another coincidence?

I turned off the lights and went to the window. I had

that brief disorienting moment of trying to decipher the black silhouettes against the white snow. I couldn't see any movement except for the pond. Starlight glinted off the water and the ice that had formed on the sides. Nothing was stirring.

Kong, my giant black cat, ambled in and yawned at me. I took the hint and changed into my Springsteen sleep T-shirt then climbed into bed. In my mind's eye, I remembered Charlie as he'd been that morning, laughing as he filled my coffee mug and teasing me about my love life. He'd been such a comfort to me when Bill was dying. The remembered grief of that time combined with the grief I was feeling now. I ached with a sharp sense of loneliness and a sense of loss I couldn't understand.

It was almost midnight before I finally cried myself to sleep.

****

I was in no mood to put up with Gus Colcannon's bullshit in the morning. I wanted answers and I wanted them fast. He wasn't going to weasel out of explanations.

The damn coward avoided me all morning. I got there early, as usual, but he didn't show up until almost nine o'clock. I heard him come into his cube then leave immediately.

Our kitchen/lunchroom was locked with yellow Crime Scene tape all over the door so I went downstairs for my morning coffee. Charlie's death was the big topic of conversation, of course, with the potluck fiasco running a close second. I overheard a couple of Suits talking about it. "Someone was sent to the hospital," one of the three-pieced ones said as they fixed their morning coffee. "Guess that's the end of potlucks for us. I thought we had it covered with the labels. How could they have gotten mixed up?'

Good question. I longed to hash it over with Denise, but Tuesday was her day for meetings and I wouldn't see her until lunch. I refocused on tracking down Gus Colcannon. I spied him in the lobby at mid-morning when I went to a meeting but he ducked away when he caught sight of me. I glimpsed him in Nelson Scott's office when I got out of my meeting then later he and John Slocum were talking, John's pudgy face creased into worried wrinkles. I listened for Gus to return to his cube, but he hadn't by the time Denise came to get me for lunch.

"I should go see how Paul is," I said as we rode the elevator down to the small cafeteria on the first floor. "It may have been my brownies that made him sick."

"Or not," she pointed out. "I couldn't see who was sick yesterday."

"I just need to check." My conscience was bugging me.

The receptionist at the front desk of the Riddenour Insurance Agency assured me Paul was fine. "They took him to the hospital yesterday as a precaution, but they released him last night. He said he might come in to work this afternoon. It's just a shame that happened, I don't know how somebody could mix up the labels like that."

I beat a hasty retreat, not anxious to admit to being a perpetrator, however innocent. As Denise and I headed for the large, glass-walled cafeteria Gus Colcannon strode across the lobby, walking toward the front doors. I made a move to intercept him then I realized his destination. The Blonde Barbie Bombshell was outside, getting out of a big black sedan as she looked into the building. I ducked behind a palm tree.

"What the hell are you doing?" Denise asked.

"It's her." I jerked Denise's sleeve to pull her behind the tree with me.

"Who?"

"The Barbie doll."

"Ooh. Where?"

I pointed toward the front entrance, where Gus was pushing through the turnaround doors as he talked on his cell phone. The Blonde got behind the wheel of the car as Gus folded himself into the front seat, still talking.

"They didn't kiss." Denise peered around the fronds. "They don't seem happy to see each other."

She was right. The other day at lunch Gus and the Bombshell been talking but not in that head-to-head, intimate way couples do. "Maybe he's just being careful. It wouldn't look good for a guy doing investigative work to be smooching some babe on the job."

"I don't know," Denise said. "It seems more like business than pleasure."

I considered her words that afternoon in the privacy of my cube. Perhaps I was jumping to conclusions. Just because Gus was seen in the company of a young, long-legged, busty blonde that didn't mean there had to be a romance involved. A man could spend time with a woman who was centerfold material and not be involved with her.

The minute the thought crossed my mind I laughed at myself. That Babe was Hot with a capital H and I'd seen that sexy little glint in Gus Colcannon's eye. I snipped at the folded paper in my hand, keeping one eye on the data scrolling down my screen and my ears tuned to Gus's cube. Gus seemed like a mild-mannered professor, but I had a suspicion that underneath all that winter gear was a man who was hot to trot. The Barbie sure looked like a girl who knew how to ride the stallion. I unfolded the paper and examined my handiwork.

"That's cool."

I almost stabbed myself. Gus was leaning in the doorway to my cube, his arms folded across his chest. Today he wore faded jeans and a dark brown sweater with little flecks of color in it that matched his eyes. His long hair was tousled and windblown.

"Where have you been?" I demanded. "I want answers, Bub, and I want 'em now."

"Really?" He sat down in the guest chair, rolling it nearer to my desk until our knees were almost touching. "About what?" He leaned close to me.

"You know. Why were you at the police station? What was that about you consulting with them? Did they tell you anything about the hunter in my yard? How come you—"

He held up a hand. "Whoa. Slow down. One question at a time."

I grabbed a piece of paper and pleated it then folded it, using my shaping tool to get a sharp edge. "Where do I start?" I considered the square of paper in my hands then made the first cut. "What company do you work for? How did John know to call you in? What kind of stuff are you doing here? Why are you so interested in all this junk that's affecting me? I can't turn around without stumbling over you." Little yellow bits of paper flew around me as I spoke.

He put his hands over mine, stilling their motion. "Jessie." His voice was very soft and gentle, almost caressing.

"What happened to Charlie? What's going on? Why are you worried about that hunter? Did my brownies kill him? What—" I suddenly realized he was holding my hands. My eyes jerked upward, to his. He was smiling, his hazel eyes alight with humor and... "What?" My breath hitched.

"Can't a guy be interested in a pretty woman?" He stared at me, his face close to mine. The soft hair of his beard around his mouth was tempting. I knew it would be smooth and silky to the touch.

"Hmm?" I was very, very close to kissing him.

He smiled, crinkle lines appearing like unfolded fans at the side of his eyes. "Jessie?"

I pulled back and regarded him. "Why?"

Now it was his turn to pull back. He released my hands. "What?"

"Why are you interested in me?"

"Well, because—uh—because—" A dark flush started edging up his cheeks.

Disappointment surged through me but I didn't let it show. "What's going on, Gus? You're not the kind of guy to flirt with a woman like me."

"Really?" I saw something in his eyes, a hint of anger or maybe disappointment. "I suppose it would be futile to argue with you."

I brandished my scissors at him. "You bet it would be. Confess."

"Sorry. I'm interested because John asked me to keep an eye on things here. And because Charlie—" I was sure I saw anger flash in his eyes. "I blew that. He shouldn't have been hurt."

"You're not very reassuring about your competence. Are you a cop or something?"

"Keep your voice down, would you?" He looked over his shoulder.

"Well, are you?"

"Sort of. I'm helping the police, let's just leave it at that."

I snipped, tiny bits of paper dropping onto the towel

on my lap, my concession to the cleaning crew. I kept my voice low. "I'm not stupid. And I'm not brave. I'm scared. So answer my questions. You think somebody in my company killed Charlie. I want to know what I have to do to make sure I'm not next." I began to sniffle. "Charlie was a nice guy. Do you know how I'm feeling right now?" I wiped at my tears. "Do you? Damn it, say something, Colcannon. Tell me why I should trust you? Tell me—"

He put a hand on the side of my face and wiped away a tear with his thumb. "It's okay. They're not going to hurt you."

I wanted to believe him. I wanted to abdicate responsibility and let somebody else do the worrying for a change, just for a little while. It had been so long since I'd had anyone to share with. I longed for that sense of belonging, that feeling of security.

I sniffled and it woke me back to reality. This wasn't a fairy story. I swallowed hard. "I'm not going to trust you unless I see some kind of badge or ID."

He jerked his hand away as if I'd bitten him. Anger flared in his eyes. "I can't do that."

"Fine." I focused my attention on the paper in my hands.

"Jessie."

I refused to meet his eyes. The chair squeaked as he stood up. There was a long pause. I know he was staring down at me.

"I'm sorry, Jessie." He touched my shoulder then left.

I raised my head, the Yellow Submarine forgotten in my hands. I stared out the atrium window, swamped by anger and a twisting sense of failure. I had no right to be so upset but I was. I had thought Gus and I were friends of a sort, united by Charlie's death if nothing else. This refusal to trust me hurt, even though it shouldn't.

A flash of light on the other side of the atrium broke my trance. Brian was sitting at his desk, his back to me. Sunlight was bouncing off the small mirror he had positioned on the top of his monitor. I wondered if he'd seen Gus and me talking.

I didn't hear Gus in his cube. He'd either gone to another meeting or left. I stared at my computer screen for a few minutes then wandered into the mailroom and grabbed magazines and some envelopes from my slot. I came back and stared some more, then gave up. I decided to pack it in and work from home that night.

I bundled up and made for the elevator. Maybe a swim at the gym on the way home would help put me in the right frame of mind.

****

An hour later, I'd done my obligatory half-hour in the pool. It was as I was lying in the sauna that it struck me. Charlie had said he would give me a copy of his presentation for the conference. Where was it?

I showered and dressed in record time, emerging from the building with my hair still wet. I pawed through my briefcase in the back seat of the car, pulling out the stack of mail I'd gotten from the office. A 5x7 envelope was inside with my name printed on it in block letters. I opened it with shaking hands and pulled out a CD.

"Holy shit," I whispered.

Chapter Six

I grabbed Barry and dialed Detective Alex Raney's number. He wasn't in so I left a message, asking him to call me later. I stuffed the CD back into my bag and raced home through falling snow, hampered by lousy visibility caused by blowing winds. I got inside my house and jammed the laptop in the docking port, putting Barry in its synch cradle. Then I dealt with the resident felines, made some coffee and came back to pop the CD into my computer.

I first made a copy of it, making a protected folder on my hard drive and copying the contents there. Then I made another two copies onto blank CDs, putting one into my desk drawer. I was probably being paranoid, but I figured it wouldn't hurt.

I took a long swallow of coffee and settled down to read.

****

An hour later I sat back. Dusk was beginning and a light snowfall blanketed the outside world. My monitor cast the only illumination in the room.

Charlie had left me a puzzle. There were ten files on the CD. One was a read.me. I'd skimmed it and he'd just listed the files, asking me to '*run my code, I can't figure out what's wrong*'. Testers often did that for programmers—sometimes a program seemed to run slow or produced unreliable results. Someone who didn't know the code well could often pinpoint the problem faster than the designer. I'd done code-checks for Charlie in the past.

Three of the other files were slides for the upcoming conference, all detailing the types of products we'd developed in the past year. They looked like typical marketing bullshit.

The others files were programs, obviously part of a

larger program. One other file, possibly two, might be needed to link them together. And one file was data—lines of names, numbers, letters, and symbols. Many of the names had colors attached to them: John Black, Jane Red, Barb White, Fatima Gold. They were mixed with the names of people at the company, including mine, John Slocum's, and Gus's. Odd.

My phone rang. I pushed aside my now-cold coffee and answered.

"Jessie?"

I leaned back at the sound of Gus's raspy voice. "What do you want?"

"Don't sound so happy to hear from me."

"You're pissed off at me, remember?" I dragged over Barry and thumbed a note: *Norma, cut*. I was getting tired of pushing my fluffy bangs out of my eyes.

"No, you're pissed off at me, remember? I wanted to apologize."

My stomach rumbled. I started toward the kitchen. "Apologize for what?"

There was a pause. I pulled open the fridge and considered my options. I hadn't been grocery shopping lately and my larder showed the effects of my forgetfulness. The freezer held several containers of frozen soup but that would require time. I gave up and took the box of Frosted Flakes down from the cupboard.

"I know it looks like I don't trust you," he finally said. "I do, Jessie, but there are reasons I can't tell you everything I'm doing."

I shook some cereal into a bowl and leaned against the counter. Far in the distance I heard the buzz of a snowmobile. Fresh snow always brought them out. "I'm upset about Charlie," I said around a mouthful of crunchy flakes. "I feel responsible, I guess. And it's just—" I munched some more, trying to decide how to articulate what I was thinking.

"What are you eating?"

"Dinner."

"Potato chips?"

"Frosted Flakes." I took a swallow of water.

"Don't you ever eat any real food?"

"I hate cooking." His mention of chips reminded me of

the bag cached away in a different cupboard. I pulled them out. "I heard you and Charlie talking. I wanted—"

"Do you want to go out to dinner tomorrow?"

"Huh?" I almost spilled my chips.

"Do you want to go out tomorrow? My treat. No, wait. I can't tomorrow. How about Thursday? We could go out Thursday night."

I pulled the phone away, shook it then put it back to my ear. "Why?"

He sighed so loudly I could hear it. "It's like a date, Jessie. Remember those?"

"Oh." I was stunned. A date? With Gus Colcannon?

"Man, don't sound so enthusiastic. If you don't want to, just say so."

"No, no, it's not that. I'm just surprised. I thought you liked blondes."

"What?"

Good Lord, why had I blurted that out? I was such a kumquat sometimes. "I've seen you with a woman, that's all. I figured you were dating someone."

"A woman?"

"You know—tall, blonde, Barbie-doll." There was such a long pause I was sure I'd offended him then he burst out laughing. It was honest, carefree laughter, too.

"She's a business acquaintance." His low voice had laughter in it and I wondered why. "So does that mean we're okay for dinner?"

"Sure. As long as it's not dressy. I don't do dressy."

"No problem. I'll cook."

I gulped. I hadn't bargained on going to his apartment. "Do you know how?"

"Yeah, I know how. Thursday after work, okay? We'll have a nice, quiet dinner."

Was it wishful thinking on my part, or did I hear an implied *and maybe a great dessert afterward*? I shook my head, trying to dislodge the lustful imaginings. "Okay. That sounds nice."

"So you forgive me?"

"I guess so. But I still want answers to my questions, Gus. I'm smack in the middle of all this and I feel like I'm working blind."

There was another long pause. "I know. I promise on

Thursday I'll answer all the questions I can. Will you wait that long? Give me another couple of days?"

I nibbled another chip. "I don't have much choice, I guess."

"You don't sound very enthusiastic."

He sounded disappointed or hurt, but to my relief, I didn't have to answer his implied question. *Blue Christmas* sounded from the den, part of Barry's holiday ring tone package. I was being summoned. "Hey, I have to go, somebody's calling on my mobile. I'll talk to you later, okay?" I started to walk toward the den.

The sound of the snowmobiler was louder now. I looked out the window toward the pond, wondering if somebody was on the trail in the gathering darkness. Then the noise shifted and I realized it was coming from the front of the house. "Damn it."

"Now what did I do wrong?"

"Not you. There's a snowmobiler." I picked up Barry from the sync cradle on my desk in the den. "I have to go."

The snowmobile was insistently loud, drowning out Gus's response. I set down my portable phone and turned, trying to listen to Barry over the clatter of an engine that sounded like it was just underneath my front window.

The snowmobile engine shut off. The silence was deafening.

"Jessie?"

I picked up the portable phone again. "Gus, I have to go. There's a snowmobile outside." The bathroom across the hall faced the street. I could see from there who was out front.

"Jessie, don't hang up. What do you mean, there's a snowmobile outside?"

I looked down at Barry, glowing in my hand. 'Chaska PD' shone on the LCD screen. "Oh, good. It's that cop. I have to talk to him. I'll talk to you tomorrow at the office." I clicked *off* on the portable phone then edged my way out of the den. I put Barry to my ear as I twitched the bathroom curtain. "This is Jessie."

"Miss Patrokus, I'm glad you called, I've been meaning to talk to you."

I recognized Alex Raney's distinctive rumbling voice. I peered through the small gap where my café curtains met in the middle of the window. The street was like a scene out of Currier and Ives, with the houses nestled in their snowy cocoons and the snowflakes glistening as they twirled past. A person was in front, sitting on a snowmobile. Whoever it was, they looked big and solid in the bulky snowmobile suit. The helmet added to the menacing appearance.

I remembered the hunter in the back yard, dressed in camo and with a stocking mask on. Now another stranger was sitting in front of my house. This couldn't be a coincidence, not with Charlie dead and the police all over the place. I hadn't had this much traffic on my property in the fifteen years I'd lived there.

I whispered into the phone, "There's somebody outside. He's staring at my house."

"What?"

"There's—" The person got off the snowmobile then walked toward my house. I backed away, tripping over the toilet as I searched my bathroom. The only thing even remotely like a weapon was the toilet plunger. I doubted any assailant would stand still long enough for me to suction him to death. "He's coming here, he's coming to my house, what should I do?"

"That's probably Officer Quinn," Raney said, his voice soothing and calm. "They had a report of a deer down in the woods behind your house. He said he'd check it and he'd stop—"

My doorbell rang.

"—to see you on the way. From the way he described it, he'd need to use a snowmobile to get to the scene."

My knees wobbled with relief. "Really?" I left the bathroom and headed for the front door as my portable phone rang. It was probably Gus, checking up on me. I'd sounded panicked before, I suppose. He could wait. I peeked through the spyhole in the front door but the snowmobiler stood on my stoop with his helmet on and visor down. "So is that what happened last night with the guy with the gun?"

"We think so. Is that Officer Quinn?"

"I don't know, he hasn't taken off his helmet. It's hard to tell who it is." I opened the door a crack. "ID?" I called out.

The figure turned, startled, then pointed to an insignia on his snowmobile suit. It was hard to see through the frost-starred glass of the storm door but I thought I saw "PD" on an appliquéd patch over the breast pocket. I started to open the inside door further, Barry still pressed to my ear but the snowmobiler must have seen me on my phone. He gave a little wave and started back toward the machine parked at the curb in front of my house.

"It must have been him." I watched as the person got on the sled. "So it was just a hunter last night?" I asked again. I felt a pang, thinking of a dead deer somewhere in my vicinity. "Was it a buck with one antler? Why would somebody kill a deer and just leave it?"

"I'm not sure about the antler. Maybe the hunter couldn't get the body out without being seen. You said it was illegal to hunt near your house, right?"

I locked the front door and wandered back down the hall. Outside the snowmobile roared to life as the answering machine in my den clicked on. *Jessie, are you okay? Give me a call when you can. This is Gus.* He recited a phone number. My computer monitor glowed on my desk, reminding me of why I'd called Alex Raney in the first place. "Listen, I called because Charlie gave me something."

"I beg your pardon?"

"Charlie asked me to look through a presentation he was going to give at our upcoming user conference. The CD was in my mailbox today." I described the files I'd been examining. "Do you need me to drop a copy of the disk off at your office?"

My landline phone rang again. I ignored it and left the den, going into the living room. In the distance I saw the snowmobile, moving cautiously along the trail at the bottom of the hill near the pond.

"I'd like to have a look at that disk," Raney said. "Hold on a second."

I peered out. The snowmobile had stopped and the rider was walking near the pond, looking down at the spot where the hunter had stood last night. I heard voices in the background as Raney talked to someone. Then I heard Gus Colcannon's distinctive, raspy voice as he said *She didn't tell me about it.*

Son of a bitch. Gus was sitting in the police station the whole time he was talking to me. Had he been there when he said that bit about *I promise you I'll answer all the questions I can?*

Another snowmobile engine intruded. This machine was coming down the trail from the opposite side of the pond. The rider at the bottom of the hill looked around, startled. He pulled off his helmet, probably trying to hear better. I caught a glimpse of the new sled as it made its way down the snow-packed trail from the opposite hill.

I looked down at the first rider. It wasn't Officer Quinn.

It was a woman.

"What the hell?" I raced down the hall to the den, grabbing my field glasses.

"Miss Patrokus, if you could please—"

"Hold on just a minute." I set Barry down on the desk and focused the glasses. Behind me I heard Alex Raney say something on Barry but I ignored it. The woman had short dark hair, but that was the only distinguishing feature I could make out given the shadows in the woods and the distance. As I watched she buckled the helmet back on and jumped on her machine.

I picked up Barry. "Detective Raney, there are two snowmobiles out here now. The one that I thought was Officer Quinn wasn't him."

There was a pause. "I'm sorry?"

"It was somebody else. A woman. Why did she come up to my house and then leave? How come she's at the pond?" I peeked out the window and saw the snowmobile disappearing around the bend of the hill. The other snowmobile, which had negotiated the tricky trail down the hill, was idling at the bottom near the pond. I focused the field glasses again and saw "Carver County" painted on the side of the second snowmobile. "This one must be Quinn, I can see an insignia on the snowmobile."

I heard Gus say in the background, *"Would somebody tell me what the hell is going on?"*

I knew exactly how he felt.

****

Twenty minutes later, I had another visit from

Officer Quinn. I told him about the first snowmobiler. "Maybe she was from the Park Service or whatever the local equivalent is." I stood in my driveway next to Quinn, who was perched on his snowmobile, the motor idling. I saw Norma peering out her kitchen window at us and knew I'd be getting a phone call as soon as the young policeman left.

"Could be." Quinn was red-cheeked from riding. I could tell he was one of those guys who loved winter. The town had designated snowmobile paths that paralleled the streets and they'd had a lot of use already this season. Quinn looked like he was itching to get back on the trails, especially with the fresh powder that just fell. "The deer carcass is just west of the pond, in a stand of trees. I tagged it, so if the carcass shows up at a butcher shop, I'll get a call."

I wondered what kind of tag they put on a dead animal that would do this but decided I didn't want the details. "I hope it wasn't Buck. It was so close to the house. We've got kids who play in the woods down by that pond." I saw his alarmed look. "They know the ice is soft. They're responsible kids. Did the deer have one antler?"

He looked confused. "One antler? No, I don't think so. I'd better check that pond and make sure it's posted for hunting and for thin ice."

"If you need access via my yard, feel free." I gave him the copy of the CD I'd made and he said he'd make sure to give it to Detective Raney, who was sending someone out for it. Then he bundled up and headed out.

Sure enough, five minutes later my phone rang. I reassured Norma that all was okay, reporting to her about the deer. The news would be all over the neighborhood in twenty minutes and the kids would be warned. As soon as I hung up the phone, it rang again.

"Why didn't you tell me about that CD?" Gus demanded when I picked up.

"Why didn't you tell me you were at the police station?" I made a bourbon drink, in preparation for my upcoming phone call from my father. Dad always called on Tuesdays at six o'clock so we could share a drink and conversation.

"Would you answer my question?"

"Would you answer mine?" I switched on the tiny kitchen TV. The weatherman was predicting what was obviously going to be an ominous blizzard. Menacing animated storm clouds were pushing in from North Dakota and edging their way into western Minnesota. I grabbed a discarded receipt from the trash and started making a grocery list. "Gus? What were you and Charlie talking about the other morning? Did it have something to do with all this?"

I could sense his irritation through the phone line. "I told you I can't tell you about that right now. Can't you wait?"

"How did John Slocum know you were available and for hire? It's awfully lucky that you just happened to be here in Minnesota at the right place and the right time. Where do you work, Gus? What kind of a company does this kind of work? Are you a cop? Is that it?"

"Don't you trust me, Jessie?"

He sounded hurt. A brief pang of guilt assaulted me but I squashed it ruthlessly. Now was not the time to be stupid. "I told you. Show me a badge and—"

"Man! Give a guy a break. When are you going to trust your instincts?"

I hesitated but decided I had to be honest. "I am, Gus."

There was a long pause. "Oh. I get it. Thanks a lot."

He slammed the phone down so hard it echoed. I winced. Before I had a chance to put the phone back in the charging cradle it rang again. "Hey, Snipper," Dad boomed out. I could imagine him sitting in his recliner in the living room of the townhouse he and his second wife, Karen, owned in Missouri, geographically halfway between his two kids.

"How's it going in the frozen North?" my brother Drew chimed in.

Oh, good—a family conference call. We had these occasionally. "Hey, boys," I said, sipping my bourbon. I wandered into the living room and turned down Iron Butterfly on the Bose stereo. "You won't believe what's happened."

"Tell all, sis," Drew said. "I'll bill you later."

Drew was a high-priced attorney in Houston. His

wife, Janice, was a financial consultant. Thanks to her I was sitting on a comfortable savings account. I flopped onto the couch next to Kong and unloaded with my news, happy to share with someone. I told them about Charlie, the police, the hunter, the snowmobiler, and, finally, about Gus Colcannon and his 'consulting' with the police department and the cryptic conversation I'd overheard.

"Spell that name," Drew demanded. I obliged. "I'll check on him. He sounds like a cop."

"Why would a cop be working at CodeBusters?" I sipped my drink, the alcoholic warmth seeping into my bones. "We just write software programs."

"For the government," my dad pointed out. "You said yourself that you had to get clearance to work on some of the stuff."

Drew barked out a laugh. "I'm still surprised you got it. Who'd you bribe?"

I laughed, too. It came in handy to have a brother who knew the law. My few brushes with the legal system had been minor but scary. "Thanks for helping, Drew."

"This guy sounds interesting. Are you going to go out with him?"

"I doubt it. I think he's pissed off at me again. Besides, he's just in Minnesota temporarily plus he's freshly divorced. No way am I hooking up with somebody on the rebound."

"You have to take a chance sometime," Dad said.

My husband and my mother had died within six months of each other. Dad and I had helped each other through our grief. When he remarried I felt nothing but happiness for him—and a touch of envy that he'd found someone again. "He's got two strikes against him, Dad."

"As long as it isn't three, he's still in the running. Don't be too quick to judge."

I appreciated the advice but I wasn't about to take it. "We'll see."

"I know what that means. Keep an open mind. You never know what might happen. I have to go now, Snipper, Karen has supper on the table. You call if you need anything. I'm looking forward to seeing you in a few weeks."

Our family celebrated Christmas at a resort in

Georgia during New Year's week. I was already planning the books I'd pack for my days on the beach. “Me, too. Kiss Karen for me.”

“Will do.”

Drew stayed on the line after Dad left. “Are you sure there's nothing to worry about with the hunter and the snowmobile?”

“The police don't seem worried, so I'm not.” I drained my glass and stood, debating on a refill. “I think it's all coincidence.”

“I don't know.” His doubt was evident in his voice. “I'll check on this Colcannon guy and let you know what I find. And hey—listen to Dad. It's time you found somebody, Snip.”

“I'm doing just fine.”

“I know you are but…” He paused. “I want to see you happy again, that's all.”

I was suddenly misty-eyed at the sincerity in his voice. My little brother wasn't often so affectionate. Whenever he was, it caught me off-guard. “I'll keep an open mind. But not so open my common sense falls out.”

“Good. And don't forgot—Andrea has her heart set on that Psychedelic Sixties wycinanki.”

“I'm working on it as we speak.”

“Take care. I'll call you tomorrow with my report on your interesting gentleman.”

“Thanks, Drew.” I hung up the phone, knowing it wouldn't matter what he found. I had the feeling there would be no hot dates with Gus Colcannon in my future.

Chapter Seven

I didn't see Gus at work the next morning nor did I hear him in his cube. I assumed he'd find me and demand to see Charlie's CD, but by noon he hadn't showed up. I set up a test program to run through Charlie's files but nothing odd turned up except for a tricky bit of coding that commented out entries in a database table. It was an intricate subroutine and very elegantly done. I made a note on Barry to run more tests using the code on some of the large data files I was using for Nelson's latest project.

Denise and I went out for lunch at the Food Court at the local mall. I told her about the snowmobiler, the hunter, and the CD Charlie had given me.

"Are the files on the disk anything he was going to demo at the conference?" she asked as we sat in the noisy space, crowded with holiday shoppers and business people like ourselves, on break from their Cube Worlds.

"They must be." I dumped hot sauce on the last of my taco. "I've run them and they're fine. They don't do much, just insert and remove information into a database table."

"Like that stuff you're testing for Nelson?"

"Yeah. I don't know why Charlie wanted to demo them. They're nothing special." Her mention of Nelson's code triggered a memory but before I could capture it, the elusive fragment vanished. "The other files are promo things for the programs we've been working on lately."

"I heard from Stacy—you know, Bob Madison's administrative assistant? I heard that the police said Charlie was murdered."

I choked on the bite in my mouth. "Really?" I'd suspected it, of course, but confirmation like this was still shocking. "How? Was it poison?"

She wadded up the paper holding the remains of her baked potato, tucking it into her empty drink cup. "I don't know. Stacy wasn't sure. Bob told her that the company wasn't culpable, though, so it must not have been poison. Otherwise somebody would try to nail the potluck on us."

I sat back, relieved. I'd had a nagging worry for days that something I'd done, even by accident, might have hurt Charlie. "Surely they'll tell us soon, won't they? I'd think they'd make an announcement."

"Or maybe you can ask him. He seems to have an in with the cops."

I followed her gaze. Sitting at a table across the Food Court was Gus and two women. The older woman was tall and slender, dressed in a soft-looking white sweater and navy stretch pants that showed off her long legs. She reminded me of that thin blonde from the movie *White Christmas*, the one with the impossibly tiny waist. The other was younger, maybe in her late twenties, with thick black hair and a smile just like Gus's.

The older one reached across the table and snatched a French fry from the pile in front of Gus. He laughed and slapped her hand. The girl said something that made them all laugh. I swallowed around the surprise that choked me. "That must be his wife," I said in as non-committal a voice as I could manage. "Maybe that's his kid."

"I thought he was divorced." Denise's sharp brown eyes zeroed in on my face. "You said he was divorced."

I shrugged. "I thought so, too."

"He looks pretty friendly with someone he's divorced from."

Slow anger burned in my gut. Or maybe it was the extra-spicy taco. Whatever it was, it made me nauseous. Denise, old friend that she is, saw it. "What?"

"He asked me out."

She looked at Gus then to me. "He did? When?"

"Last night." I described Gus's assertion that he'd confide in me if I just gave him a little more time. "He said he wanted to make me dinner tomorrow night. He said he was busy tonight." I fumed, ramming the greasy taco papers into my empty paper cup. "It looks like he's busy, all right." I tapped a finger on the table. *Love in Vain* by the Rolling Stones. Love? I shook my head angrily. "Obviously he's a guy with a waiting list."

"I told you that other babe is probably nothing," Denise said. "But this one..." She frowned. "I don't know. They look chummy."

"He said the other one was a co-worker or something."

"There you go." Denise peeked past me. "I'll be curious to see what he says about this one." I shook my head. "You're not going to ask him? I thought you guys had a date?"

"Nope. I doubt I'll talk to him again. He got all pissed off when I said I wanted some answers and an ID. I don't think our date is still on." Now that I'd seen him with yet another woman, I *knew* the date wasn't still on. I didn't want to get involved with anybody who had an ex he was so happy with. I stood up, stealing another glance. At that moment Gus looked up and saw me. The shocked look—the widening of his eyes behind his glasses and the way his cheeks got red—told me everything I needed to know. I jerked my eyes away from his. "Let's drop by Radio Shack. I want to see if they have that game thing my nephew wanted for Christmas."

"Good. I need to go to the bookstore and it's on the way." Denise pulled out her ever-present shopping list. "My daughter wants this book from Oprah's Book Club."

I made a face. "It'll be depressing."

Denise laughed. "Lisa will laugh it off. Kids that age don't know from depression."

No shit, I thought as we joined the crowds. *Jingle Bell Rock* chimed from my purse, telling me Barry was paging me. I glanced at the caller ID. It was Gus. I turned it off. Denise gave me an inquiring look.

"Nothing important," I lied.

****

My brain went on autopilot all afternoon. I don't know why I felt so hurt. What did it matter to me if Gus had a wife or ex-wife plus a girlfriend? Yeah, yeah, yeah—he said the girlfriend was a work colleague. I didn't believe him. Women like that had jobs in modeling or sales. They didn't work in companies that did...

That made me wonder exactly what it Gus did. I'd seen him hanging out with programmers, sitting in meetings, and talking to other people, but I hadn't seen him sitting at a computer, working.

I looked at my test machine, a clunky desktop model enhanced with more memory and speed. It was churning through test routines as I sat and would email me the results in another hour or two. My laptop was occupied with running the scripts I'd set up to verify Nelson's code. I suppose it didn't look like I was working since I was busily snipping on my design for my niece, but in fact I was working. Sort of.

I peered out into the atrium, looking through the windows at the outside world. The sky was clouding up and the first telltale flakes were starting to drift downward. If the forecasters could be believed, we were in for a whopper of a storm overnight. I maintained a healthy skepticism honed by years of faulty weather reports but I wasn't an idiot. I'd stop for some groceries and fill up the car with gas before heading home that night.

At two o'clock I had a status meeting with Nelson, Brian, and four other programmers in the Lake Minnetonka conference room. All eyes turned to the bank of windows that showed the snow falling outside. "YASS," Brian muttered.

We all nodded. Yet Another Snow Storm. He smiled at me and winked. He was only a few inches taller than me and stocky, with wiry black hair, a beaky nose, and dark blue eyes behind horn-rimmed glasses. He was almost cute, in a nerdy way.

I hadn't seen Nelson Scott since Charlie died. He wasn't a handsome man to start with, but now he looked ill. I suppose he'd caught the Bug that always seemed to drift around CubeLand. His thick brown hair looked grayer than a few days ago. Nelson was about my age, in his early fifties, but his pasty complexion, five o'clock shadow, and bags under his eyes made him look like an old man today.

"I heard there's a Memorial Service set up for Charlie for Friday," Gary said. He'd worked closely with Charlie before Charlie had transferred to TieLand. "I'll send out email about it. I thought we could go as a group."

"We should send flowers, too, I suppose." I knew Charlie and his wife hadn't had children, so I wasn't sure who was planning things. "Where is the service going to be held?"

"Are you about ready to wrap up testing, Jessie?" Nelson's change of subject left no doubt that he wanted us to move on to business matters.

I looked up in surprise from the square I was snipping. "I thought I had two more days. John told me we weren't shipping until—"

"The deadline changed." Nelson's voice was flat.

Deadlines always changed but one thing that never changed was testing. Nothing released until Quality Assurance said it did. "I don't know," I said. "I just started trolling the code. There are some complicated routines in there that I wanted to revisit and re-test."

"There probably won't be time. Just check the overall functionality. Don't worry about the timings or efficiency. You need to move on to the Fairfield project, they want that as—"

"Are you sure?" I was snipping mulberry paper, which had a high rag content so it was tough to get a clean cut. I focused on the pattern in my hand. It wasn't until I felt the silence in the room that I raised my head. Nelson was glaring at me, his face mottled with anger. "What?"

"It would be nice if you could concentrate on one task at a time. I'd like to think I have your attention."

"I can do two things at once." I'd been snipping designs for years. Some people crocheted or knitted during meetings. It was no big deal. Everybody knew you didn't need one hundred percent of your brain during status meetings.

"But not very efficiently. Wrap up testing on the database project and get ready to take over Fairfield."

"I don't think that's a good idea," Brian said. "I just finished my part of the interface and Jessie will need time to test it thoroughly."

"That's not your decision, Brian, it's mine."

"But I don't—"

"Quit defending her. Jessie doesn't need or want your help."

All eyes swung to Nelson. "I don't appreciate being put on the spot like this," I said. "You know we have to pass government standards in order to ship that code. If we don't then—"

"Wrap it up, Jessie. Now. I'll expect test results on my desk tomorrow morning." Nelson's face was hard and I saw rage boiling beneath the surface.

I looked out the window, where fat snowflakes were spiraling down. "That might be tough. I may end up working at home tomorrow."

"Don't."

"That's not company policy." This was from Lim, another programmer. "Company policy states that in inclement weather we can work at home unless we have meetings or—"

"We have contracts to meet. Forget policy." Nelson glared at me. "Do you understand?"

I stood up, my knees shaking. "Sure. I understand." I made for the door.

"We're not done with this meeting yet."

I turned. "I am. I have testing to do." I left before he could speak, my hands trembling so badly I could barely fumble the door open. What the hell had gotten into Nelson? Had his temporary promotion to manager awakened a beast in him?

I stumbled into my cube and sank into my chair, staring at the test results on my screen and trying to order my chaotic thoughts. I had two days of testing left, no matter what Nelson said. And I wasn't going to lie when it came time to sign off on the project.

I turned to my test machine and queued up two more test programs that could run overnight—as long as the power stayed on. Then I focused on my laptop, making a to-do list. If I worked all night I could make a dent in what remained. I glanced over my shoulder at the skylights and the windows that formed the atrium. Snow was coming down heavier now. I'd probably already missed my chance to make a clean getaway. I settled my headphones on my head and put *The Wall* in my CD player. Pink Floyd was good for crisis times.

Twenty minutes later Brian peered around my entryway. I pulled off my headphones. "That was a good demonstration of why Nelson shouldn't be a manager." He leaned on my cube doorway, his glance flickering to my computers and the screens I had open. “You're not going to try to wrap up the testing tonight, are you? You need to get going, the roads will be hell.”

“You heard Nelson. I need to make a good stab at this. Maybe I'll stay here tonight, it might be easier than trying to get home.”

He pushed his glasses back up on his nose then jammed his hands into his pockets, hunching his shoulders. “I hope you can test my code.” I thought he'd scuff at the carpet with a boot in a minute. “I'm sure it needs it.”

“I'll try.” Interface testing was always time-consuming and couldn't be relegated to canned programs. I'd need to sit at the monitor and stare at the screen, making notes on what I found. I always put it off because it was so tedious.

“Where's your buddy?”

“Hmm?” I followed his glance to the cube wall. “Gus? He's not my buddy.”

“I've seen you guys talking a lot the last couple of days.” Brian's dark blue eyes were guileless but I thought I saw a hint of suspicion there.

“We've been talking about Charlie. You know, about what happened.” I grabbed my test machine keyboard and typed some commands as one program wrapped up. “I don't think he's here today, or if he is, I haven't seen him.”

“He's here,” Brian said. “I saw him with John earlier.”

“Well, I haven't talked to him.” I swiveled back to my laptop. “I don't mean to be rude, Brian, but I've got a heap of work to do.”

He nodded and pushed away from the wall. “Don't stay here too late tonight. It could get messy.” As he turned, he paused. “Is your friend okay? That guy from the potluck?”

It took me a second to figure out what he was asking. “Paul? I guess so. I think they caught the mix-up in time.” I glanced up from my computer screen. Brian looked confused. “I haven't talked to him in a while, but I did check to make sure he was okay when I thought maybe I'd screwed up my labels.”

“I thought you and he were, well, you know—close.”

Brian's shoulders were so hunched he looked like he was shrugging.

"Nah. We just went out a couple of times." My computer pinged and I turned to view the results scrolling past on the screen.

"But Charlie said that you and he were—"

My head snapped around. "Charlie said what?"

Brian turned away, his face red. "Nothing. He must have been joking. Talk to you later."

I stared after him then was distracted by the sight of the snow lashing against the windows in the atrium. I could barely see the freeway beyond the windows. It was, indeed, going to be a hell commute.

An hour later I pushed away from my desk and headed for the kitchen. I needed some coffee if I was going to stay all night. John Slocum was standing at the windows that looked out onto the freeway. He turned when I entered. "What are you still doing here?"

I joined him at the window. The road was snarled with traffic. What had once been three lanes was down to two and just one in spots. The plows couldn't compete with blowing snow and traffic. "Nelson wants that government database project wrapped up by tomorrow. I'll probably just stay here tonight and work."

John stared at me in amazement. He was a small man, just an inch or two taller than me with large brown eyes and a big, booming laugh. "That's crazy. We got an extension on that project. They're not expecting it for three weeks."

"What?"

He made a shooing motion. "Go. Get while you can. And don't worry about coming in tomorrow. From what the weathermen are saying, this is a bad one."

Stress drained out, leaving me lighter than air. "Really?"

"Go." He smiled at me. "I only live a mile away so I'm not worried. Heck, I can walk home if I have to. You're out in Victoria, aren't you?" I nodded. He looked back at the freeway. "At least you can take city streets."

"Thanks, John." I hurried back to my cube to pack up. I was stuffing Barry into its traveling case when Nelson appeared in my doorway.

"Where are you going?"

I unhooked my laptop from the docking port. "John told me to take off."

"And I told you to stay." Nelson was glaring at me, his hands flexing. If I didn't know better, I'd have said he wanted to hit me.

I took a step back in surprise, my snipping-paper cascading to the floor. That was the final straw. "No offense, Nelson, but John's a VP and you're just a manager. What John says goes." I bent to pick up the paper. "I'll finish all the testing but not tonight."

When I straightened, I was surprised to see a look not of anger, as I expected, but fear in his eyes. "I told you we have to ship. The deadlines changed and—"

"We got an extension," John said from behind Nelson. He edged his way into my cube around Nelson, who was partially blocking the entrance. "I told you about that." His eyes were sympathetic. "Nelson, I'm sorry about your brother and the stress it's causing for you, but you need to focus on work. You can't ask Jessie to stay tonight. The roads are terrible. She'll have trouble getting home as it is."

"My brother has nothing to do with this." Nelson's face whitened so fast I was afraid he'd pass out.

"I know what it's like to worry about a family member," John said in a soothing voice. "You're letting it interfere with your work, though. Why don't we talk about it?" He smiled apologetically at me. "Jessie needs to get on the road."

Nelson's gaze flickered first to me then to my laptop. I decided to take advantage of the distraction and slipped my laptop into its case. By the time I'd suited up for the outside world, John and Nelson were walking away, talking in low voices. I beat a retreat, slipping out the back door and down the stairs, glad to be away.

What was normally a twenty-minute drive took me more than an hour with two narrowly missed slides into the ditch, almost joining other cars I saw there. I stocked up at the grocery store then spent another excruciating thirty minutes negotiating the mile of dark, slick roads to my house.

As I approached the turn for my street, I saw a

pickup truck nosed off in the ditch, hazard lights flashing. Some testosterone-enhanced driver probably tried to take the curve too fast. The front of the truck was tilted forward and I didn't see anyone inside. I considered stopping but didn't dare lest I join it in the ditch. I crept along the last quarter-mile then turned on the hill that led to my house and inched the car downward. There was a sharp turn at the bottom and it was easy to slide.

I was just starting to breathe a sigh of relief when my headlights illuminated a man trudging down the road in front of me. I flashed my brights at him and he careened off to one side, obviously surprised—and snow-covered. It looked like he'd taken a tumble because he was white from head to foot.

There were only two houses at the bottom of the road, Tom's and mine. I slid around the corner and into my driveway, turning in the seat to look back at the figure barely visible through the swirling snow. He was walking with his head down and hands jammed deeply into his coat pockets. It made my bones ache just to watch him. I could tell from the stiff way he moved he was cold through and through.

I drove into the garage and was just getting out of the car when the man walked up my drive. My motion light came on and I peered through the dense snow.

"Jessie," he called out, his voice barely audible above the wind. He walked into the light and I saw who it was.

Chapter Eight

"Gus, what are you doing here?" I hurried toward him.

"My truck went off the road up there." He jerked his head to one side. "I couldn't get it out." From the looks of him he'd tried shoveling or maybe pushing—and failed. He was coated with snow from his hatless head to his soaked jeans.

"Come inside." I grabbed my laptop and purse from the back seat of my car then led the way up the steps into the kitchen. He followed, pausing to kick snow off his boots then standing on the entry rug, shivering. I took one look at his white face, ice-coated hair and canvas gloves then made a fast decision. "Get out of those clothes," I said, dropping my bags on the floor.

"Huh?" He stared at me, his eyes and his glasses fogged with cold.

"Get undressed." I kicked off my snow clogs and went into the laundry room, pulling down two bath sheets from the linen closet. "Here." I thrust them at him. "Wrap these around you. You need a warm shower. I'll toss your clothes in the dryer." He stood there like a snow-covered statute. "Oh, for heaven's sake." I dropped the towels on the boot bench and unbuttoned his coat, which was heavy and stiff with snow. His flannel shirt underneath was wet at the collar and I winced when I saw his blotchy, chapped skin. I tugged off the coat and started working on the shirt when he seemed to wake up.

"I can do that," he said through chattering teeth.

"Good. You get undressed and I'll find you some clothes." I went through the kitchen to the hall, pausing in the bathroom to turn on the shower and adjust the temperature. Then I went into the spare room closet for Bill's old XL sweatpants and his Monty Python "*It's Just a Flesh Wound"* sweatshirt, thankfully clean and folded. I dug out the socks I'd been meaning to use for my Sock Monkey projects and put them and the sweats in the bathroom.

Gus was staggering down the hall, wincing at the cold floor. He had the towels clutched around him and was visibly shaking, looking around uncertainly. His bare legs and feet were white with big splotches of dark red skin. I hoped it wasn't frostbite.

"This way." I shoved him into the bathroom. "Don't change the temperature," I warned as I closed the door behind him. "Don't make it hotter."

"Okay." I heard the shower curtain open then clink shut on its rings. Satisfied that he wasn't going to die on me, I went back to my bedroom and stripped out of my work clothes, switching to Pink Floyd flannel lounge pants and my "*Chocolate: The catnip of the female world"* sweatshirt.

I paused at the bathroom as I walked back to the kitchen. "Are you okay?"

"Yeah." He sounded tired. It was probably the aftermath of almost freezing to death. "I'll need to get a tow."

"Not tonight. There are a billion accidents and they were closing the Interstate as I came home. You're stuck here, sorry."

"Maybe I can get the truck out once I warm up."

I moved down the hall. "We'll talk later. I'm going to put some soup on to heat." He said something but I didn't catch it. I went into the kitchen where Kong sat like an implacable black Buddha. I could almost see the thought balloon over his head: *Food. Now.* Faye looked warily around Kong's bulk at the bathroom door where the Boogie Man was showering.

"Okay, okay." I dished out the Kitty Kibble then grabbed some chili out of the freezer and nuked it to start the thaw process. After stacking my CD player I unloaded the groceries and turned my attention to making biscuits.

Gus came out as I was setting the table. His hair was fluffy, like he'd toweled it. The sweatpants that I wore over my exercise shorts to yoga class fit him nicely. "Are you okay? Did you warm up?"

“Yeah. The shower did the trick.” His gaze swept my small, plain kitchen, resting on the two framed Lowicz wycinanka on the wall near the window. “What's that?” He examined the intricate multi-colored silhouette scenes, one the classic 'rooster and heart' repetitive design and the other a multi-layered flower. Each was nearly a foot tall and almost as wide.

“That's wycinanki,” I said, pulling biscuits out of the oven. “My grandmother did them. That's a particular kind, made with multiple layers of paper.”

“How did she...” He stared closer. “Good God, that's amazing. She made all the different layers and then glued them together?”

“Yep. They're her design, too.” I dumped the biscuits onto a plate. “I told you, it's an art form. It's not just snowflakes and teddy bears.” I saw his chagrined look. “So did you take the turn too fast?”

“Nope.” He watched as I dipped out the chili. “Did you cook that?”

“I told you—I know how to cook. I just don't like to.” I handed him the soup mug and nodded towards the dining room. “Go ahead and sit down.”

I dished out my own mug then joined him. He spooned cautiously at the chili. “This is good.” His face was flushed above his beard, his high cheekbones tinged with color.

“How fast were you going? That curve can be bad in snow.”

“I was going about two miles an hour. I wasn't sure where the street was for your house so I was looking for the turn. Then I saw a stop sign and slid.”

“Stop sign?” I buttered a biscuit as I reconstructed where I'd seen the truck. “There aren't any stop signs there.”

“Yeah, there is. A small one.”

I grinned. “That's a snowmobile sign.”

“What?” He stared at me, his hazel eyes incredulous. “Those little signs I saw?”

I nodded. “They mark where people can ride. They're smaller, closer to the ground.”

“I thought it was a regular sign. I could barely see anything between the wind and the snow.” He glanced past me to the windows that overlooked the deck. “It felt like something maybe snapped. I couldn't see anything, there was too much snow and it was too dark.”

“Snapped?” I added some Tabasco to my bowl then shoved the bottle to him. He added a generous amount.

“Hard to describe. It felt like the wheel twisted all of a sudden. I'll need to call a tow.” I started to speak but he didn't give me a chance. “I know, I know, nobody will come out tonight. But at least I'll get on the waiting list.” His eyes flickered to the living room. “The couch looks comfortable.”

“I've got a spare room.” I stifled the brief disappointment I'd felt at his immediate assumption he'd sleep on the couch. Then I gave myself a mental slap on the head. “What the hell were you doing out here, anyway?”

“I tried calling you all day.”

“You did?”

“Check your messages.”

I thought of Barry, turned off all afternoon. “I thought you had plans tonight.”

“I canceled them.”

“You didn't answer my question. Why are you out here?”

“You have a real problem with trust, you know that?” He buttered a biscuit with angry little stabs. “Listen to yourself—you're not exactly making me feel welcome.”

I dropped my spoon with a clatter. “I have a problem with trust? Me? What about you, Mr. 'I'm here on a secret assignment'?” The accumulated pressure of the day started to bubble up and began a slow eruption. “Man, between you and Nelson, I'm on the way to having one of the more stressful days of my year.”

“Nelson? Nelson Scott?”

The sharp look in his eyes told me I'd struck a nerve. “Yeah. He read me the riot act before I left work about how I had to wrap up my testing. Luckily for me John Slocum was around and told him to back off.”

“What do you mean, wrap up your testing?” Gus bit into his biscuit, his eyes never leaving my face.

“He told me to skip going deeper into the code. Apparently this new contract coming up is important or something."

"But John told you to stay on the government testing?"

"Yeah. And you're lucky he did, too. Otherwise you'd be sitting on my front step in a blizzard because I'd still be at the office, working." I glanced at the windows. "Even Minnesotans don't go out on nights like this. I wonder what the deal is with Nelson's brother."

Gus's face stilled then he resumed spooning his chili. "What about his brother?"

"John mentioned something about problems with Nelson's brother. I thought maybe that's why Nelson was acting like such an asshole."

"I don't know." Gus took a grape from the dish on the table. I was beginning to recognize his stalling tactics. He knew something about Nelson that he wasn't sharing. It was just one more secret Gus Colcannon was keeping from me.

"I came here because I wanted to apologize," he said, spooning at his chili. "I know how it looked today, at the mall." When I started to speak he barreled on. "Elaine is—was—my sister-in-law. That's who I was lunching with. Elaine and Darla, my niece."

"Your sister-in-law?" I didn't try to hide my surprise. I had thought he was alone in town. Then I remembered his ex-wife. "Your wife's sister?"

He hid his surprised look by focusing on his chili. "Yeah. My ex-wife's sister."

"I figured she was your ex," I said. "Something about the way you guys were acting toward each other made me think—" I shrugged. "I don't know—you seemed close."

"Why do you think I'm carrying a torch for my ex?"

I couldn't interpret his expression. Confusion, amusement, and—anger? Exasperation? "You've only been divorced a few months. Nobody gets over an ex that fast."

"What do you mean, a few months?"

I sighed, praying for patience. "You said you moved here for her job then you got divorced. And this is your first winter."

"Why do you think it's my first winter here?"

"Look at your clothes." I gestured toward the laundry

room. "You don't have a warm winter coat or boots, you don't have a hat and those gloves are fine for driving but they're shit when it comes to keeping out the cold. If you were here last winter, you'd have bought winter gear. Therefore, you've only been here since spring at the earliest. That means you're freshly divorced."

"Uh—" He seemed stumped by my logic.

"You don't owe me any explanations." I hurried on, wondering why he looked so confused. "Except one thing, maybe."

"What's that?" His voice was cautious.

"How did Charlie die?"

Gus sat back. "Do you ever stay on one subject at a time? We've bounced between about a dozen topics here in the last five minutes."

"So?" I drained my beer. "Want a refill?"

He looked at the windows. "Yeah. I'm not going anywhere."

I went into the kitchen, calling back over my shoulder, "How did Charlie die? Nobody's said anything. I figure you and that cop are such buddies, you should know."

Gus waited until I came back to the table to answer. "He was stabbed."

I sat down with a thud. "What?" My thoughts were whirling. "You mean it wasn't an accident? He didn't get sick and—"

"It doesn't appear that way."

"But there wasn't any blood, was there?"

"He bled internally."

"What did they use? There wasn't a knife around, at least not a sharp one. It's an office, for cryin' out loud. We just have bread knives and plastic silverware." This was surreal. People didn't get stabbed in high-rise office buildings in suburbs in the middle of the day. They got stabbed in gang killings or in prisons.

Gus held out a hand and I passed him the two bottles of Rolling Rock, which he opened with the church key on the table. He slid one across to me. "It was a small skewer, like the kind used for barbecues. Whoever did it knew just where to stab him."

"So it was just coincidence about my brownies." I

absorbed the words as I sipped my beer. "And it wasn't someone at work who did it." I blew out a sigh of relief.

He paused, beer bottle upraised. "Why do you say that?"

"I doubt we have any assassins on the payroll."

He set down his beer, untasted. "You know, you should be a cop. You're making a lot of good assumptions here."

"I'm a tester. That's what we do. We look at a product and figure out if it's doing what it should. If it doesn't, we figure that out, too." I thought of Charlie's code, which I'd skimmed the day before. There was something in there that needed to be figured out. There was something there… The thought slipped away. I sipped my beer, surprised how relieved I felt. "I suppose you can't tell me any more." I saw the answer in the way he avoided my gaze. "That's okay."

He raised his eyes to look directly at me. "No, it's not okay." His voice was weary, like he was holding back some emotion. "I owe you a lot of explanations, about what happened to Charlie, about me, about—" He hesitated for a long second, "—about a lot of things. I promised you and I meant it. I'll explain everything I can as soon as I can."

Barry chimed out *Rockin' Around the Christmas Tree* from my bag, still on the bench in the laundry room. Gus shot me an accusing look. "I just turned it on," I said. "It'll bounce to voice mail. Do you want more chili?" I got up. "I've got more. You—"

He grabbed my hand, pulling me to a halt beside him at the table. His hand easily encircled my wrist as he gazed at me over the tops of his glasses. "What are you running from?"

I tugged my arm away from him. "Nothing."

He stood, pushing the chair back so he was standing very close to me. "Are you sure?"

I couldn't think clearly. He was too near. I could see his chest rising and falling in the faded sweatshirt. If I peeked up—I did and saw him watching me, serious and searching. "You're as good as married." It was the first thing I could think of.

"I'm not married." His hand moved to cup my face.

“I'm not in love with anyone. I'm not living with anyone. I'm not seeing anyone.”

“But you're just divorced and—”

He bent his head and kissed me.

My first thought was, *This tickles.* I'd forgotten what it was like to kiss a man with facial hair. Gus's mustache and beard were soft but I felt the little hairs on my chin as his lips moved on mine. My arms automatically went around his neck and I was pulled against him, feeling the long, hard expanse of his body on mine. His lips were firm, as were other parts of him—male parts that I remembered with aching memory. Warmth, need, loneliness, longing all swamped me. It had been so long since I'd had this feeling, it had been so long since I'd felt this overwhelming need to touch and be touched. I longed for—

My Blackberry rang again, dragging me back to reality. “Leave it,” he whispered, his beard soft against my neck. “Jessie, leave it.”

“No.” Common sense intruded. “I need to answer it.”

“Jessie.” He held my face pinned between his hands, staring at me with an intensity that made me want to cry.

“I can't, Gus.” I prayed he'd see my explanation in my eyes. “I can't.”

He released me. I went to the laundry room, sick with longing and regret. I had to lean against the wall to fumble in my bag for Barry.

“Jessie?”

I took a long, shuddering breath. “Hey, Drew.” I sank down onto my boot bench, forcing my tears away. “I forgot you might call.”

“I heard you were getting a blizzard.”

“Yeah, we are.” I glanced out into the kitchen. Gus was clearing the table, bringing the dirty dishes out to the sink. Kong was watching him from his spot near the heating vent, obviously curious about this unknown male in his territory.

“Listen, I ran a check on your Gus Colcannon.”

Gus leaned down and patted Kong, who sighed with pleasure and rolled over, exposing his plump tummy. Laughing softly, Gus obliged with belly rubs while Kong stretched. I envied my cat his simple pleasure, wishing I could so easily expose my affections. I turned my gaze to the window and the streetlights flickering in the blowing snow outside. "What did you find?"

"He's in the government, but I couldn't pin down exactly what he does. He's a 'Nam vet and he's ex-career Army intelligence, an oxymoron if ever there was one. When he got out he worked for the FBI for a while, and now he's on so-called special assignment."

My depression started to give way to curiosity. "What's that mean?"

"I'm still checking. I've got a buddy at the State Department, with contacts in the Pentagon. I asked him to dig for me. My guess is Colcannon is working for the cops or a government agency. What is your company working on? Anything big for the government?"

I looked at my laptop, still sitting in its case on the boot bench. "Maybe." I remembered the 'ghost program' Charlie had included on his CD. Did that have something to do with it? "I'm not sure, Drew. I'll have to do some checking."

"Okay. I can tell you this for sure—he's single, he's fifty-four, and he lives in Las Cruces, New Mexico. What the hell is he doing in Minnesota in the middle of a blizzard?" Drew laughed. I wondered what he'd think if he knew Gus was sharing the blizzard with me.

"Yeah, how about that?" I saw Gus's boots, sitting next to mine on the Welcome mat. The prosaic sight made my heart constrict. "Listen, I've got to go. Thanks for doing that."

"No problem. I'll call as soon as I find out any more. Stay warm there, Snipper."

"Will do. Thanks, Drew." I closed Barry's case and leaned back on the boot bench, still so shaky I wasn't sure I could stand.

"Everything okay?"

Gus was in the doorway, looking at me. I nodded and got up. "Yeah, fine."

He moved toward me. "Jessie, I—"

I held up my hands. "No, Gus. It's not going to happen."

He stopped as though I'd hit him. "Why? What's wrong?"

I brushed by him, going into the kitchen. “I don't need the grief, Gus.”

“Huh?”

I whirled to face him. “You're temporary, remember? You're moving home as soon as you can.” I hurried on before he could protest. “I've had enough grief to last a lifetime, Gus. I'm not going to set myself up for more.” I picked up a glass and stared at it, struggling to articulate what I was feeling. “I'm not good at casual relationships and I'm not going to let myself get involved with somebody who isn't going to be around long.”

I saw the anger and exasperation in his eyes. “Can't you just trust me about this? Please? I'm not going to hurt you. I don't have to...be temporary.”

I set the glass down so hard I heard it crack. “What's that supposed to mean?”

“I can't tell you.” He crossed the kitchen in a couple of strides. “Jessie, please.”

I met his eyes. “I can't.”

He held my gaze for a long minute then he closed his eyes before opening them again. I saw the sadness I was feeling reflected there. “From the minute I met you, I knew I wanted to get to know you better.” His laugh was shaky and soft. “You walked into my cube and started talking to me and I sat there in shock. You just so—you're just so—” He shook his head, his face confused, angry, and sad, all at once. “I'm sorry you can't trust me.”

I considered two different responses, knowing that I was making a commitment one way or the other.

“I'm sorry, too.”

Chapter Nine

His face seemed to freeze. “I think I'll check on the truck.”

I recognized the need for escape when I saw it so I didn't argue. “I've got a hat you can use.” I went to the boot bench and pulled out a warm hat, scarf, and heavy gardening gloves I wore over my knit gloves when I shoveled. I held them out to Gus.

“Thanks.”

“Your clothes are probably dry.” I gestured toward the laundry room. “If you want to change, just toss your jeans back in when you come back.”

“If I can get the truck out, I'll leave.”

I heard the controlled anger in his voice. I put a restraining hand on his arm. “You're welcome to stay. Don't take chances. It's bad out there.”

He turned on me but his expression softened when I met his eyes. “Okay.”

I stepped back into the kitchen. A few minutes later I heard the door from the laundry room to the garage open then slam shut. I peeked out the kitchen window and saw him struggling up the hill, leaning into the wind with the hat pulled low and my scarf high around his face. I put a pot of coffee on to perk and busied myself with kitchen cleanup. I didn't want to think about what had just happened. I didn't want to examine my actions. I'd made a choice. Now I had to stick with it.

Thirty minutes later he came back in. I was hunkered on the living room couch under my afghan, watching my little black and white portable TV because my satellite reception was on the fritz. I had my snipping tray on my lap. I was working on Andrea's wycinanki, but wasn't having much luck. I'd given up on the Yellow Submarine and was aiming for a collage of silhouettes:

Hendrix, Joplin, and Morrison in a variety of papers with the Fillmore in the background. My *Rolling Stone Illustrated History of Rock and Roll* was open on the coffee table for reference.

I heard Gus fix himself a mug of coffee while chatting in a low voice with Kong. Then both males came into the living room.

"Any luck?"

Gus sat down in the chair opposite me where Kong took up position on his lap. "Not tonight," Gus admitted. "I could barely find it again. But it does seem like the snow is letting up. Maybe once the plows come out I can get a tow."

I nodded. "I called triple-A for you and got you on the list. Was that okay?"

"Great. Thanks."

I nodded toward the little TV. "They're saying we got about eight inches, with maybe an inch or two more to come. Apparently it's blowing and drifting pretty bad, though. Most schools are canceled tomorrow. I'll work at home, now that John said I could." I considered the paper in my hand and said casually, "So you don't know what's wrong with Nelson's brother?"

He shook his head. "Nope."

Another lie. I wondered what else he was fudging the truth about. "How long have you been here in Minnesota?"

He sipped his coffee. "Just a month or two. I'm borrowing an apartment in the West Wind complex, over by the office. I wasn't sure how long I'd be here."

I considered this. "So you were lying about coming here because your wife had a job?"

He almost choked. "Let's just say I wasn't being strictly honest."

I counted to five, which was as far as I could get without the need for movement overtaking me. I got up, balancing my tray. "I made up the bed in the spare room downstairs. There's an attached bathroom so you'll be all set."

"Jessie."

I paused, looking back at him.

"I *will* explain it all to you."

He looked sincere—and pissed off. I shrugged. "Whenever." I went into my den and sat at the desk, staring at my laptop screen. Nothing made sense any more. Gus had kissed me, I wanted him, he was lying, I was afraid to be with him—nothing made sense.

Faye looked up from her spot on the ratty old blanket on the futon where she'd fled at the sight of the Strange Man. I knew how she felt. I longed to bury my head in the blankets, too, and ignore Gus's intrusion into my life. I wasn't sure if I was angry or sad—angry that he continued to lie or sad that I'd turned him down. I didn't want to examine my motives or his. I turned my attention to my computer. Maybe work would help put things in perspective.

I had an email from John Slocum: *Jessie, you know you can work at home tomorrow if the roads are as bad as I think they'll be. Don't feel you need to come in. I spoke with Nelson.*

I was impressed. John was a V.P. but he'd taken the time to deal with my problem. I replied with a quick *Thanks, John. The roads stink out here so I'll stay home.* He wouldn't read his email until morning, but I wanted to let him know I appreciated his intervention. I considered telling him that Gus Colcannon was sitting on my couch but decided against it. I trusted John, but rumors had a way of getting out. I had taken enough teasing about my brief coffee date with Brian as it was. I scanned the rest of my email but it was all office business or the usual SPAM. My online admirer had either given up or was taking a break.

I brought up the test programs I'd run that afternoon and checked the results. The overall program did what we'd promised and the timings were on the mark, but several pieces of Nelson's main program needed to be examined. I extracted the code fragments in question and brought them up on my screen in separate windows.

Something looked familiar. I skimmed through the dense lines of code, looking for keywords or recognizable blocks. The basic logic of the first fragment seemed to ring a bell in the depths of my brain. I peered closer, running my hands into my hair and tugging to jumpstart my thought processes. I'd seen logic like this recently.

Granted, there was a limited amount of logic variety in computer programs—all programs were, at heart, a series of sequential instructions with branches to other routines at various points in the program. But something about this was like something...

I heard Gus speaking in the living room. I got up, careful not to let my chair squeak, and tiptoed to the door. He'd turned off the TV, so the only competition his voice had was the wind outside.

"I'm going to need a car. My truck is completely messed up." There was a pause then he said, "I know. It must have been done after I left CodeBusters but before I got here. That means someone was following me." Pause again. "Grocery store, liquor store—just a couple of stops. It was hard to tell in the dark, but I think the axle was twisted. That means somebody—"

He paused again, probably listening. I crept into the hall, straining to hear.

"Look, I know that, but I thought it was important to see her and find out what she knows about Charlie Gordon's files. I'm getting the feeling she's crucial to all this, more than we suspected. I thought it was worth a trip to the boonies to talk to her." He paused again. "Yeah, yeah, I know Alex would have come out but I wanted to and—"

I peeked around the doorway. Gus had his back to me, sitting on the couch and staring out the window with his cell phone pressed to his ear. Kong lounged on top of the couch cushion behind him, one black paw idly toying with Gus's hair. He seemed oblivious to the touch.

"I don't care what Alex thinks. You know how he is. He can't believe a man and a woman can be alone without having sex. I can restrain myself." Gus made a disgusted noise.

My ears burned with indignation. So much for Gus Colcannon's kiss and avowals of interest in me. It was all just business. I wondered who he was talking with.

"I don't care." I heard the exasperation in his voice and when he leaned forward I saw his free hand clench and unclench on his knee. "We don't have much time to find it. Charlie thought he was close. I'm betting he handed it off to her. Charlie trusted her. He said she was the best tester they had. He swore she'd find it. We just need to buy her more time."

Gus stood. I pulled back. He went to the window, staring out into the howling blackness. "No, I'm not going to tell her what's going on. If she knows too much she's liable to tip off the people doing this. She can't tell a lie to save her soul."

Bullshit! I could so lie. Then his words soaked in. Who was involved in what? What was he looking for? I took a chance and peeked around the corner.

He swung around. I ducked back, just in time.

"I'll see if she can give me a ride to my apartment in the morning, as soon as the plows come through. Just have a car there and waiting for me."

I strained to hear.

"Damn it, I don't care what he says! Just have the car there waiting for me. I'll deal with him later."

I heard the mobile phone snap closed. I scurried back into the den just as Gus went into the kitchen, passing by the doorway where I'd lurked just seconds before. I flopped into my chair, unmindful of squeaks, sorting through everything I'd heard. I pulled over Barry to jot down some notes but my brain was so full of questions I stalled, unable to move. Thoughts and fragments jumbled through my brain.

Gus and Alex Raney were obviously more than recent acquaintances. And there was some kind of animosity between them.

Gus thought someone had tampered with his truck.

Charlie was supposed to have given me something.

And I was supposed to figure out—

What?

Barry rang out under my hand, *Holly Jolly Christmas* startling me out of my immobility. I checked the Caller ID. Why was Paul Henderson calling me?

"Hi, Jessie, how's it going?"

I kicked back in my chair and switched on my Bose stereo with the remote. Bruce Springsteen started singing to me as I picked up Andrea's wycinanki. "Paul, how are you? I heard you'd been sick from the potluck. That was a terrible mix-up with the signs." Had it been a mix-up? Or was that email right—did somebody do it on purpose?

“It wasn't bad. I was just sick for a bit then felt fine. Luckily we caught it in time.” He laughed, sounding embarrassed. “That's why I'm calling. I got this odd email today at work. It came just as I was leaving the building.”

My stomach dropped. “Really?”

“Yeah. It was from somebody apologizing for the screw-up at the potluck.”

Relief washed over me. “Who? Somebody at CodeBusters? I suppose they sent it to everybody who attended or—”

“No, it wasn't that. It's anonymous. And it came directly to me. Or at least, that's how it looks. Let me read it to you. I forwarded it to my home account.”

“Better yet, forward it on to me. I’m online now.” I put aside my snipping and opened the email program on my laptop. “I can read it while we talk.”

Movement in the doorway made me look up. Gus was watching me, two beers in his hand. I gestured him into the room, covering Barry to speak softly. “It's Paul Henderson. He said he got an email that—” My email program pinged me. I spoke into the phone again. “Here it is. Let me look at it, Paul.”

Gus came closer, setting the beers on the desk. Faye jumped to her feet and would have slunk out of the room but he plucked her up and came to stand by me, holding her against his chest and rubbing her head. She was so stunned she sagged in his arms, a petite pile of beige fur with twitching black paws. If it hadn't been so pathetic it would have been amusing. “She doesn't like strangers,” I whispered. “Don't be surprised if she claws.”

“I’m not worried.” He peeked over my shoulder. “What do we have?”

“I'm sorry, Jessie, did I interrupt something?'

Paul sounded surprised. He probably hadn't thought that I'd have a man in my house. “Not at all, Paul.” I opened the email.

Sorry about the potluck. My signals as well as the signs got mixed up.

“That's odd,” I said.

Gus leaned closer. His face, and Faye's, were just inches away. Her startled green eyes were starting to look panicked. I held out my arms and Gus relinquished his hold but remained leaning over me, reading my computer screen. I tried soothing the tubby little cat but she'd have none of it and soon jumped down, stalking out with one indignant backward glance. I recognized that territorial flick of her tail. She was headed for the laundry basket where she would pound my sweatpants into submission.

"Isn't she a fussy little thing," Gus muttered. He turned his head to stare into my eyes. "Like her mistress."

I rolled my eyes in exasperation. "No one is the master—or mistress—of a cat."

"Uh—Jessie?"

Damn. I'd forgotten I was holding the phone. "Sorry, Paul. I was distracted."

Now Gus rolled his eyes. "Yeah, right. Like I could distract you. So when did he get this email?"

I touched the 'conference' button on Barry. "Paul, when did—"

"I heard." Paul sounded peeved now. "I got it at about four this afternoon. I left early because of the snow. I just thought you'd like to know about it. I heard about the guy who died in your office and I wasn't sure if this was connected."

I stared at the computer screen. "I think we should tell Detective Raney about this. He's the policeman who's investigating Charlie's death. I'll call him and let him know that you got this. I don't know if it's connected but he should know about it." I felt better as soon as I said it. I liked dumping my problems on a cop.

Gus straightened up and I could tell he was irritated. It looked like I was batting a thousand, pissing off all the guys around me. "Thanks for calling, Paul. I appreciate it."

"Will you be in the office tomorrow? Maybe we can have lunch."

Gus jammed his hands in his jeans pockets and glared at me. I ignored him. "I doubt it, Paul. The roads look bad. But I should be in on Friday."

"Okay. I'll give you a call. Good night."

I hung up, putting Barry into the cradle to charge and synch. Gus stared past me at my computer screen where Charlie's files were displayed in individual windows. "Now that your love life is back on track, can I ask you a question?"

"My love life, such as it is, was never off the track, thank you. And yes, you can ask me a question." I checked my screen, where results of one program were scrolling. There was a long pause. I figured Gus was counting to ten before answering. I printed the email that Paul had forwarded to me then checked the pile of papers on my desk for Alex Raney's business card.

"Did you find anything on that CD that Charlie gave you?'

I tapped the screen. "I'm looking at it now." I gestured to the hassock. "Pull up a seat, if you have a minute."

The wind howled outside. "I'm not going anywhere." Gus dragged over the faded green hassock and looked around my arm at the screen. "What do you have?"

I opened Barry. "Let me call Alex Raney first and tell him about the email."

"I'll tell him," Gus said. "I have to call the police later anyway."

I hesitated, my hand on my Blackberry. Gus looked at it then at me. "Don't you trust me, Jessie?"

I met his eyes. His gaze was direct, unwavering, and, I thought, honest. "Yes." My ears turned hot with...embarrassment? Longing? Fear? I wasn't sure. I jerked my eyes away from his and back to the computer screen. "Charlie gave me ten files. Four of them were easy—slides for the conference. One file looks like a data file but it's not the canned data we use at work."

"Canned data?" Gus picked up a beer from the desk where he'd set it and sipped.

"We have data files we use in the QA department. When I test, I download the parts of the data I need—you know—name, address, city, state, zip, or fake social security numbers and occupations. That's the kind of stuff we almost always need to test with." I leaned back. Gus slid the other beer over to me. "Charlie's data file is different than the data files we use."

"So? Does that matter?"

"I'm not sure. Plus there's one other thing." I moused open a new screen and showed it to Gus. "Charlie burned this CD about twenty minutes before the potluck started."

I pointed to the date and time designators on the file listing. “Why did he take the time to download a data file, too? A data file isn't that important. I mean, it's good to have a comprehensive set of data to test against a program, but it's not critical. The program files are critical.”

Gus stared at the screen, one elbow on the corner of my desk, propping up his chin. His hazel eyes were sharp and thoughtful. “Maybe he just copied a lot of files all at once and the data file was one of them.”

“Maybe.” It didn't seem right to me, and my doubt showed in my voice.

“Why not?” Gus's gaze flickered to the doorway. “Looks like someone found their courage after all.”

Faye ambled into the room, acting as though she hadn't just pulled a Chicken Little minutes before. She paused near the futon, giving Gus a quick up-and-down glance. He held a hand out low and she wandered toward him, ostentatiously casual. “I guess some women in this house can overcome their fear,” he said as she rubbed against his fingers.

I considered and discarded several replies. “As I was saying…” I tapped the screen.

He looked up at me, that mischievous expression in his eyes. “I'm paying attention. Continue.”

“I don't think the data file was just one of many. He downloaded files of several different types—slides, a text file, and the compiled program files. None of them were obviously related, so I doubt they'd all be stored in one central location. He had to pick and choose file folders to download them from.” Faye jumped into Gus's lap, purring. “Little slut,” I muttered.

“Now, now. Don't be jealous.” He began to pet her, staring at the screen. “So why did Charlie include that file? That's what has you worried?”

“I wouldn't say worried but it's odd. Just like the program files.” I opened a new window and brought up a piece of code from the program I was testing for Nelson. “Some of these subroutines look like the ones in Charlie's file. They use the same basic logic. But it's impossible to tell for sure. I haven't been able to test everything in Nelson's program and I don't know if I can.” I sipped my beer, trying to articulate the nagging doubts I'd been having.

"Why not? I thought you had scripts that went through and tested everything?"

"Not everything. I like to think of programming as a series of houses. When you start, you go into house 1. You do something inside. Depending on what you do, you leave the house by door A or door B. Depending on which door you leave by, you might enter house 2 or house 3. You keep doing this, going through a series of sequential steps."

"What about parallel processing? I've heard about computers that let programs work in parallel."

"That's a bit more complicated. It's still a series of sequential steps, but now there are threads added—pieces of the program that branch then come back." I shook my head. "That's not happening here. This is a straightforward series of about eighty subroutines that fire off other subroutines. There's maybe a couple of hundred subs, total."

He grinned. "Straightforward? A couple of hundred?"

"I've tested programs that have more than that, believe me."

"So what's the problem? What are you seeing?"

"The program is executing fine, but it goes into one subroutine—one house, if you will—and nothing happens. It goes in, it comes out. But nothing happens while it's there. And I can't get a handle on what's supposed to be happening."

He stroked Faye, who simpered with pleasure. His hands were large, with knobby knuckles. I wondered what it would feel like to have them stroke me. "So why don't you look at the code and figure it out from that?'

"Do you know how many lines of code are in that program?" He shook his head. "I don't either. But I do know it's about two hundred pages, printed. And that's not to say that every routine is being printed. There's no guarantee of that." I stared at the test results on my screen. "My programs go through, test each subroutine they can, and print out what happened going into the routine and what happens coming out."

His hand paused on Faye's back. "What do you mean,

'test each subroutine it can'?"

"That's what I'm saying. There are some routines that aren't firing—they aren't being accessed. And I can't figure out why. Have the police analysts figured anything out?"

"Police?"

"Come on, Gus. You and Alex Raney are buddies. What does he say?"

"We're not buddies." Gus straightened and Faye jumped down. "I don't think the police have come up with anything, either. We did find one thing, though."

"What?" I took a swallow of beer.

"The files were erased on Charlie's computer. As far as we know, you got the only copy." He looked at me, his eyes curious. "Which might explain the hunter outside your house the other day. I wonder why Charlie gave you the files?"

Chapter Ten

I choked on the beer. “Erased? Can't you recover them?”

He shook his head. “They're gone. Whoever did it used a program that screwed up Charlie's computer. So the copy you have—that's it.”

“Whoa. I'm glad I made so many backups.”

“Backups?”

“Sure. There's a copy on Barry, because it's synched. There's a copy on my laptop and Raney has one and there's one on a CD and—”

“Barry?”

I pointed to my Blackberry, sitting in the synch cradle. “My life is on Barry.”

Gus grinned. “Interesting. So if I stole your PDA, I'd have you?”

“In a manner of speaking.”

“You tempt me.” He stood up and pushed the hassock back, brushing against my arm in the process. It felt like an electric spark jumped from him to me. “In more ways than one.”

I jerked my eyes away from an examination of his mid-section and the interesting bulge in his jeans. “Are you going to call Alex Raney now?”

He nodded toward the printer. “Can I have that copy?”

“Sure.” I sipped my beer. “I'm going to turn in soon. Do you need to get up at any particular time tomorrow?”

After taking the paper from the printer, he hesitated by the door. “No, not really. I'm an early riser.” He looked down at the floor then at me, as though he'd come to some decision. “I didn't mean to offend you or back you into a corner earlier. I guess I forgot about your husband. I can understand why you're not ready to move on yet.”

I started to protest this description then realized if I did, it might seem like an insult since I'd turned him down earlier. I nodded.

"I hope you know—" He shook his head. "I care about you. I care a lot, probably more than I should. I meant what I said. From the minute I met you I've been trying to figure out a way I could—" His cheeks flushed. "Anyway, it's hard to meet people in my line of work and you—"

"Gus, you don't have to say anything." He looked so embarrassed I was embarrassed for him. "I told you—I just don't want to set myself up for grief. You're leaving as soon as you can. You said so yourself."

"Me and my big mouth." He looked at the window and the snow outside. "I could be talked into staying with the right incentive. I hope you'll consider it." He held up a hand when I would have spoken. "Just think about it, Jessie."

I was sorely tempted. My wild, reckless youth beckoned to me. Memories of short-term affairs and lovers were suddenly vivid, feeding my brain with lust. "I will, Gus."

Hope flared in his eyes. He blew out a long breath. "Good. I'll see you tomorrow."

"Good night." I watched him leave, Faye a silent shadow at his heels.

What was I thinking? I propped my head in my hands on the desk, glaring down at my keyboard. There was no way in hell I was going to embark on any kind of a relationship with Gus Colcannon. That way lay potential heartbreak, and I'd had months of excruciating heartbreak when Bill got sick then died. I wasn't going there again. Never.

I heard Gus in the living room, turning on the TV and talking, probably to one of the cats. Or maybe he'd called Alex Raney. I was exhausted with worry, emotion, and the events of the last few days. I saved my files then closed my laptop for the night. I stared out the window for a long time at the trees moving in the wind and the snow piling up on the pond. Then I shook myself out of my hypnotic trance and went to get ready for bed.

I tossed and turned but finally fell into a light doze. I was at that in-between place between deep sleep and waking when I heard the landline phone in the living room ring. Gus answered, his voice low and rumbling over the sound of the TV. I snuggled back into the bed and was just drifting off again when the door pushed open.

"Jessie?"

Gus's voice was very soft. His silhouette was backlit by light from the living room, down the hallway.

"What? Is something wrong?"

He came into the room and stood next to the bed, holding out my portable phone. "It's your brother, Drew. He wants to talk to you."

I sat up, conscious that my hair was a tangled mess and I was wearing my old "When pigs fly" flannel shortie-sleep shirt and boxers. Luckily the room was mostly in darkness so Gus wouldn't see. I took the offered phone. "Drew, what's wrong? Is everything okay?"

"Damn it, Jessie, why the hell isn't that guy in bed with you? He's nuts about you, you stupid idiot. Where's the big sister I knew, the one who took chances?"

I almost dropped the phone in surprise. "That's not fair, Drew, and you know it."

"You listen to me for a change, Snip. It's time for you to move on. Nothing in life is perfect. I talked to my buddy in Washington and he says this guy is legit. I can't get any more details because it's classified, but Colcannon has gotten some commendations and some awards. He's a good guy, Snip. Yeah, you and he will need to work out the whole New Mexico and Minnesota thing, but you can." He laughed. "Hell, you used to date a guy who lived in Alabama when you lived in Maine. That worked for years."

"That's the point, I don't want—"

"You won't know what you want until you try. It's not fair to ask somebody to commit to a lifetime based on a few days' acquaintance. But it's also unfair to not give it a chance." I could almost imagine Drew standing with the phone in his hand, stabbing at the air as he made his point. Drew was always given to hand gestures when he talked. "Trust your gut instinct on this, Jessie. That's what you always tell me to do—trust your gut."

I clutched the phone, my face red with humiliation. Drew wasn't modulating his voice and I was sure Gus could hear every word. He stood next to the bed, staring down at me but I couldn't read his expression in the dark shadows of the room.

"Snip? You want to, don't you? I know you. And I've talked with this guy. He's okay. Damn it, talk to me."

"It's a bit tricky, Drew, since he's standing right next to me." I ran a hand through my hair, longing to hide under the blankets.

"Well then, quit talking and start doing." He hung up.

Gus held out his hand. "Sorry about that. He demanded to talk to you. I thought it might be important."

I gave him the phone and he started to leave. "Gus?" My voice was shaking.

He paused by the doorway.

"I just don't know, Gus."

He put the phone on my dresser and came back to the bed. "Do you want to talk about it?" He leaned over, his hand on my shoulder. Then he slid his palm upward and under the collar of my shirt until he was cupping my neck. His thumb rubbed along the angle of my chin, the rough skin of his palm sending tingles through my body.

I scooted over in the bed. "No. I don't want to talk." My heart was beating so hard I was shaking. I was suddenly shy, not sure what to do.

He sat down on the edge of the bed. He'd taken off his flannel shirt, revealing a black T-shirt. I touched his arm, feeling the hard, inflexible strength in it. The little hairs pricked up at my touch. He turned to me, bringing his leg up and leaning so one arm was near my left side. "I'm a bit out of practice with this kind of thing," he whispered as he bent to me.

"What kind of thing is that?" I put my arms around his neck, tugging him closer.

His lips hovered near mine. "You know—romance."

"I think you're doing good. I barely know you and I'm about to invite you into bed."

"Really?"

The soft hairs of his beard tickled my chin. "Really." I pulled him and his arms moved around me, drawing me closer. I felt the hard lines of his chest against my soft breasts, a feeling I'd forgotten in the years since Bill had died. Good Lord, it had been almost ten years since I'd been with a man in anything like an erotic embrace. It all felt so new and yet so familiar, so comforting, natural and exciting. Emotions and sensations rush through me, as though a part of me that had been dormant was rampant and alive again. I ran my hand down his back, exploring hard, straining muscles.

"Jessie?" His lips grazed mine, teasing me with an electric tickle.

"Hmm?" I angled my body. One of his legs slipped between mine and I felt that familiar tightening in the base of my belly, that incredible expectation that started to build. He moved his leg upward, rubbing gently against my pubic bone.

"Nothing," he murmured against my lips. "I just wanted to say your name." He pulled back to look down at me, then fumbled his glasses off, setting them on the bedside table. The reflected light from the living room highlighted the angles of his face. His eyes were memorizing me, flickering from my chin to my forehead then back to my eyes. He started kissing me—slow, delicious touches along my cheek, my eyes, my neck, and my chin. He rubbed his beard against my neck as his head moved lower. "It's been a while since I've tried to seduce a woman," he whispered, his tongue flicking over my collarbone as he tugged at the buttons of my shirt.

The old flannel was loose and the buttons gave way easily. He opened the fabric and his hand cupped my breast, his thumb flicking over my nipple with tantalizing slowness. A shocking burst of warmth shot from my nipple to my vagina and I wanted to be far, far closer to the man next to me. I slipped a hand down to his belt. "Let's get rid of some clothes," I suggested.

He laughed, his breath warm on my nipple. "I guess that means I'm doing okay."

"How out of practice are you?" I lifted my hip and felt something satisfyingly hard press against me. "Not all parts of you feel out of practice."

"It's been six years since my divorce and I haven't had much action since then." His lips fastened on my nipple, sending hot sensations of anxious need through my body. “Not much action at all.”

“You lying rat.” I leaned back, tugging at his belt buckle. “I thought you were freshly divorced.” He helped me slide his jeans down. I sighed with satisfaction as his erection sprang out at me. I wrapped my hand around him.

“Will you forgive me?” he whispered as he pushed my boxers off.

I pushed against the questing hand that was sliding up my thigh. “Maybe. If you're good.”

Gus peered up at me, his eyes dark and mysterious. “I'll do my best.”

He certainly did.

****

I awoke soon after dawn, marvelously bruised and as satisfied as a cat dunked in a bowl of cream. I knew immediately that Gus was next to me. It felt natural to have him with me. I luxuriated in the feel of a long, naked man lying next to me, his breath soft and warm on my shoulder. I loved the sensation. I felt like a part of a pair again.

His hair was flyaway, the gray and white strands shimmering in the light from the hallway and the streetlight outside. I wanted to touch him, to run my hands over his body and wake him for yet more fun, but he was so peaceful and calm. Without his glasses he looked younger and vulnerable despite the gray beard and mustache.

I slipped out of bed and padded to the bathroom, dragging on my robe as I went. I considered a quick shower but decided to wait—maybe I could convince Gus to join me. I smiled at the thought as I washed my face and tamed my hair before going out to the kitchen and regarding the winter white world beyond my window. The plows hadn't come through yet so no tire marks showed where the road started and the yards ended. We wouldn't be going anywhere for a while.

Faye joined me, emerging from whatever hiding place she'd found while the Boogie Man slept in her spot on my bed. I soothed her with a good brushing and she eventually consented to sit with me on the couch to watch the morning news. We'd gotten almost ten inches of snow and most schools and some businesses were canceled for the day. A new terrorist alert had been posted, bumping America to Orange Level, whatever that meant. On the home front, a snowmobiler had gone through the ice on Lake Minnetonka and been rescued from certain frozen death, there'd been a multitude of car accidents overnight, and the local parks and ski slopes were doing a booming business.

The sun was edging up when I budged from the couch to make a pot of coffee. I glanced in the bedroom. I could see the top of Gus's head poking out from the covers. Kong was nestled against Gus's stomach, his paws twitching as he snored. Typical men. Sleep in while there were chores to do.

I dressed in sweatpants and shirt then put on my outerwear and went to the bird feeder, filling the seed bin and scattering peanuts for the squirrels. It was a startling clear morning although the wind was eddying the snow into little tornadoes. I went to the front of the house and saw the plows at the top of the hill, working on the street there. It would be another few hours before they got around to us. I got the mail from the box and sorted it into the recycle bins in the garage, then came inside.

I shucked out of my coat. The coffee smelled great and I made a beeline for the pot just as Gus came wandering in the kitchen wearing the sweatpants and sweatshirt I'd given him the night before. I wasn't sure what to say—it had been a long time since I'd had hot sex with a guy and woken with him the next day.

His hazel eyes were bright behind his glasses. “Hey, princess.” He crossed the room and enfolded me in a warm hug.

I hugged him back, smelling warm, musky man. It was comforting, erotic, and enticing. “We're still snowed in,” I mumbled into his shirt.

“Good. That means we don't have to go anywhere soon.” He kissed the top of my head. “Can I fix you breakfast?”

“Really?” I snuggled against him. “I think you could talk me into that, if…”

“Hmm?” His voice sounded dreamy.

“If I could talk you into showering with me.”

He slipped his hand down the back of my sweatpants. “Why, Jessie. You're not wearing any underwear.”

“I was waiting for you to get up.”

He pressed hard against me.

“And I see you are.”

He laughed. “Take me to your shower.”

****

Gus made a fabulous breakfast of French toast with powdered sugar and bananas in some kind of gooey caramel syrup. He moved around my kitchen with confidence obviously born of long acquaintance with pots and pans.

“Where'd you learn to make food like that?”

“It's a hobby,” he said as he stacked plates in the dishwasher. “Where does this go?” He held up a sticky fork. I gestured toward the silverware bin. “Which slot?”

“Huh?”

“Don't you sort your silverware?”

I'd never even heard of such a thing and it must have shown on my face. “It saves a lot of time when you empty it.” He bent over and separated the knives, forks, and spoons into their own little compartments.

“Sort now or sort later, I guess.” I grabbed some stale bread and went into the living room to peer down at the pond. Because of the overhanging trees it wasn't totally snow-covered. Two of the neighbor kids were playing near the edge. I pushed open the door out onto the deck, grabbing the shovel I kept nearby to clear a path to the rail. The small figures below me looked up at the sound and waved.

“No school today?” I called out to Teddy Baxter, the larger of the two.

“Nope. How about you?”

Gus came out, wrapping his arms around me and pulling me against him. “Nope, no school!” I leaned against him, savoring his warmth. “Be careful on the pond, you know how it is after snow! Clear the path to the tree, would you?”

They waved acknowledgement and moved off into the woods.

“What happens to the pond when it snows?” Gus asked, leaning his chin on my head and peering past me.

"The snow acts as an insulator so the ice never thickens. It was thin to start with, so I wanted to make sure they didn't go out on it." I watched as Teddy led his little sister through the trees, kicking a path to the Rescue Tree where the rope, axe, cowbell, and shovel hung. Satisfied that we'd be able to get to the equipment quickly if needed, I turned into Gus's embrace.

I heard the rumbling noise on the street that signaled the plows. "Looks like we'll be able to make our escape soon."

"I wish we could stay snowed in a bit longer," he whispered. "This has been one of the best nights of my life."

My heart swelled at the raspy words but my spirits started to nosedive. "We can have a few more until you leave," I said, trying to sound casual.

His arms tightened around me. "I'd like that. No—I'd love that."

I drew back to look up at him. "I would, too, Gus."

He kissed the tip of my nose. "Let's get inside. I'm not cut out for this weather." While he went back into the living room I picked up the bread I'd dropped and frisbeed a slice off the deck toward the bird feeder at the edge of my yard, wishing I could toss my problems away so easily.

We shoveled the plow boulders out from the driveway as Tom blew out the snow with his blower. Then the tow truck called, and we drove to the top of the hill to meet it. Gus had a huddled conference with the driver then came back into my warm car, carrying some things he'd pulled out of the glove compartment.

"They'll tow it to the dealership near my apartment," he said as we drove back to my house. "At least they don't need a flatbed. I was afraid they would." He plugged a phone charger into my car's cigarette lighter and pulled his cell phone out of his pocket. "I'm getting low," he said as he attached the charger to the phone.

"How bad is the truck?" I negotiated the turn at the bottom of the street and we slid the last few feet into my driveway.

"Bad. The front axle is cracked. It looks like some of the lug nuts loosened on one of the tires just enough to pull the axle. I'll need a rental. I called a friend last night, so that's taken care of, at least." He looked tense, the easy-going lover gone in the cold light of day.

I put a hand on his where it rested on his thigh. "I'll drive you there, okay?"

He relaxed visibly under my touch, taking my hand in his and running his fingers over my palm. "Thanks. I appreciate—" He paused for a minute then said, "No, 'appreciate' is too weak a word." The gold flecks in his eyes seemed to glow as he stared at me. "Jessie, I can't tell you what it means to me that you took a chance on me like this. I know how it must look to you, the fact that I can't tell you everything. But you trusted me, and that means a lot to me. A lot."

"But—?" He hadn't said the word, and he didn't have to. I knew it was there, waiting.

"But I need some more time. I can't tell you what's going on and I can't explain things even though we had last night together. I need you to trust me just a bit more."

I looked at the shining new world, blanketed in snow. Until he'd said it, I hadn't realized how much I wanted him to come clean and tell me what he was doing. It hurt that he wouldn't.

His hand tightened on mine. "Just a bit more time. Please."

I nodded. "I trust you not to hurt me, Gus. I may not know much about you, but I think I do know that."

He kissed me. "I won't, Jessie. I promise."

I wanted to believe him but before I could ask for more reassurances, his cell phone rang. He opened it and looked at the tiny screen. "Sorry. I kept it off all night because the battery was low. I need to take this call."

I turned the car key to 'accessory' and opened the door. "Come in when you're done. I'll be ready when you are."

"Thanks." He put the phone to his ear. As I went inside I heard him say, "Yeah, I'm here. What's happening?"

I wished I had an answer to that question myself.

Chapter Eleven

We left the house at mid-morning. The roads were snow-packed but passable, although there were some abandoned cars in ditches. As we approached the Interstate, I saw it was jammed, so I took the county roads instead, where traffic was lighter.

Gus was staring out the passenger window, one finger tapping time to Jethro Tull on my CD player. I was struggling with regret tinged with astonishment. I couldn't believe I'd spent the night having sex with a relative stranger. That was the sort of stunt I used to pull when I was thirty years younger. Here I was, fifty-one years old and I was going through all the agonies of 'will he call me', 'should I call him', and 'will he still love me tomorrow'?

Love? No one had mentioned that. The topic never came up. I shook the idea away. “What did you and Drew talk about last night?” I asked as we wound our way through city streets toward the office.

“Who?”

The surprised look told me how far away his mind had been. “My brother, Drew. Remember? He called last night before you came in and accosted me in my bed?”

“Who accosted who?” He reached over to give me a tickle.

I laughed and squirmed away. “What did you talk about?”

“He wanted to make sure I was good enough for his big sister. He gave me the third degree. Just typical brother stuff.”

“Do you have a brother?” I turned onto the stretch of road that led to the local mall and from there to the office building.

He was quiet for a long minute. “I did,” he finally

said. "He was killed."

"I'm sorry. Was it recent?" The hushed tone in his voice told me that there was still a wound there, unhealed.

"Six years ago. It was—" I glanced at Gus. His face was averted. "It was a sudden death. It caught us by surprise."

As we crested a hill, I saw a pickup truck ahead of me, skidding toward the right side of the road. There were no houses here, just a park on the left down a steep embankment and the scar of a subdivision under development on the right. "Another accident?"

The truck swerved. Someone rolled down a window and tossed out a box, which landed in the soft snow of the road shoulder. The truck fishtailed then took off ahead of us up the hill. "What the hell?" I slowed and looked at the box, which had tipped on its side, spilling the contents. Several kittens were emerging from the cardboard carton, blinking in the bright sunlight then tumbling into the snow.

"Son of a bitch!" I skidded to a stop, torn between helping the little critters or going after the assholes who'd done it.

"I got the license number," Gus said. "Pull over."

"But they're getting away—they shouldn't—"

Gus was unbuttoning his coat. "Pull over." He looked at me. "Trust me. I'll make sure the cops find them."

I eased my Subaru to the side of the road, grateful there was no traffic immediately behind me. Gus flung open his door and was out of the car before I stopped. He tore off his coat, tossing it back inside. Then he quickly unbuttoned his flannel shirt and righted the cardboard box as he headed for one of the kittens who'd tumbled down the bank. Luckily the thick snow had stopped its progress before it had gone completely into the ditch. I put on my flashers and got out, slipping on the pavement before reaching the embankment. Two kittens were still in the box, crying. Gus had taken off his flannel shirt and had one kitten tucked into its folds, pressed against his black T-shirt. A tiny black and white kitten was tottering around the shoulder, perilously close to dashing out onto the pavement. I scooped it up, cradling it against my chest as I looked at the tracks in the snow, wondering if there were more.

The kittens in the box were scrambling against the sides, threatening to tip it. I grabbed the container and added my captive, looking down at three frightened, cold faces peeking up at me. Gus approached me, his shirt bunched in his arms. "Got two. I think that's it." He held out the shirt. "Put the others in here."

I nabbed the wiggling babies and dumped them into Gus's warm shirt. He closed it gently and put all of them back into the box, shirt and all. "Let's go to my apartment," he said, getting back into the car with the box in his arms. "It's closer."

I slid back to the driver's side and got in. Gus was gently parting the shirt and peering down into the box. "Who would do this?" I demanded, wiping away my tears as I got the car moving again.

"Motherfuc—" Gus took a deep breath. "Stupid assholes." He reached into the box.

"How old are they? Will they live?" I made the turn onto the city street that would take me to the apartment complex.

"I don't know. They look healthy and they're good sized. Maybe they're weaned." He glanced up at our surroundings. "Is there a Humane Society around here?"

"There's one out by my house for the county. I can take them home tonight, after work, if we can leave them at your apartment this afternoon." I turned into the parking lot. There were three buildings in the complex. "Which one?"

"Down there. Park near the center door." He pointed to the end building then reached to the floor, fumbling in the pocket of his coat to pull out a set of keys. As he lifted them, one of the kittens grabbed for it and he laughed. "Sure. We can leave them here for now." He batted at the tiny paw. "Feisty little booger." He unplugged his cell phone and charging cable from my lighter socket and handed them and his coat to me. "Let's go."

He led the way into the three-story building, unlocking the outer door with a key. We went up one short flight of stairs to a long corridor with six doors on either side. Gus went to a middle door and opened it with his keys, juggling the box in one arm. "Where should I put them? I've never owned kittens before."

I looked around. We were in a living room/kitchen/dining room combination, the kitchen separated from the other areas by a low counter. The décor was muted beiges, warm browns, and deep golds with two big expensive-looking couches, a fireplace with a marble mantle and large windows that led to two balconies beyond. "Is there a spare bedroom with a bathroom? Bathrooms are usually warm."

Gus led the way to a short hall, which led to a T intersection. He went left into a small bedroom that held a desk, futon, easy chair, and end table. Through an open door I saw a bathroom to the left. "Perfect." I took the box from him. "We'll need a litter box of some kind. A low tray and some torn-up paper will do for now. And some water bowls." I looked down at the scrambling kittens, all jumbled together in a pile in Gus's black-and-white flannel shirt. "I don't know if they can eat anything or if they're on milk."

One small tuxedo cat yawned, exhibiting a surprising amount of pink tongue and tiny, sharp teeth. "Maybe some shredded meat," I said, thinking out loud.

Gus went back the way we came. I set the box down near the heating vent on the floor then tossed my coat on the futon and gently tipped the box on its side. Kittens came tumbling out, although two dug in to stay inside the box. Gus's shirt covered one little lump and I laughed as it started to move, trundling across the floor with deliberate purpose.

I flipped off the shirt. A small tabby cat sat down and peered at me, eyes wide with wonder. I took inventory. We had two tabbies, two tuxedos, and one all black kitten with long, silky hair. One of the tuxedo babies looked like a twin of my Kong. They all appeared unharmed, well fed and healthy. Whoever had kept them hadn't abused them, at least.

Gus came in carrying what looked like a 9x12 glass baking dish with a newspaper in the middle on which sat two bowls. He handed it all to me before closing the door behind him. I filled one bowl with water from the bathroom. The other held small chunks of cold chicken, which I tore into tiny pieces as Gus shredded the paper and put it into the tray.

"You'll need a new baking dish," I said when I set the makeshift litter box near the toilet in the bathroom.

He followed me carrying one squirming tuxedo kitten, whom he deposited in the middle of the tray. "They're cheap." We both watched the kitten sniff at the papers then promptly squat and piddle, tail quivering in the air. Gus laughed, his hand on my neck, caressing me. "That was easy."

"I hope they're all that smart." I watched the kitten hop out of the tray, amble into the other room and proceed to join its siblings in an exploration of the new territory. Two had already found the dishes that I'd set in the bathroom corner on a towel. I breathed a sigh of relief as they tore into the shredded chicken. "That answers that question, at least."

Gus's mobile phone rang, startling us all. He pulled it from the clip on his belt and left the bathroom, the phone to his ear. I stepped over the kittens, following him. "Yeah, I saw the keys," he said into the phone. "Thanks. I'll—"

I picked up one of the tabby kittens and put it in the sunlight that was streaming in through the window.

"What?"

I flinched at the sharp tone in Gus's voice. He strode to the bedroom door and jerked it open. "That's bullshit—you know it is! I have to be there. Who knows—" His voice faded as he left the room, slamming the door behind him.

I pulled a blanket off the futon, putting it on the floor in the sunlight. Two of the kittens settled on it, their purrs loud in the stillness. I picked up each one, checking for any sign of injury, but everyone seemed okay. I made sure they'd all found the food and water then I grabbed my coat and left the room, closing the door behind me. Gus was leaning on the kitchen counter, speaking into the phone. He'd pulled on a black sweater from somewhere. It outlined his hunched shoulders as he tapped on the countertop with a pencil. I wandered to the window that looked out on the balcony.

"She's full of crap and you know it. I'm not going to put up with this." I looked over my shoulder at him. Gus was watching me with an odd expression, his eyes sad and angry at the same time. “This is wrong. We can't do this.”

I held his gaze and watched his face change. It hardened, as though ideas were running through his mind that he had to hide from me. He nodded once. “Okay. I will. Make sure you don't screw this up, though. If you do, I'll kill somebody, probably—Just don't screw it up.” He snapped the phone shut. I thought he might throw it across the room but he controlled his anger, running a hand through his hair before turning to me. “Sorry about that. Business.” He took a long, deep breath then crossed the room to put his arms around me. “I'm not going in to the office. Something's come up that I have to deal with.”

I leaned into his solid warmth, the deep thump of his heart loud in my ear. “My offer still goes. If you'd like a repeat of our evening, I'd be glad to have it.” I waited, barely breathing, for his reply.

He tilted my head back. “I'd love a repeat. But I'm going to be busy for a couple of days. I'll call you tonight, though.” His eyes were concerned. “I think Alex may assign someone to stay with you for a day or so until we wrap this thing up.” He put a finger on my lips when I tried to speak. “Just cooperate with him, okay? For my peace of mind if nothing else.”

“Why don't you just stay with me?” I tried to make it sound off-handed and light.

I saw the hurt and anger in his eyes before he bent his head to kiss me. “Can't right now.” He put an arm around my shoulders as he led me away from the window. “I've got to get going.”

I looked back to the bedroom door. “What about the kittens? I'll need to pick them up later. They can't stay here if you won't be around.”

“I don't have an extra key, I loaned the spare to somebody.” He picked up the car keys lying on the kitchen counter. “I'll talk to the manager. Just call him before you come over and someone will let you in. Alex has the number.”

Questions were struggling to get out but I restrained myself. “Okay.” I put an arm around his waist and let him lead me toward the door.

He picked up his coat from the couch where I'd tossed it, bundling up as we walked down the hallway and out to the parking lot. We paused by my car. “Be careful,” he said, looking down at me.

I touched his face, surprised by the worry I saw there. “I always am.” I smiled. “Except when I let certain guys stay overnight with me.”

He hugged me. “I’m glad you weren't careful about that.”

I pulled away from him. “Gus, what's going on? Why can't you tell me about it?”

“It's confidential.” His fingers were cold as he caressed my cheek. “Trust me.”

“I've got no choice on that.” I got in and started my car. I saw him in my rear view mirror as I drove away. He watched me until I turned onto the main road and was out of sight.

Something terrible had just happened but I didn't have a clue what it was. That last phone call—who had it been from? What had Gus so angry he looked ready to spit bullets?

I drove to the office but couldn't get a spot underground and had to park in the exposed lot on the first level that had been roughly plowed. As I dragged my bags out of the car, I tried to bring my mind into focus on the here and now. It was impossible, though. My thoughts kept going back to last night and how Gus had treated me. Okay, it had been a long time since I'd been with a man but I could have sworn there was more than just lust with him. I could have sworn there was…affection.

I didn't dare voice what was nagging at the back of my mind. Was it…love? What was I feeling? Could I even articulate it? Maybe I was over-reacting, so happy to just be with someone again. Maybe I was blowing it all out of proportion. We'd had a fun night together and that was that. No big deal.

I tried to convince myself as I rode up in the elevator and came into CubeLand. It was almost one in the afternoon but the area was quiet. Apparently many of my co-workers had decided to take a snow day along with the school-age population of Minneapolis/St. Paul. I had just plugged in my laptop and gotten settled down with my first cup of coffee when John Slocum poked his head in my cube.

"I'm glad you made it safely, the roads are a mess."

I looked out into the atrium and the windows beyond. The freeway was still at a crawl. "No kidding. I appreciated your email yesterday." I rolled my eyes. "I guess Nelson's feeling the pressure."

"About that..." His glance flickered to my test machine, where data was scrolling past from the programs that ran the night before. Then his eyes moved to my laptop, which I'd just opened. "We've had to make some shifts in our priorities. I'll need you to give me a truncated wrap-up of the database project today then I want you to move to the Fairfield work."

"What?" This was contrary to what we'd talked about just a day before. It wasn't like John to shift gears like this.

John was watching me with a stare that was unlike his usual, laid-back casualness. "I think it would be best if you stop testing Nelson's code."

I hesitated in mid-sip of coffee. John was telling me something more than what his words implied. There was a message there—maybe. "You do?"

His bald head shone in the light from the atrium as he nodded. "I do. Give me your final report today." He stared at Gus's cube wall. "We think it would be best."

"Okay." Was John telling me that he and Gus had talked and decided on this? Or was I over-reacting again?

"Just give me a broad outline of results. I don't need details." He looked again at Gus's cube wall then smiled as he left. I could have sworn I saw him wink as he turned.

I swiveled in my chair and stared into the atrium, picking up my craft paper. This made no sense. Why was John telling me to move on to a new project when I wasn't finished with Nelson's work? I snipped out a snowflake-chain, thinking as fast as my scissors cut. Gus and John must have talked and decided that I should move off the project. That meant there wasn't a problem, or else the testing wasn't needed or maybe...there was danger?

I put down my scissors. Danger? From Nelson? Nerdy, gangly, overworked Nelson? It was impossible. But a week ago I wouldn't have believed that someone would kill Charlie, either.

I was probably over-reacting. I turned to my laptop and my email queue. Denise had sent me a message from home. I wasn't surprised she hadn't made it to the office, she lived in a southern suburb and her kids were probably home from school. I replied, telling her *We have to talk tomorrow, much to tell you.* Our Friday exercise session would be interesting. She'd probably go ballistic when she found out I'd slept with Gus. I briefly debated not telling her but knew it would be impossible. Denise had a way of worming my secrets out of me.

I picked up my scissors, going back to the Yellow Submarine theme I'd abandoned earlier. I opened the Beatles' CD cover on the desk in front of me. I decided to do overlays of several of the characters using the vibrant-colored mulberry paper that was such a hassle to cut. Grabbing my magnifying glass, I peered closer at the artwork, wondering how I'd manage the lettering.

A brisk knock sounded on my cube wall. I swiveled again to find Alex Raney standing in my doorway. It was the first time I'd seen him in days. I realized my initial assessment of him had been right. He was studly in a Marine-no-nonsense, body-builder sort of way. His face was weathered with stubble, dark and light, on his cheeks. He wore a short leather jacket, faded denims, and big, chunky boots. Unlike Gus, Alex Raney seemed to ooze masculinity in an aggressive, out-there sort of way.

I decided I preferred Gus's type of masculinity. I forced a smile. "Detective Raney, Gus said you might stop by."

He froze, his scowl deepening. "What did he say?"

"Just that you might assign someone to—"

Raney leaned over to stand close to me. "Keep your voice down, okay?"

I looked up at the ceiling, Gus's wall, my other wall where the empty cube sat, then at the window. "Okay. So what's up?"

"I just wanted to check what time you're leaving today. I'm following you home and I've made arrangements for a policewoman to stay at your house tonight."

"Care to tell me why?" I regarded him with what I hoped came across as cool assessment. I was not the shy, worried office worker who'd quaked in front of Alex Raney three days ago. Oh, no. The last few days had changed me. I chose a sheet of purple paper that exactly matched Paul McCartney's coat on the album cover and considered how best to cut while trying to worm information out of the bulky cop in front of me.

"You don't seem too worried," Raney said in a low voice.

"Of course not. John just told me to move on to the Fairfield testing. That must mean that whatever was such a concern is in the past." I snipped slowly, incorporating John Lennon's pants into my pattern. The same paper could be used for the Apple Bonkers and Sgt. Pepper. If I was careful, I could minimize the number of pieces I'd need to assemble.

"What?" He leaned over further.

I shifted in my chair. "You're in my light."

"Would you put that down and pay attention?"

I looked up. His narrowed glare and clenched hands told me how pissed off he was. "I'm on a deadline for this Christmas present, so I'm not putting it down. I can snip and think at the same time." I finished with the purple and selected blue paper for, of course, a Blue Meanie. "You heard what I said. John told me quit working on Nelson's code." I ventured a glance at him.

"Damn it. Colcannon's behind that." He stabbed a finger toward me. "Stay put."

"Me? Stay put?" I shook my head. "That doesn't happen. I'm known for my inability to sit still for longer than—"

"Humor me." He spun around and went out.

I put down my Meanie and looked at the album cover again. Something about it was bothering me, some little aspect...Under the title was tiny lettering. *Nothing is real.* No kidding. I knew how that felt. My gaze went to my computer screen. I opened the data file that Charlie had given me. The data there certainly looked real enough. It was full of names, addresses, ID numbers and—

What kind of ID numbers? One column looked like

social security numbers but another was a sequence of digits with alpha characters at the end. What were those?

I pushed speculation aside for the moment and turned my attention to typing a report for John. I had test results, so it was simple to plug the facts into a pre-set matrix that we used. Some of the sections were empty, of course, because I hadn't finished a total set of tests. But I was able to compile a somewhat complete report, giving the project my okay to release with the understanding that I couldn't endorse it one hundred percent.

It was almost four o'clock when I finished. The lobby lights had come on in the atrium and I saw headlights on the freeway. Brian and Bobby were apparently out today, but then so was half the company. I started packing up my craft project, tucking my finished and unfinished pieces into the special compartments in the accordion portfolio I used for the purpose. I stared at the CD cover a minute before it followed my Blue Meanies into the pocket.

Raney materialized by my cube doorway just as I was kicking off my office sandals. "Ready?" he asked, watching as I packed up my laptop, Barry, my portfolio and my briefcase.

"Yep. We have to stop at Gus's apartment on the way, He said you'd call the landlord and make sure I could—"

"I took care of it." He grabbed my laptop bag. "Let's go."

"What's your rush?" I put on my coat then stuffed Barry into my Sak. I followed him to the elevators.

"I've got things to do." He jabbed the button.

"I'm sure there's no reason for you to have someone stay with me." I'd thought about it all afternoon. "I didn't find anything in Charlie's files and since John has me working on a new project, there probably isn't anything to find."

"I've been told to play it safe, just in case."

The man was a communicative as the rock he resembled. "So who is this policewoman who will be—"

"She's meeting us at your house." He led the way out of the elevator on the first floor and out to my car. He must have scoped it out ahead of time because a dark sedan was parked next to it. “I'll follow you to Colcannon's apartment.” He handed me my laptop and got into his car.

Just to piss him off, I took my time getting under way. I drove the quarter mile to Gus's apartment making a mental list of questions that I would insist having answered. When we pulled in, I wondered how we were going to get in the building. But Raney went to a small intercom and pressed a button, speaking into it before I could reach him. He jerked open the door when a buzzer sounded and strode up the steps, two at a time. I followed more sedately. We were halfway down the hall when Gus's door opened.

The Busty Barbie Blonde looked out at me.

Chapter Twelve

She acted like she owned the place. Her expensive-looking black leather topcoat lay on the couch and she had a cup of coffee in one manicured hand. Even her clothing was perfect, matching the furniture in tones of beige and brown, all of it tight and stylish.

She held the door open. “Come in. Gus said you'd stop by.” Without waiting for me to move, she walked into the kitchen area. “Want some coffee? I made a pot.”

Raney pushed past me. “We don't have time. We're meeting Officer Moran at Jessie's house.” He glanced back at me.

I was rooted to the spot, shocked at the casual way the Unknown Hussy was making herself at home in Gus's kitchen. Part of my brain was noting how svelte and slender she looked in her stylish getup. I felt like a dumpy little country cousin in comparison. My jeans were faded and baggy, my sweater came from Target, and my supposedly windswept hair was really just curly and unruly, not fashionable. But another part of my brain was clamoring for attention, reminding me of Gus's affectionate words that morning, the way he'd treated me last night, and the tender way he'd cared for the kittens.

I raised my chin, squared my shoulders, and entered. “I don't believe we've met.” I strode to the kitchen counter and stuck out my hand. “I'm Jessie Patrokus.”

I saw her surprise before she hid it behind a cool smile. “Barb Severson. Gus and I… work together.” She hesitated. I thought for a minute that she wouldn't touch me then she gave my hand a brisk shake.

There was just enough pause in her words to make it sound like she and Gus did more than just work. My heart started hammering hard. “Really? He's never mentioned you.”

"Hmm." She shrugged, her large breasts doing a complicated dance in the tight sweater. "That's surprising."

"Let's get those kittens," Raney said. "Where are they?"

Barb-the-Babe sipped her coffee. "In the back room. They were crying earlier but they've shut up now. Honestly, I'm surprised at Gus. He's got better things to do than rescue a bunch of stray cats."

I opened my mouth to blast her but Raney beat me to it. "Yeah, well, you know as well as I do that abuse of animals is just one step away from abuse of humans. He called me with that license plate number. We'll get those assholes on neglect if nothing else."

I appreciated Raney's defense. He sounded almost sincere. I walked past the Hussy to the short hallway. "They're in here."

"I'll be there in a minute. You go get 'em ready."

His tone of voice didn't allow me to argue. I went into the spare bedroom. Three of the kittens were sleeping on the blanket. I peeked into the bathroom. It looked like the litter tray had been used and the food dish was empty. The cardboard box was still on the floor. The other two kittens were nestled inside, using Gus's flannel shirt for warmth. We could use the cardboard box for transport, but I'd rather have something sturdier. I opened the closet, but all I saw was spare bedding on a shelf and a couple of coats on hangers. I left the room to search for a container.

"Why'd you do that? You know as well as I do how Gus feels about her. Why try to make her think he's cheating on her?"

Alex Raney's voice was angry. I closed the bedroom door behind me to prevent kitten escape and sidled closer to the hall that led to the living room.

"And you know as well as I do he'll be lucky to keep his job," the Barbie said.

"It's not that bad."

"Bullshit. He's going to blow a twenty-five-year career just because he can't keep his dick in his pants—and for what? Some software geek he barely knows."

Software geek? Me? I longed to smack her, but she

had six inches on me and I had good manners. I leaned closer instead.

"Maybe he's in love."

"Oh, for cryin' out loud, that's shit and you know it. He's got the hots for his sister-in-law. He's always had the hots for her."

"Now wait a minute, that's—"

"Shove it, Raney. Just because you want to get in her pants doesn't mean Colcannon hasn't been there already."

I clenched my fists. Somebody really needed to hit that bitch.

"You're the one who's full of crap, Severson. I know Elaine. She's not sleeping with Gus. He's like a brother to her. You don't know the difference between love and lust, that's your problem."

You go, Alex Raney, I silently encouraged. *You tell her.*

"Lust is going to ruin Gus Colcannon's career in the FBI, I know that. I can't believe anybody would be that stupid."

FBI? Gus was in the FBI? And sleeping with me had ruined his career? Holy shit.

Rage was simmering in Alex Raney's voice. It was cold, not hot, but it was rage nonetheless. "That just proves you've never been in love."

"I've never wasted my time like Colcannon has, if that's what you mean."

That was it. That was the straw that broke this camel's back. I rounded the corner. Alex Raney turned, his eyes wide. Barbie-doll Severson was leaning against the kitchen counter, her long legs crossed in the tight stretch pants. She eyed me coolly. "Hear enough?"

I stalked up to her, so mad I wanted to kick. Instead I took a calculated risk. "Listen to me, you silicone bimbo," I spat. "Just because Gus turned you down doesn't mean you have to demean other women in his life."

The ugly red flush that leapt to her face was my answer. My arrow had hit home. "I don't know what you're talking about."

I looked her over from the tips of her pizza-toed boots, past the stretch pants and the tight sweater to her oh-so-blonde hair. “Care to tell us how *your* career is going? What a pity there's such a double standard in the world. A woman can sleep her way to the top but if a man sleeps with someone, he's—”

She lunged at me but I dodged her, ducking behind Alex Raney. “Whoa there.” He held out his arms. “Slow down, Barb. Come on.”

I peeked under his arm. “Bitch.”

He turned. Only I saw the grin on his face. “Cool it.”

“Because of you, Colcannon is ruined,” she said in a low, venomous voice, looking over Raney's shoulder. “You've ruined his career.”

I stuck my tongue out at her. “We'll see who's ruined. You don't know what you're talking about.” I silently prayed I was right. “You underestimate me.”

She narrowed her eyes. “That's shit.”

“Try me,” I taunted.

“Ladies, ladies.” Raney put an arm around my shoulders and turned me. “Go get those cats ready for transport.”

“I'm not done here. I'm going to—”

“I'll handle it, Jessie.” He gave me a little shake. “Go.”

I straightened my shoulders, brushing his arm off.

“Slut,” she whispered in a low, caustic voice.

I strode to the hall. “Witch,” I said over my shoulder. I ducked into the master bedroom, across the hall from the spare room where the kittens were temporarily housed. My hands were trembling and I was all hot and cold, but I'd stood up to her. I was proud of myself. For once I hadn't fled from confrontation. It felt surprisingly good. I should do it more often.

I hesitated as I entered the bedroom, not sure what I'd find—evidence of a hot sex party? Signs that Barbie Bimbo had slept here? I looked around the spacious room. The king-sized bed was made, no clothes littered the floor and there was no reason to believe anyone had recently been here, much less anyone who had sex on their mind. I breathed out a sigh of relief, until that moment not realizing how much I wanted to trust Gus and how unsure I was if I could.

I went into the master bathroom, looking for

anything I could use to transport kittens. Like the bedroom, this room was neat and appeared unused except for the toothbrush, toothpaste, and hairbrush all aligned together on the clean countertop. I thought with chagrin of my own bathroom counters, littered with hand lotion, face lotion, toothpaste and brush, hairbrushes, and other assorted things that never found their way into the vanity drawers.

I touched the hairbrush. Was Gus's career on the line because of me? Was he in the FBI? He didn't look like an FBI agent. All I had to go by were TV shows and the agents on TV were all about thirty years old with movie-star looks and killer physiques. Gus looked like a college professor—one with a sexy smile and a look in his eyes that made my bones turn to mush. And I had no complaints about his physique. It had satisfied me very well the previous night.

I went back to the bedroom and into the walk-in closet. A meager assortment of clothes was in the cavernous space, but there was also a basketball and a tennis racquet next to a brown wicker picnic basket on the floor. I pounced on it, expecting to find plastic dishware inside. It was empty, though, except for a discarded wine bottle and two sticky plastic wine glasses. I tossed them into the bathroom wastebasket and went into the spare bedroom.

I put Gus's shirt and the kittens into the basket. They were curious and squirmy, so I latched the basket with the leather loop and button closure. I rejoined Alex Raney, who was standing near the kitchen counter. “Where's what's-her-name?” I asked. “The witch. Is her name really Barb?”

“Yeah. So what?”

I shrugged. “Barbie doll.”

He snorted as he took the basket from me. “She's no doll. Is this them?” He hefted it experimentally. “They don't weigh much.”

“They're babies. Of course they don't weigh much.”

“Will they be okay in there? Can they breathe?”

“They'll be fine. It's not that far to my place. You didn't answer my question. Actually, you didn't answer several questions. Where is Barb? Who is Barb? Why is someone staying with me tonight? Will I see Gus tonight?" I followed him out the door, glancing back once to the apartment. Barb-the-Hussy had left her mug sitting out on the counter. The half-full coffeepot sat out on a trivet. I smiled smugly. Gus wouldn't appreciate that.

"Barb had to leave." Raney strode down the hall, swinging the basket.

"Unless you want a bunch of puking cats, you'd better quit that."

He stopped so fast it was comical. "Shit. I forgot." He almost tiptoed ahead of me, looking like a bull terrier trying to be surreptitious.

"So why did that...person try to make me think she was sleeping with Gus? Is it really just the woman-scorned thing or is there something more to it? And why is someone with me tonight? Gus and I were supposed to have dinner tonight. Does that mean it's canceled?"

"I'm not sure why she's acting that way. She had some trouble in New Mexico and—"He stopped and turned slowly. "Gus told me you were sneaky but I didn't believe him. That's really good, what you do."

"What?" I tried to sound innocent.

"The way you pile up the questions like that. It's effective. And sneaky."

I slipped past him and down the steps. "I wouldn't call it sneaky. I'm simply curious, that's all. My mind tends to wander sometimes. It's what makes a good tester." I held the outside door for him. "You can put the babies on the passenger seat, it's warmer there."

He placed the basket with such care I knew he took my 'baby' remark seriously. I got into the driver's side. "Are you going to follow me?"

"Yep." He leaned down to look in the car, the parking lot lights illuminating his face in the dusk. "Gus isn't sleeping with her. Or Elaine."

"His sister-in-law? His ex-wife's sister?"

Raney pulled back, surprised. "His brother's widow. I know Elaine." His flushed face told me that he knew Elaine well. "They aren't sleeping together."

I patted his hand. "Don't worry about me, Detective. I can take care of myself. I trust Gus no matter what that floozy said."

He smiled at me, the first time I'd seen a smile crack his face. Years fell away from his age and he looked like a teenager. "Yeah, I'll bet you can take care of yourself. To answer your question, I want someone to stay with you as a precaution. You were one of the last people to see Charlie Gordon alive and he left you those files. I'd feel better knowing you're safe. And as to Gus—" He shifted from one foot to the other. I recognized an upcoming lie when I saw it. "He probably won't see you tonight. He's sort of...busy. I'm glad you're trusting Gus. He's a good guy—except he is a bit over-protective of his sister-in-law."

I waved a hand. "Let me work on him. I'll see what I can do. Perhaps he just feels responsible for her. He and I can discuss it. Now go—I'll drive slow so I don't lose you."

He gave a short laugh. "I've heard about your driving. Thanks."

"Are you implying I'm a speed demon?"

"No, I'm saying it."

"Well, now I have friends in the police department. I trust you to ignore any small infractions. After all, I have small animals here who need a warm home."

He hurried to his car as I turned on my engine. I was glad to have the time alone. I had a lot to think about. I slipped John Prine into the CD player to soothe the crying babies and headed out into the night, going at a reasonable speed—or at least, a speed that was reasonable for me.

The roads were in far better driving condition than they had been that morning. A day of sunlight and zealous road crews had done the trick. I passed the spot where Gus and I had rescued the kittens. I remembered how he'd scrambled in the snow, chasing the little tabby cat. He'd sacrificed his shirt for them. Here was a man who hated winter and he was slogging through a snow bank in a T-shirt picking up wet and cold baby cats.

What a guy.

So Elaine was his brother's widow? I wondered if she'd moved here after the brother's death or if they'd lived here. I dragged over a pad of paper and scribbled a quick note since Barry was out of reach on the back seat. If Gus was in the FBI, was that Barb person in the FBI, too? She must have been the one who dropped off the car keys. That would explain why she had a key to his apartment. I decided I liked that explanation better than an obvious one, such as infidelity, hot sex, or lust.

Wait a minute. Infidelity? Gus and I weren't lovers with a lasting commitment. We were two ships who passed in the night. We were spontaneous combustion. We weren't a slow, long-lasting fire, just two warm bodies colliding in the middle of winter. He really didn't owe me any explanations about the busty Barb. I doggedly repeated that to myself, all the time whining inside. I wanted an explanation about her and her implications.

One thing he did owe me was an explanation about what was going on with Charlie, Charlie's files and CodeBusters. He'd promised to tell me what he could tonight, when he made dinner for me. Would that still happen? Where was Gus? Would I see him tonight? He said he'd call, but he hadn't mentioned dinner. I'd been looking forward to a return engagement with him.

Would I see him again?

That question preoccupied me so much for the remainder of my drive that I looked around, surprised, when I pulled into my driveway. Once again, I'd driven home on autopilot. I parked in the garage and got my laptop and briefcase from the back seat, dumping them inside the house on the boot bench then coming back out. As I came around to the passenger side to unload the picnic basket, I heard a snowmobile in the back. With all the fresh snow I guess it was to be expected, but it was dark now. It would be hard to traverse the area around the pond without hitting a shrub or, God forbid, going in the water.

Curious, I left the kittens in the warm car and went outside just as Raney's car pulled in behind me in the drive. His headlights illuminated my way as I minced along the shoveled but icy path at the side of the garage. I was in time to see a bobbing light in the distance, down the hill and near the pond.

Alex Raney followed me. “What is it?”

“Someone's out there on a snowmobile.” I moved forward. The snowmobile lights were fast disappearing into the darkness. My exterior Christmas lights had come on, illuminating the yard. I saw a line of tracks through the snow, leading from the hill's edge to my back door. “That doesn't make sense.”

He knew what I was implying. Obviously he'd grown up in Minnesota. “Is the trail well marked in back?”

“No, it isn't. And look.” I gestured to the tracks through the snow. They stood out in stark contrast to the whiteness. My blinking red and green lights that outlined the eight-foot tall snowman on the side of the house added a festive touch.

“Wait here.” He slid along the path to my back door, moving cautiously but fast. I hesitated then followed. I paused by the deck, peeking around the corner of one of the deck support posts to watch. He approached the back door, moving in a slow, careful way that told me he was examining everything before he put one foot in front of the other. He tugged on the storm door handle. I was startled when it opened.

“That should be locked,” I called. “I always keep that door—”

He glanced over his shoulder at me. I could barely see him between the posts of the deck, over the top of the tarp-covered lawn implements I stored under there. “I told you to wait. Get back, would you?” He pulled a gun out from some hidden holster at his back without waiting to see if I'd obey.

Holy shit. A gun. I ducked behind my riding mower and my wheelbarrow, bobbing up to peer over the top to watch. He inched forward, gun up and leveled at the closed door. As he turned, he saw me. “Would you get out of here?” he whispered.

I ducked out of sight but popped up again when I heard him move. He pushed open the interior door and disappeared inside, his gun drawn.

“Oh my God.” I had visions of Kong being shot by Alex Raney as he crept through my house in cop mode. I dashed to the front of the house, snatched the mewing kittens out of the front seat of my car, and caromed into the kitchen.

“Kong? Faye?”

“What are you doing? Get back outside!” Raney's voice called up to me from the basement where he was prowling around, getting ready to shoot my pets. He sounded pissed off. I ignored him, going back to set the kittens in the laundry room and moving through the kitchen to the living room entryway.

My interior Christmas lights were on, the white glow outlining the windows that looked over the deck and the back yard. There was no movement except for the blinking reflection of the lights in the window. Everything looked as it had that morning.

"Faye? Kong?" I don't know why I was whispering and especially whispering to cats, of all creatures. If anyone could ignore me with enormous sangfroid, they could. I tiptoed my way toward the hallway that led to the bathroom, den, and bedrooms. I peered around the wall in my best James Bond imitation and almost had a heart attack when Kong came sauntering out of the spare room at the end of the hall, yawning. Faye followed behind, stretching languorously then sitting down to bathe with one pale beige paw.

"I guess that answers that question." I ducked into the bathroom and glanced around, but everything was untouched in there. I was just getting ready to call out to Alex Raney that the coast was clear when I glanced into my den.

The three drawers in the corner file cabinet were open and file folders lay strewn around on my braided rug. The desk, which faced the doorway, had been jumbled. There was no other word for it. The various accessories—Eric Clapton mug of pencils, dancing Mr. Peanut doll, M&M tape dispenser, souvenir plastic lobster business card holder from Boston, cupped hand in-and-out baskets—none were where I'd left them that morning. I flipped the light switch, turning on the desk lamp.

As I ventured into the room, I saw that my desk drawers had all been opened. I was just reaching out a hand to move the file folders in one drawer when someone grabbed my arm.

Chapter Thirteen

"I told you to wait outside," Alex Raney said, giving me a shake.

"I almost peed my pants! Give a girl some warning, would you?" I slid out of his grasp and went to the desk. "Damn. They got the disk."

"What?"

"Charlie's CD. I had a copy here in the drawer."

"What?" He strode to the desk and looked at the open drawers. His hands clenched and his icy blue eyes got even icier. "Shit."

"It's gone."

"Damn. That means we have the only copy. I'd better call this in."

I started to correct his mistake but he was already moving. He went out into the hallway, putting his gun behind his back, into some spot along his waist and securing it with a snapping noise in the hidden holster.

I followed to face the resident felines. Faye had long since disappeared, probably traumatized by yet another Strange Man. I'd be lucky to lure her out from under my bed, assuming the dust bunnies didn't overpower her. Kong gave me a long-suffering look then headed for the kitchen, a cat with priorities, a man with a mission—food had precedence over reassurance.

"Do you ever follow orders?" Alex Raney pulled out a cell phone, pacing behind Kong, who refused to be rushed. Kong is a large cat and when he wants to, he can take up a lot of space. The disdainful flick of his fat black tail told me how pissed off he was. There was no way he was going to let Alex Raney set the speed limit in his house.

"No, I don't follow orders." I stalked past the human to the kitchen and the laundry room beyond where Kong was sniffing at the picnic basket and its crying occupants.

I looked toward the basement steps. “So what happened?”

Raney was speaking into his cell phone. Seeing no answer there, I turned my attention to the situation at hand. I went into the living room and found my phone book. I dialed the Humane Society only to find they closed at six o'clock. Since it was five-thirty and I was probably going to have cops in my house, a trip there was out for the evening. I'd have to keep the cat kids for the night.

Raney came in. “Anything else missing?”

I looked around. My bookcases were intact, my stash of cutting paper was still on the coffee table with the rock and roll picture books I'd consulted sitting next to them. “It doesn’t look like it.” I picked up the picnic basket then went to the spare room, followed by Kong, anxious to verify that these crying intruders weren't dangerous. That room was untouched, too. My Nordic Track ski machine was still in the corner gathering dust and the old couch still sagged in the other corner. The closet door was ajar, but I probably left that open when I dug into it and got out the sweatpants and shirt for Gus last night. It looked like whoever had come into the house had found what they were looking for and left, leaving my home and my pets unharmed.

Faye, alerted by mewing noises, dashed into the room behind me with glances over her shoulder at the Boogie Man in the living room. She pawed at the wicker basket. I considered keeping the kittens separated from the grownups in case the kittens had a disease or, God forbid, fleas. But before I could make up my mind, Faye managed to hook the basket with one claw and tip it over. I flipped the latch and kittens came tumbling out. Kong approached the small creatures, his puffed fur making him look like a black football on toothpicks. I really had to put him on a diet.

Faye's puzzled double-take between Kong and the small kitten who was his twin was so hilarious I laughed. Kong sniffed each kitten in turn then went to the doorway and sat in the middle with his back to us, his hulking presence preventing anyone from going or coming. I appreciated his blocking tactic as the two tabbies made a break for it.

I corralled the kittens and put the wicker basket on

the floor near the heating vent, propping it on its side so they could easily go in and out. Then I nudged Kong as I picked up Faye and left, closing the door behind me. The kittens would have to fend for themselves while I fended with the police.

I set Faye down in the bedroom and went toward the voice I heard in the living room. Raney was still on the phone. I went into my den and surveyed the mess there. Desk drawers were pulled out, the printer paper was scattered on the floor and my docking station had been moved. I peered into the side drawer. Yep. The copy of Charlie's CD was gone.

Kong was glaring at me from the hallway so I went into the kitchen to address his needs. I opened the kibble cabinet and pulled out two cans of cat food. I decided everybody needed a treat tonight. I was just doling out the first tablespoon of food when Raney came in the room.

"Hey, what are you doing? We need to process the scene." He strode toward me and jerked the can out of my hand. "Would you cooperate?"

"What scene? The burglars were in the den. And they probably escaped by snowmobile." I snatched the can back. "And anyway, I think I've been amazingly cooperative."

"I meant with me, not with Gus Colcannon."

My face burned with anger. "That was uncalled for. You apologize to me, right now. I don't care if you are a cop, you can't get away with crap like that."

I don't know if it was my glare or Kong's that did the trick, but he relented. "You're right. I'm sorry. This case has me crazy. I shouldn't take it out on you."

I divvied up the food between four saucers, watering down the contents of two saucers for the kittens then I tossed the cans in the sink. "What case? Charlie's murder or the other one?" I handed him two of the saucers.

He wrinkled his nose at the smell. "What do you mean, 'the other one'?"

"Oh, please. I'm not a moron." I led the way to the spare room. "You and Gus have been in cahoots since Day One and I'd like to know what it's about. It obviously has something to do with Nelson's code, but for the life of me, I can't figure out—" I stopped, using the opening of the door to cover my hesitation.

Could I figure it out? Nelson's code had to be at the heart of this. Something in his code had Raney and Gus anxious and interested. I still had a copy of Charlie's program fragments, stored on my laptop. What if I could figure out why he'd given that to me?

I maneuvered through the anxious four-legged carnivores who wound around my legs, setting my dishes down in a corner. “Come on,” I told Raney. I picked up Kong and we left the kittens to eat in peace. Kong angrily jerked in my arms until we got the den. “There.” I pointed to a spot in the corner. Raney put down the dishes and Kong sprang into action, muscling me out of the way so fast I was breathless.

Raney looked around the room. “Anything else taken?”

I heard sirens in the distance. “Oh, man. You didn't tell them to use sirens and flashers, did you? I'll be the talk of the neighborhood.”

“Cooperate,” he snarled.

He left before I could come up with a snappy comeback. I picked up one of the food dishes and put it in the bedroom, closing the door behind me. The way things were going, poor Faye wouldn't emerge from under the bed for hours. At least this way she'd have some food to sustain her as she waited for events to subside.

****

It was two hours, to be exact. The police were only there for one, but it took Faye another hour before she came out to glare at Elizabeth Moran, the policewoman assigned to 'watch' me. Faye hissed then ran away again to hide, probably so far behind my bed she would find the prehistoric dust creatures lurking there. With my luck, she'd inhale toxic allergens and come down with some disease.

Officer Moran was unfazed by that feline welcome. She was a homely woman with coarse skin, short red-black hair bundled behind her ears, and a slender although lumpish build emphasized by her loose, mannish clothing. She and Raney talked in low voices for a long time then he came to speak to me where I stood in the living room.

"Officer Moran is staying here tonight. Since the disk has been stolen I'm guessing that means you won't have any more problems, but I'd like to error on the safe side."

I secretly endorsed his caution. "I've got a spare room downstairs where she can stay." I gestured toward the staircase. "It's all ready."

Raney raised one eyebrow. "Is that where Gus slept last night?" The sly look in his blue eyes told me he knew the answer.

I gave a haughty shrug. "None of your business. Or anyone's business, for that matter." I tugged on Raney's sleeve to pull him out of the hearing of the sour-looking Ms. Moran. "Is he really in trouble because he stayed here last night?"

For an instant the hardened cop vanished. Raney's face softened and a rare smile appeared then disappeared. "We'll see."

"If I need to testify at a trial or something, you'll let me know, won't you?"

"Don't worry about it. Let's get this case behind us then we'll consider that."

I was reassured by his use of 'we'. Perhaps he was on Gus's side after all. "Keep me in the loop," I insisted.

"Sure. I'll talk to you tomorrow. And...try not to worry."

Try not to worry, he said. Easy for him to say. He didn't have a dour policewoman parked on his couch, a pissed off female cat cowering under the bed, a pissed off male cat pacing in front of a spare room door where five crying kittens alternately clamored for attention or were ominously quiet. Oh, and let's not forget an AWOL lover, a murdered colleague, an email stalker, a ballistic boss and work deadlines that wouldn't go away.

To my relief, Officer Moran pulled out a laptop computer, plopped it on her knees, and started typing as soon as Alex Raney left. At least that meant I wouldn't have to entertain her. I went into the spare room. The kittens were all in a pile, snoozing in the picnic basket. One of the tabbies blinked at me, yawned then snuggled back in with her siblings. I closed the door and tiptoed to the den where Kong, a large black lump, was snoring on the futon.

The fingerprint people had focused their efforts on my desk, the file cabinet, and the doorway so I didn't have much cleanup to do. I wiped away their dusting power with the cleaning solution the CSI tech had left for me then loaded up my CD player and sat down at my desk. I retrieved Charlie's files from my laptop, curious about the idea I'd had earlier. I had just started to examine the first set of code when Barry chimed *Jingle Bell Rock*. I answered and heard Gus's voice.

"Jessie, are you okay? I just heard about the break-in. I'm sorry I wasn't there with you, I got tied up at the office."

"It's okay. They just took Charlie's CD and didn't touch anything else. Are you in trouble, Gus? Did I get you in trouble?"

He hesitated so long I thought the connection was lost. "Who told you that?"

"I overheard Barb Severson talking to Alex Raney. They were arguing about it." I held my breath, waiting for his response.

"What did that stupid—" He paused. "What did she say?"

"That you were in the FBI and you were in trouble because you stayed here. Is that true? Are you in the FBI? Are you in trouble?"

"Damn it."

"They also said something about your sister-in-law."

"I suppose Barb implied that I'm sleeping with her." He made a disgusted noise. "I swear, that woman has sex on the brain. I suppose it's because she was reprimanded."

"Reprimanded?" I perked up. This was juicy gossip. "For what?"

"Sexual harassment."

I almost dropped Barry. "What? She harassed somebody?" This explained why she'd lunged at me when I made that crack about sleeping her way to the top. Man oh man, I'd really hit the nail on the head with *that* one.

"Yeah." I could imagine the worried look in his warm hazel eyes. "She used to be based in Albuquerque but she got into trouble and was transferred to Minneapolis."

"Oh." I suppose it made sense that Minneapolis would seem like a demotion if you lived in the southwest, but it still pissed me off that we were considered a 'step down' on a promotion ladder. Wheels were churning in my brain. "Is that how you met her? In New Mexico?"

He hesitated again. "It's complicated, Jessie. We'll talk about it when I see you."

Complicated? What did that mean?

He must have sensed my question. "Jessie?"

"Hmm?"

"Trust me."

Oh, God. There it was again. Trust. Images flashed through my brain: Gus in bed with me; Gus cradling a kitten; Gus kneeling next to Charlie's body. "I do."

"Besides, I'm not in that much trouble."

"What does that mean—'that much trouble'? That means you're in trouble, right?"

"It's nothing to do with you. Don't worry about it."

"Damn it, everybody keeps telling me not to worry. It's not that easy. I can't just turn my worry on and off. I am worried and I'm going to stay worried until all of this crap is done with."

"It won't be long now, I'm sure of it. We're getting close to a solution. I'm glad Alex listened to me and assigned someone to you tonight. It makes me feel better, if nothing else." He gave an unconvincing laugh. "Humor me, okay?"

"Did you have something to do with asking John to pull me off Nelson's project? Alex seemed pissed off about that today."

"Alex is always pissed off. Don't wor—" He stopped, which was good. If he hadn't, I was going to whack him the next time I saw him. "Sorry. I seem to be saying that a lot lately."

I decided to be magnanimous. "Knowing when to apologize is a good trait in a man."

"Then I'll do it often. I'd like to impress you."

I smiled. "You have, Gus."

His voice softened, caressing me across the phone line. "Jessie, I—"

I waited, my heart hammering so hard I was sure he had to hear it.

"I loved last night. I really did. I want to be with you again, as soon as I can. It might be a day or two, though."

I let out my breath in a whoosh. "I loved it, too."

I could hear the grin in his voice. "Nothing like dancing around making a commitment, is there?"

I laughed out loud. "I guess we're older and wiser."

"Maybe." He sounded wistful now. "I did love it—and I want to have more time to get to know you, to find out how we both feel."

"Me, too." My email icon pinged on my laptop. I clicked it open. "Let me know if I need to do anything to get you out of trouble. I'd hate to have your career on the line because of me."

"It would be worth it." I heard voices in the background behind him. "I have to go now. Jessie, be careful, okay? I just found you and I—I mean, keep on your toes. We're getting close to the end on this thing and—"

An angry voice in the background said, 'Wrap it up, Colcannon.' It sounded like Alex Raney but he'd just left. "Gus, is everything okay?"

"Just be careful, Jessie. I'll call you as soon as I can."

He hung up. I sat back in my chair, still aglow from his almost declaration of love. I wasn't sure how I felt but I felt...good. I pulled over my Yellow Submarine project portfolio. A few minutes of snipping might be what I needed to get my thoughts in order.

My landline rang. I glanced at the caller ID before picking up. "Hey, brother."

"Hey, Snipper. Did you take my advice last night?"

Trust Drew to get right to the point. This was the brother who used to spy on me from the upstairs window when my dates brought me home. Drew had a rating system for my boyfriends based on the intensity of kissing he witnessed. I'd never forget the time he fell out of the window holding up a placard with a big '10' on it when Mark Buford and I were caught in the bushes near the house.

"None of your business," I said.

He laughed. "I know what that means. I hope you had fun."

I had to laugh, too. "I did. Thanks for the advice."

"Glad to return the favor—you did it for me enough all these years." His light tone changed. "I got some more information about what might be going on there. It could be bad, Jessie. If what my friend found out is true, you could be in danger."

My stomach lurched, either from fear or hunger, or a combination of the two. "Tell me."

"There's a guy in your office, Nelson Scott."

"I know. He's my temporary boss." I pulled out my Yellow Submarine CD cover and my magnifying glass.

"Well, your temporary boss might be in trouble. His brother is missing." I started to speak but Drew talked over me. "His brother was in Saudi Arabia. He married a native woman and was working there for an oil company, doing research. He's gone missing."

I set down the Yellow Submarine snip in my hands. "What do you mean, missing?"

"My friend in the State Department said that they think Robert Scott was kidnapped by terrorists. They're demanding that the American government remove all advisors from the area."

I started pleating some scrap paper. "Was it on the news? I didn't see anything. The local news would have been on that like dirt on dogs if a local family was affected."

"The terrorist demands came directly to the State Department. No one is talking much about it. Listen, Jessie, my friend said that whenever someone is kidnapped like this, the family members are always watched. That's why Colcannon was assigned to your company. He's watching Nelson Scott."

"Watching for what?" I snipped the purple paper in my hands. "What could Nelson do? He's just a programmer. He doesn't...oh. Wait." It started to make sense. "Nelson's a programmer and we're working on a government program. Do they think he's—"

"Let's just say it's standard procedure. You said that you were looking at Scott's code. That puts you in the firing line. You need to be careful."

"I was pulled off the project today." I unpleated the paper to look at what I'd wrought. The silhouette in my hand looked like either a lopsided Blue Meanie or Osama Bin Laden. Now that I considered it, I realized that a lot of Muslim terrorists looked like Blue Meanies. Had the

Beatles been prescient? "But Gus is from New Mexico. Why was he assigned? Couldn't they assign someone from here? Minneapolis has an FBI office."

"Colcannon's brother used to live here. Maybe he requested it." I heard the crackle of papers, presumably in Drew's hand. "His stepbrother was a cop, killed in the line of duty. There was a scandal, you must have heard about it. The stepbrother's name was Danny Chisholm. He was an undercover cop, shot during a drug bust. The defense said Chisholm was drunk, but his partner said Chisholm was drinking just to fit in with the undercover operation they were working. But it still looked bad."

I vaguely remembered the story. It had led the news one summer, several years ago. "Gus said his sister-in-law and his niece lived here."

"Her name is Elaine Chisholm. The niece, Darla, is a brainiac. She started college at age thirteen and got a Ph.D. in physics when she was only twenty. Colcannon was close to his stepbrother. Maybe he volunteered to come here to see how his sister-in-law is doing."

"Who was Chisholm's partner?" I pleated another piece of fluorescent yellow paper and started snipping lightning bolts. I knew the answer before Drew said it.

"Alex Raney. He quit the Minneapolis force after Chisholm's death and went to work in the suburbs."

"In Chaska, to be precise. I've met him." I unfolded my lightning bolts and overlaid them on the Osama Bin Laden. If Alex Raney had been here, I'd have hurled them at him. "I think Gus came here as much to check on Raney as he did to check on Elaine."

"Really? Sounds complicated."

I remembered Gus's comment about Barb Severson. "Yeah. It's all complicated." I pulled over the Submarine to examine it again. "Thanks, Drew. I appreciate the update."

"Colcannon isn't the only one who's close to his family. I'm worried about you, Jessie. I don't like all this crap happening around you."

I thought of Officer Moran, plunked down on my couch like a lumpy bulldog. "I'll be okay. Thanks for calling."

"Call me if you need anything, anything at all. You're

the only sister I've got."

I dropped the phone back in the charging cradle. So Alex Raney and Elaine Chisholm's husband had been partners. That was interesting. No wonder Gus was so suspicious of Raney. I glanced at my email screen and froze when I saw the subject line of the email message there.

Hello again, Jessie.

Damn it! My unknown email admirer was back. I put down my snipping, then dragged my laptop closer. I clicked open the message.

Did the snowstorm keep you home? Rumor has it you had company last night—you like older guys, is that it? Are they more your speed? Maybe a woman like you should be happy with an old man like Gus Colcannon.

Holy shit. I stared at the screen, my jaw sagging. He knew about Gus and the snowstorm. This had to be someone I knew, someone I worked with. Nobody else knew about Gus except my brother. Who the hell was this guy? It was time for me to find out.

I clicked my mouse pointer on 'reply' and raised my hands to type.

Chapter Fourteen

Hello, asshole. Long time no message. No, the snowstorm didn't keep me home. Why—did you let a little snow ruin your day? And yeah, I do like older guys. They know how to please a woman.

I sent it and sat back, my stomach lurching. No matter how much I disliked confrontation, I was sick of this guy bugging me. It was time to figure out who he was. I picked up my scissors but I was too fumble-fingered. I'd do more harm than good if I tried to snip. It didn't take long for the answer to come back to me.

I don't know why I bother. I'll never find a match. No one can match me.

Was this arrogance or self-pity? *Why?* I typed. *What makes you so unique?*

I got up to get a beer and a bag of corn chips. By the time I got back, he'd answered.

I got my first Ph.D. when I was fifteen, my second when I was twenty-two. All I knew growing up was study, study, study. My mother stayed home to raise us kids while Dad worked in an insurance office—talk about your normal life! I'm so tired of being normal. I'm tired of being Mr. Nobody.

I thought of Gus's niece. That would be a match made in heaven. *It's not normal to stalk someone through email,* I pointed out. *Or to lie about yourself like you did on the survey. Why did you bother filling it out if you weren't going to tell the truth? Why did you waste the fifty dollar fee and take the time?*

I finished my beer, staring at the computer screen and waiting for his answer. When none came immediately, I popped Led Zeppelin into the CD player and turned my attention to the conundrum of Charlie's files. I wasn't an experienced programmer, but I had enough background to realize I might be able to plug Charlie's code into Nelson's program and, with some customization, get it to run. I settled down to work.

Zoso had wrapped up and Pink Floyd's *Dark Side of the Moon* was well underway before my email icon dinged. I opened the new mail.

I didn't pay the fee. I borrowed your survey.

I jerked my mind away from programming problems and back to the puzzle of my email stalker. How could he have borrowed my survey?

"Everything okay?"

I jumped, tipping Barry out of the synch cradle. Officer Moran filled my doorway like a glowering black snow cloud. I righted my keyboard and rescued my scattered wycinanki project parts. "Fine. Everything's fine. No problems."

Her disgusted look spoke volumes. "Yeah, Detective Raney said there wouldn't be any problems but some FBI guy raised a stink about protection." *FBI guy* sounded like it rhymed with *pig sty*. So much for interdepartmental cooperation.

"I guess Raney was right. This will be an easy assignment for you." I peeked at my email screen, itching to close the betraying window. I didn't dare. Officer Moran didn't appear intelligent but some smarts might lurk behind her loutish façade.

She made an unpleasant snorting noise, like a rooting pig. Or else I just had pigs on the brain. "Easy assignment—just because I'm a woman."

"I doubt that had anything to do with it." I opened Charlie's data file with all the casualness I could muster. "I'll bet they felt it was more appropriate to have a woman guard me than a man. I don't think sexism was involved." I wondered if someone had used that argument about Gus's stay last night.

"And I don't think you know much about it," she snarled. "I'm going to check the locks." She lumbered back the way she'd come, her booted feet echoing in the hall. Elizabeth Moran must have called in sick on the day social graces were being handed out.

Forgetting her for the moment, I brought up my email screen again, re-reading what my asshole admirer had said. It didn't make sense. How could anyone 'borrow' my survey answers?

I pulled out my cache of mulberry paper and selected a pink to use for John Lennon's shirt and my next snip session. As I considered the paper in my hand, I re-ran the memory of my involvement with Silver Harmony. I'd filled out the survey at home, on my desktop system. It was a two day process, too. When I finished it, I brooded over my answers, going back and changing a few here and there. I finally printed the whole thing at work, re-read it one last time then launched it and my dating hopes into cyberspace with the Send key, following the instructions to send each section separately.

I looked at my email screen and typed the first thing that came to mind. *I don't believe you. How could you do that?* If the guy were a hacker, he'd have to tell me. Hackers were notorious for bragging, often to the wrong person.

I yawned. To my surprise, I saw that my Felix the Cat clock said it was almost midnight. I finished editing a subroutine I was examining then plugged it into the copy I'd made of Nelson's program. I set the whole mess to compile overnight and run, if run it would. There was no guarantee I wouldn't wake up in the morning and see a list of error messages scrolling down my screen. I was too tired to deal with it now, though. It and my asshole admirer would have to wait.

I went into the kitten room, encouraged to see that they'd used the impromptu litter tray I'd made out of the lid from a packing box. I had a panicked moment when I only counted four kittens but soon found the missing one chasing a binder clip in the closet. I refilled the water bowl then spent a few minutes with them, petting and playing, before heading off to bed.

Kong and Faye both joined me on the bed that night, seeking reassurance about the intruders, both feline and human. The sheets smelled like Gus, a warm, musky odor that brought back all my memories. That and the purr of my companions sent me into dreamland.

****

I awoke to the sound of Officer Moran stomping around my living room. I lay in bed a moment and took inventory. It was Friday. I had to check the programming I'd done the night before, start work on the Fairfield contract, and try to get in touch with Gus. I also had my exercise session at noon with Denise and I needed to make a stop at the Humane Society as soon as possible. I nudged Faye off my hip where she was dozing and emerged from my bed cocoon, a butterfly ready to face her day.

Officer Moran was as surly in the morning as she had been at night. Her wrinkled blue pants and shirt indicated she'd slept in her clothing, although perhaps that was her habitual style. I showered, dressed, then called the Humane Society, their message machine confirming that they didn't open until noon on Friday. The good news was they stayed open later at night, so presumably I could turn over the kittens to them after work. I pounded some dry cat food into kitten-size chunks, grabbed a full water bottle and went to do my duty.

Kong was camped outside the kitten room, his implacable glare telling me that there would be no escapees while he was on duty. I sidled past him, greeted at the door by clamoring felines who clawed up my leg in anticipation of the tasty chunks. I divided the food into the empty food dishes, refilled the water bowl and scooped the Tootsies out of the litter box. I slipped out while they were distracted.

After appeasing the resident adult feline gods, I checked my laptop. A couple of error messages were displayed on the screen but not as many as I'd anticipated. I shut it down then loaded it and Barry for work. Moran almost vibrated with impatience, glowering at me from the kitchen as I came out of the den. “Are you ready?”

I looked with longing at the cold coffeepot. “Are you going to work with me?”

“No way. I'm just following you. Raney will have somebody waiting for you.”

“How reassuring.” I led the way out of the house where bitter cold hit me as I stepped into the garage. The thermometer in the garage read zero, which meant it was probably below zero outside. Once again someone had opened a door to the Arctic and let the cold air into

Minnesota.

Moran made that rude noise behind me. "Don't ask me. I just do what I'm told."

Probably a good thing, I thought. I certainly didn't trust her to use her intelligence to make decisions about my safety. She backed out of my drive and got behind me as I drove down the street, my car protesting the cold weather. It was stiff and unresponsive, the seats without any springiness and the shocks creaky and hard. The sun, bright on the snow pack, made it look warm but I saw the wind whipping the loose snow on the street into clouds. The wind chill factor had to be double digits below zero. I fumbled on my sunglasses, once again driving on autopilot as my wandering brain took over.

There was too much to assimilate. My thoughts bounced from one thing to the next in my mental inventory. Gus, our night together, the email asshole, Charlie's death, the hunter in the yard, Gus, the snowmobile outside my house, the break-in, Nelson Scott's brother, the potluck, Gus, the brownies, the kittens, Gus...Images of Gus filled my mind. My memories of him naked, memories of his body with mine, memories of the sweet, soft caressing tone in his voice as he talked to me all seemed to fill the car as I drove.

It had been years since I'd felt like this. Exhausted, giddy, happy, worried, frightened, exhilarated—all at once.

In love.

I argued with myself all the way to the office, trying to talk myself out of being in love. I didn't succeed. I was ninety-nine point nine percent sure I was and there was nothing I could do about it.

I got a close-in parking space in the lower lot. Moran followed me but didn't park, just pulling up to the front door and watching as I unloaded the car. The icy wind hit me as I started toward the door. The blast funneled through the parking garage like a wind tunnel. By the time I'd gone three steps my eyes were tearing and my vision blurred. I staggered the last few steps, gasping with shock. I glanced back and saw Moran watching me. Her duties apparently didn't extend to helping me schlep my belongings into the building. My last sight of her was of her sour frown as she drove away. Her lack of concern about my safety was reassuring. If there were any threat, she'd have been on me like a pig in slop. I entered the warmth of the foyer, stepping over the pile of newspapers that had arrived earlier that morning. I was slightly later than usual but still had to swipe my way in with my security badge because the building didn't officially open until eight a.m. As I rode up to the fifth floor in the elevator, I tried to prioritize what I had to accomplish that day.

No matter what I told myself, my main priority was getting in touch with Gus. I had to see him again and talk with him. He was the man with answers to all my questions, not the least of which was what kind of a relationship could we have if he moved back to New Mexico and I stayed here. Was there a chance for anything long-term with us? New Mexico. I knew nothing about it except what I'd seen in movies or on TV. What would it be like to...

I didn't dare articulate the thought, even to myself. I swiped my way into the office suite, hit the lights, and negotiated the rat's maze of cubes to my desk. I was unpacking my laptop when I heard the *whirr-thunk* of the security door to the stairwell as it opened. I hesitated. This was how it had all started, just four short days before. Charlie and Gus had come through that door, talking, and the juggernaut of adventure had begun.

I stilled, straining to hear footsteps. All I heard was the white noise of the ventilation system as the heat kicked on. I should have heard someone as they stepped on the tiled floor outside the stairwell door. I should have heard the swish of a winter coat or the clump of a boot.

The clunk of the stairwell door closing was like a gunshot in the quiet room. I jumped, catching Barry's synch cradle in time to keep it from skittering to the floor. As I righted it, I looked in the atrium window and saw a reflection of lights going on in the cubes behind me. I breathed a sigh of relief when I saw that it came from John Slocum's office. I reminded myself of Officer Moran's cavalier security measures and gave a shaky laugh.

After getting my computer unpacked and set up, I headed for the kitchen. John was already there, pouring a cup of coffee into a CodeBusters mug. He held out the coffeepot when he saw me. "How's it going today, Jessie?"

I held out my Garfield mug. "Good. I suppose you heard about last night."

"The break-in? Yeah, I did. Alex Raney called me. The good thing is it looks like the police aren't concerned any more. He told me they figured the thief got what they came for so we shouldn't have to worry any more."

I dumped the contents of a couple of creamer tubs into my mug. "But what about Charlie? Do they have a lead on that?"

"I got the impression they do." John's eyes flickered to the doorway behind me. "It sounds like they're wrapping it up."

Nelson Scott came into the room. I hadn't seen him since he'd chewed me out a couple of days before. It looked like he'd aged a decade. I remembered what Drew had said about Nelson's brother, but I wasn't sure what to say—*oh, sorry your brother is being held captive by terrorists.* Somehow I didn't think Nelson would want to be reminded. I knew how I would feel if Drew was threatened in any way or, God forbid, hurt. I'd be a bundle of nerves and a snappy wreck, or else I'd be a weepy mess. I was amazed that Nelson could even walk around, much less form coherent sentences. His earlier outbursts, his odd behavior—it all made sense now.

I smiled at him. "I see you survived the snowstorm."

He looked at me, a blank expression in his eyes. I doubt he'd even noticed the storm. He nodded, his head making little jerks as though he was having trouble controlling his movements. It was probably exhaustion. "I'm sorry I jumped on you, Jessie. I've had some things on my mind and—"

"No problem. I understand." I sipped my coffee, glancing from him to John. "I gave John that report on the database project and I'm moving on to the Fairfield contract now."

"Good." Nelson stared around the room. I don't think he processed what I was saying. His attention shifted to John. "I heard you say the police are wrapping up this investigation."

John nodded. "That's the impression I got."

"It'll be nice to get back to our old, boring lives, won't it?" I asked.

"So they know who killed Charlie?" Nelson asked, his gaze focused on John. What did I see in his pale green eyes—fear? Relief? Hope?

John picked up his mug and started toward the door. "I'm not sure. But I got the feeling that Alex Raney isn't worried about it any more. That tells me they must have a good idea who did it." His attention moved to me. "Do you have a minute? I'd like to go over some of the Fairfield test parameters with you. Some things came up at the last minute that I'm not sure how we want to handle."

"Sure." I grabbed a stir stick and followed John out the door, conscious of Nelson's gaze on us as we left.

"I meant what I said," John said as we went toward my cube. "It sounded to me like Alex Raney was wrapping up the case. I don't think there's anything else to worry about."

I glanced back. Nelson was hurrying through the blue cube aisles, his head visible above the partitions. "That's good to hear. Let me know if you need more details about the database project. I've got a couple of things I'm still testing."

John's plain face creased into a smile. "I figured you would be. Between you and me, we'll revisit that code next week, when things quiet down. But for now—" He looked beyond me, to the spot where Nelson had vanished into his own cube. "For now, you're on Fairfield." He left me at my cube doorway. I watched as he disappeared into the open space that was Cubeland.

I booted my laptop and sat down, sipping coffee as I waited for it to start. I had the feeling that someone was playing a big charade for Nelson's benefit—and mine. But what was it? Alex Raney wasn't going to back off this case unless he was sure he had a good suspect. That meant that they truly were close to solving it. But what weren't they telling me?

I considered calling Gus but it was still early. He'd called me late last night. Would he be at home? Did he have to stay in the office last night? I wondered if Raney and Barb the Barbie were right—was Gus in trouble? I glanced at my computer screen. The log file from last night's computer programming session popped open. I looked at the error messages. All the boo-boos were easily correctible. Of course, that didn't mean new ones wouldn't crop up once this batch was fixed. Such was the axiom of programming: *Software means never having to say you're finished.* I slipped Guns 'n' Roses into the CD player. Time to hack.

Two CDs later, I sat back and picked up my scissors and a piece of brown construction paper. I'd corrected all of the errors and the completed program was now running with the test data I normally used for database programs. I watched as the logic of the program progressed, dipping into those 'houses' I'd described for Gus—the subroutines that never fired.

This time they did fire. I'd substituted Charlie's code for those odd routines that never appeared to be used. Now the data went into the routines. I got a feedback message, indicating data had entered the loop.

But nothing happened. The data went in and it came out. The routine was being used, but it wasn't doing anything.

I sat back in frustration. I had been so sure that I was on to something. I was certain that Charlie's programming fragments would make Nelson's code do...something. I adjusted my headphones and stared at the screen. There were no error messages, no glitches, no problems. The programs all fit together like they'd been made for each other.

Why weren't they working? Why weren't they doing anything?

I pulled over my stack of snipping paper and selected a rich gold for George Harrison's Nehru jacket. I started to snip, glancing at the CD cover to refresh my memory.

Nothing is real.

The words teased me. I still didn't have any idea how I was going to do the intricate lettering on the cover. Of course, I didn't have to do the lettering. Anyone seeing the big yellow submarine and the four Beatles would know what the cover depicted. But if I didn't do the lettering, there'd be a big black blob in the foreground of the picture. The lettering and the submarine broke up the blob and added color.

Color.

Something added color.

I stared out into the atrium, trying to will the nugget of information to ferret its way out of the depths of my brain and to the forefront. I saw Brian at his desk, his glasses like Little Orphan Annie disks glinting in the sunlight. I made a mental note to tell him about Nelson's apology. Poor Brian had looked so upset the other day when Nelson chewed me out. He'd be relieved to know that Nelson was back to his old self...sort of.

I looked down at the gold paper in my hand.

Gold.

Color.

I looked back up at the data scrolling past on my screen.

Charlie had given me two types of files on the CD. Most of them were program files. But he'd also left me a data file—a data file that had color in it. He'd used the names of people in the data list with last names that were colors.

I opened a new window on my computer screen and brought up his data file. I opened another window and compared the standard data file I used for testing next to Charlie's.

They were different, not just in content but in structure. Each file was a long list of individual lines of numbers, letters, and symbols. But Charlie's file had extra words at the end of each line. The extra letters were preceded by a series of symbols: ##@##. I counted the list of entries. He'd included fifty entries. It looked like none of them repeated.

I looked at the program subroutines again. A database is essentially a series of rows and columns. Each row was a record and each column was another piece of data that went into that record. The databases that Nelson worked on were far more complex than that, but at their heart they were simple matrices—endless rows with corresponding columns. A database update program, like the one I was testing, went into the individual rows and updated the information in the columns. When I'd customized the subroutines to use Charlie's code, I had included what I thought were enough columns for each row. But looking at the data file that Charlie had included, I now realized that an additional column could be added—the one after the odd series of symbols at the end of each row of data in Charlie's file.

I put down my snips and started coding again.

It took almost the entire *Wall* CD before I finished. While the program compiled I opened up the corporate mail directory and scanned it, then dialed Gus's home number. The call bounced to his answering machine. I left what I hoped was a breezy message: *Hey, give me a call. I'm working on those files Charlie gave me and I've got a great idea on how they work. So call me as soon as you can.* I wanted to add something like "...and tell me how you feel so I can tell you how I feel and we can talk about how we feel..." but I decided not to be pushy.

The program finished compiling, which meant it was theoretically ready to run. I accessed Charlie's data file, setting it to be read into the program. I sat back and watched the results.

I was right. There was something there.

Chapter Fifteen

The subroutines fired. Data flowed into the loops, sat there, was manipulated, and flowed back out. I stared at the log files scrolling on my computer screen, fascinated.

Updated information marched in tidy rows on the monitor. Each line started with a ten-digit number followed by what looked like a name, a date, more numbers, and a two-letter abbreviation, then more numbers, letters, and symbols, like this:

```
9817263032EL-AMIRSCOTT01060612302030NW##CC3211
7718291820WHITEIZAKMU'EED01110600000830UA###FD10913
1930484372GREENFATIMA01210611302000BA###CC4763
```

The list went on with the final two letters often repeated. The other information changed, though, except for the two digits in the second set of numbers: 01. There was one other noticeable thing—the names were all unusual, containing special characters not normally found in American or European names such as apostrophes and hyphens. Charlie's subroutine had handled this anomaly flawlessly, which told me he'd anticipated this oddity.

The program finished running through the data Charlie had provided. I stared at the mix of numbers and names then went back to the original list. I created a quick little subroutine that would output the information before it went into the subroutines, then while it was in the subroutines, and at its final destination. I inserted the lines of code, compiled the program then set it to run while I went for a potty break.

When I came back a stack of folders was sitting on my desk. I opened the top one and saw the specs for the Fairfield project. John must have dropped them off when I was in the bathroom. I pushed them aside and sat down.

The program was churning away, data scrolling down the screen then being stored into a file I'd set up.

I looked at the initial set of output and on a whim, opened up a Google window in a new window on my computer. I typed in NW##CC3211. Nothing—just an error message—"*Did you mean* NW##C3211?" Following that link took me to the web page for a law office, somewhere in Southern California. I tried another tack and typed in "NW." Northwest Airlines was the first item on the results page.

I typed "UA" and got results for United Airlines, the University of Alabama, and the United Association of the plumbing, pipefitting, refrigeration and fire sprinkler industry. Interesting. I cleared the screen and typed "BA" in the search pane.

The first item on the search results page was British Airways.

Three airlines? I skimmed through the rest of the file and saw initials for KL, SY, DL. I typed each into the Google search pane. The only one that didn't return an airline as the first result was SY. I had to scroll to the bottom of the page before I found it—Sun Country.

KLM, Delta, Sun Country, United, Northwest, British Airways. All were airlines that flew out of Minneapolis. Coincidence? Was Charlie's data going through and accessing something to do with people associated with the airline industry?

Holy shit.

Drew had said that kidnapper terrorists were holding Nelson's brother hostage. Nelson's program had something to do with the airline industry. One plus one equaled—what?

I pulled over my phone and dialed Gus again. Once again I got his answering machine. I left a more excited message this time: *Call me, Gus. I think I've found something in Charlie's code. It's important. Call me at work.* Then I dug out Alex Raney's business card and called the number listed there. A bored-sounding woman informed me that he was out of the office and she'd see that he got my message to call him.

I was itching to talk to somebody about my discovery. I didn't have long to wait. My phone rang almost as soon as I replaced it. “Ready to exercise? Sounds like we have a lot to talk about,” Denise's laughing voice said when I answered.

I thought of all that had transpired since I'd last seen her—seeing Gus at the mall, the snowstorm, Gus staying with me, finding the kittens, finding the Busty Barb at Gus's apartment, Officer Moran on my couch—good heavens, a lifetime had passed in just a few short days. “No kidding. I'll be there in a minute.” I snatched up my gym bag stored under my desk, set the screen saver on my computer and was gone in a minute.

Fifteen minutes later, Denise and I were on the treadmills in the building's small gym, doing our weekly 'walk'. In better weather we'd be outside, but with sub-zero temperatures and a fresh two inches of snow on top of the ten inches we'd gotten earlier, we opted for warmth and non-slick surfaces.

“So tell all,” she demanded as we paced sedately for our warm-up. Eight treadmills were grouped together in one corner near two elliptical machines and three exercise bikes. We took the two machines closest to the wall near a window. We had a prime view of the snowy outside world and the city street that wound in front of our office.

I glanced around the small room. Sarah Diver, an administrative assistant in Sales, was on the Nautilus machine. Bob Davies from Customer Support was working out with the free weights. They were far enough away that no gossip would reach them above the music piped in from a local radio station. The other three people in the room were strangers, probably from one of the other offices in the building.

I told Denise about Gus coming to my house. She almost fell off the treadmill when I said, “And he had to stay overnight because of the storm.”

“He what?” She righted herself in time but had to jog to get back in pace.

“Shh.” Sarah looked over at us and smiled. I gave a wave in return then said in a low voice, “Keep your voice down. I don't want the whole company to know.”

“So did you two—you know—did you like—” Denise panted, adjusting to the pace her treadmill was setting. “Did you do it?”

"Well, duh. Yes, we did."

"Holy cow. I thought you said you weren't going to let him get within a mile of you. His dick isn't that long, is it?"

"Denise!" I looked around but the person nearest to us, another woman on a bike, appeared oblivious to our conversation. Her short iron gray hair conflicted with the energy she was putting into her workout. She appeared in her sixties but her body said thirty.

"I can't believe you did that," Denise said, her green eyes wide with shock. "You slept with him? You barely know him!"

"I'm older than the age of consent." The treadmill started to speed up according to our pre-programmed routine. I was glad for the distraction. "Hell, Denise, I'm older than dirt—why shouldn't he and I—well, you know?"

"Honestly, you're so naïve."

"Naïve? Me? What are you talking about?" I was starting to get angry. I'd figured she'd be surprised, but… "Naïve?"

"This isn't the Sixties," she said in a low voice, finding her stride on the machine. Her red-blonde curls vibrated with energy. "It's not all peace, love, and rock and roll. For heaven's sake, you can't just go around sleeping with people in this day and age. There're all kinds of perverts out there. He could be a serial killer and you wouldn't know it. You are so trusting, I can't believe you did that. What about diseases or—" Her eyes widened. "You did use something, didn't you? A condom?"

"Just shout it out why don't you?" I looked around. Luckily some angry hip-hop music was blaring out on the overhead radio, so no one noticed Denise's outburst about prophylactics.

"You did, didn't you?" She began to jog. Denise is so thin she doesn't jiggle when she jogs. "You used something?"

I, on the other hand, jiggle when I run, so I don't jog. But I did set a hard pace for my workout. "Yes, we used something."

"Did he bring it?"

I nodded, not willing to admit that I had a small

stash of condoms tucked away in a bedside drawer, bought in a fit of optimism.

"He must have been planning it then." She was finally starting to gasp, which cheered me. I hated it when she jogged effortlessly as I struggled with a measly three-and-a-half miles an hour on my machine. Then I realized she was probably gasping because of outrage, not physical exertion.

"What do you mean, planning it?"

"He came prepared. He was probably angling for you all along. I doubt if men just carry condoms with them all the time unless they hope to get lucky."

I hadn't thought of it that way. True, Gus had brought along a couple of condoms, which we'd supplemented with the ones I'd purchased. As it turned out, I was glad I'd done my shopping that day at Wal-Mart. "Maybe he was hopeful."

She gave a short laugh. "I can't believe you did that, Jessie. That's such reckless behavior."

I was starting to get pissed. "I'm a grown-up. I can make my own decisions."

She must have heard my anger. "I know, I know. It's just that the world has changed so much since you were single. I guess I've gotten paranoid now that Lisa has started dating." She made a face. "I can't believe I have a daughter who's a teenager. I can't be that old. Dear God, there's so much to worry about now. You hear about girls being snatched off the street or taken from a parking lot in a mall. And then you're telling me you slept with this strange guy. I'm sorry, but it's just scary."

I laughed, my irritation forgotten. "Thanks for the concern. But I'm not worried. Gus is a nice guy. I trust him."

She shot me a shrewd look then refocused on her moving treadmill. "Is that all? Was it just some temporary thing? Is that how you feel?"

I didn't want to examine how I felt, so I changed the subject. "That's not important now. What is important—"

"Not important?" She grabbed her water bottle and took a swig. "Holy moly, you sleep with some guy—the first guy you've even gone out with since your husband died, and you say that's not important? I'd say that's momentous."

I waved a hand. "Not important. Listen, Gus is a cop. He's in the FBI."

This time she had to grab the support rails to keep from tripping. "He's what?"

Her voice carried over the TV set. Sarah and the strange woman both shot us a curious look. "It's okay," I called out. "I just tripped." I leveled a glare at Denise. "Keep it down, would you? That's Sarah over there—she works with the Suits. I don't want everybody in Tieland to know my business." I looked over my shoulder at slender little Sarah, who was defying gravity in a yoga pose near the wall of mirrors in the stretching area. "You heard me, he's in the FBI."

"How do you know?"

"My brother Drew called a guy he knows who works in the government."

Denise digested this news for a minute. "Okay, I take back what I said about you being naïve. That was smart, having Drew check the guy out."

I decided not to tell her that Drew did the research without my prompting. "I'm not a total idiot. The interesting thing is that Gus is here because of something weird going on at CodeBusters. Gus thinks there might be something the government needs to look at. You know, conspiracy stuff."

"Oh, for—" Denise tapped some buttons on the treadmill. "If you keep giving me these shocks I'm going to kill myself." Her machine slowed until she could walk. "Now tell me what the hell is going on." She dabbed at her sweaty neck with a towel.

I sketched out the basics of the code Charlie had given me, the code Nelson had written and the weird output I'd seen when I put the two together. "Alex Raney thinks whoever is behind it was the one who broke into my house last night."

"Broke in?" She tapped some more buttons on the machine. "That does it. What the hell happened? Who broke in?" Her machine slowed to a crawl.

I told her about the hunter, the snowmobiler, and Alex Raney, who had the hots for Gus's sister-in-law, widow of Gus's dead stepbrother. When I finished, Denise was staring at me, her mouth agape. “Good Lord, I don't see you for a couple of days, and look what happens!” She gulped some more water, almost choking. “Did you tell them about the code? About using Charlie's pieces with the other stuff?”

I shook my head. “I just figured that out, so no, I haven't talked to anybody about it. I tried, but nobody was there. I left messages.” I glanced around the gym again. The lunchtime rush was starting. My machine started to slow, going into my cool-down. “I can't believe Nelson had anything to do with it. This is Minnesota, for heaven's sake. We don't have terrorists here.”

“Remember that guy who was training at the flight school here in the suburbs right before 9/11?” Denise whispered, leaning close to me. “Believe me, it can happen anywhere.”

“Yeah, but he was a foreigner. He wasn't Nelson Scott, who grew up in Mankato and went to the University of Minnesota.” I gulped some of my water. “I can't believe CodeBusters is involved in anything so earth-shattering. Besides, if there were something serious going on, Alex Raney would have somebody on it like a duck on a June bug. There are no cops around, he's not returning my calls, and that cop who spent the night on my couch said as much. She said there wasn't anything to worry about. And John said the same thing. He said the police were wrapping it all up and we wouldn't be bothered again.”

Denise hopped off her machine and went to the stretching area, taking a spot on the far side of the small space. I followed her and began my standing stretches. “I still say it must be something. All those airlines must mean something.” She looked around as Sarah joined us. “You used to work for the airlines, didn't you?”

Sarah was a cute girl in her mid-twenties with honey-colored hair and a waist the size of my thigh. Besides being pretty she was also nice. “I was a stewardess for a couple of years.” She began a graceful series of moves, stretching to one side then the other.

She didn't look old enough to have even been working for a couple of years, much less have been in a career that required training. “What was that like?” I asked, trying to mimic her movement. I did a credible imitation for a middle-aged woman.

"It stunk," she said cheerfully. "It's like working on a Greyhound bus any more. Some of the passengers were so rude. And the pay was lousy."

"Really? I thought it was sort of..." I hesitated. "I don't know, fun."

"That's the way they make it seem, but it's just a lot of hard work. You know the crew only gets paid once the plane leaves the gate, don't you?"

"What?" I thought of the long check-ins I'd experienced and the time spent sitting at the gate, waiting for the plane to take off. "Really?"

She nodded, reaching her arms over her head then drooping down to touch her feet. "The crew gets paid from the time the plane leaves until it docks." She spoke from her upside-down position, her voice muffled. "It's complicated. Your rate of pay depends on seniority, how many passengers you have, the size of the plane, whether it's a domestic or overseas flight...It's just about impossible to calculate your salary every month."

"Yeah, but you get all the flying privileges," Denise pointed out as she plucked an exercise mat from the stack and tossed it down to continue her stretching from the floor.

"True. And that's fun for a while. But when you live at a hub airport the way we do, it's cheap to fly just about anywhere." Sarah wrinkled her nose as she stared at herself in the floor to ceiling mirror. I faced away from my reflection, not wanting confirmation of my creaking joints and not-so-svelte self. I flopped down on my own mat, next to Denise.

"Did you ever have any security scares?" Denise asked. "Did you ever have something happen on a flight that was spooky?"

"Not really." She laughed. "A guy once brought on a box of frozen goat steaks. Goats!" She shook her head. "Like goats don't grow in Jamaica?"

"He got on the plane with that?" I asked.

"No, they stopped him at check-in. He was on the No Fly list, so he would have been stopped anyway the minute he showed his ID. That kind of crap happened all the time." Sarah sat down next to us to continue stretching.

"What's the No Fly list?" I tried to imitate her foot-in-the-crotch-and-bend position but couldn't manage it. I just didn't have that much bend any more.

"The government has a list of known criminals, suspicious people, foreign nationals—people like that. And each airline has a No Fly list, too. It's got people who caused a fuss on flights, or drunks or people who've gotten in trouble on the airline for some reason or another."

I sat up. This sounded useful. "How does it work? Do you check everybody's ID when they check in? Does the gate person do that?"

"They're supposed to compare the ID to the person then compare the ID to the list. And the computers do a lot of pre-screening, too."

Denise and I exchanged a conspiratorial look. "Pre-screening?"

"Whenever you book a flight, your name goes into a database and is checked against the list. That kind of screening doesn't worry me so much, though."

"How so?" Denise worked herself into a complicated yoga pose that made my thighs ache just to watch.

"The government is so worried about screening passengers, but they don't screen the staff at the airports as good as they should." Sarah got up to prop one leg on the ballet bar, draping gracefully over her knee. "You've got the pilots and the cabin crew and the cleaning crews, not to mention the guys who bring in the food. Then there's the ground crew—the guys who schlep the luggage and haul around the gasoline and prep the plane." She shook her head, her long ponytail bobbing with the motion. "Everybody is supposed to be screened and secure, but who knows for sure?"

"Don't they have to wear ID badges?" I remembered seeing people with colored badges at the airport.

"Some of them don't." Sarah eyed herself critically in the mirror. "Take the cleaning crews, for example—most of the crew are immigrants who just have green cards, so they don't have any permanent ID here in this country. They're supposed to be supervised by someone who has security clearance, but a lot of times I'd see them in the cabin, cleaning, and I'd never see a supervisor anywhere nearby." She frowned at her reflection.

I followed her gaze and saw a slender girl with worried brown eyes. Then I saw her eyes move to someone behind us. Paul Henderson had just come in to the room, looking tall, dark, and anchor-guy handsome. Sarah's cheeks reddened and she ducked her head. *Ah ha,* I thought. *Another girl falls for a pretty face.* I waved to Paul and he came to stand near us.

"Jessie, I meant to call you again." He smiled at Denise, whom he knew and Sarah, who was sidling away, dabbing at her sweat-soaked face.

"Thanks for sending me that email, I gave it to the cop in charge of the case." I leaned back to stare up at him from my spot on the mat. "By the way, do you know Sarah Diver? Sarah, this is Paul Henderson, he works on the first floor."

Sarah stopped as though pole-axed. "No, we haven't meet."

Paul's attention swung from me to Sarah. "Hey, Sarah. Nice to meet you."

Poor Sarah looked like she wanted to melt. I longed to tell her she looked cute and sexy in her Spandex and T-shirt even though she wouldn't have believed me. But I think she must have seen something in Paul's appreciative look, because she straightened her shoulders and held out a hand, flashing him a big smile. "Nice to meet you."

He held her hand just a tad bit too long. Denise waggled her eyebrows at me. I hid over my knees in a stretch to disguise my grin. I heard them talking in low voices for a minute then Paul said, "Did that email have anything to do with that cop who came to see me?"

I straightened up. "Cop?"

Paul grinned. "Yeah. A tall blonde with an attitude."

I rolled my eyes. "Barb the Barbarian," I said to Denise.

Paul nodded in confirmation. "She's interesting, all right. She talked to me earlier this week about the potluck." He glanced at Sarah. "I have an allergy and had to go to the hospital."

"That's awful that the signs got mixed up." She began

to saunter toward the locker room. “I need to get back to work now. It was nice meeting you.”

Paul followed her. “Nice talking to you, Jessie,” he called over his shoulder.

“You betcha.” Denise and I watched as they walked toward the doors leading to the showers and the locker rooms. “Well, how about that?” I muttered.

“How about that indeed?” Denise took a swig of water. “What do you think about that No Fly list thing? Do you think that's what Charlie's program was doing? Was Nelson's code mucking around with that list?”

“I don't know.” I scrambled to my feet and tossed my mat toward the stack. “But I'm going to see if I can figure it out.”

Denise followed suit. “You'd better call the police again. This could be dangerous.”

“What? Nobody knows I'm hacking on the code and hardly anybody knows Charlie left me that CD.” I shook my head. “It's just an interesting intellectual exercise. And if I can figure something out, well, so much the better.”

She grinned. “There's nothing a tester likes better than a puzzle.”

I thought about that as I showered, dressed, and grabbed a sandwich from the cafeteria before returning to my cube. Was that why Charlie had left me the data? We hadn’t known each other long, but had become close while going through our grieving. Had Charlie entrusted this information with me because he knew I'd try to solve it?

I sat at my desk and stared out at the freeway beyond the building. Charlie had given his life for this. Despite all that had happened, I couldn't lose sight of that fact. Charlie. Was. Dead. And he was dead because of something he'd found out.

Slow anger started to burn in my gut. He didn't deserve that. Charlie was a good guy who was trying to do the right thing. He didn't deserve to be murdered and forgotten like this. I was as guilty as the next person. I'd successfully managed to push aside the awful knowledge of his death, relegating it to 'spooky, scary, and won't happen again'.

Well, it damn sure wasn't going to happen again. I

was going to figure out this puzzle and make sure whoever killed Charlie got what they deserved. I wasn't quite sure how I was going to do it, but he wasn't going to die for nothing.

I could almost hear his laughter in my ear as I turned to my computer to examine the data that had been processed while Denise and I exercised. Cheered by this ghostly presence, I settled down to work.

Chapter Sixteen

Before I got far, my blinking message light on my desk phone distracted me. I retrieved the voice mail, relieved to hear Gus's voice.

"Jessie, I'm going to be tied up today, but I'm hoping to see you tonight. Stick with the officer that Alex has assigned to you, just to be on the safe side. I'm not sure what's going on, I've been—" He hesitated. I wondered what phrases he was trying out in his head, considering and rejecting the wording. "I've been reassigned. But I'm trying to stay current with the case as well as I can. Anyway, like I said, make sure to stay with the officer Alex has with you. That way nothing will screw up. I miss you, Jessie. I can't wait to see you again."

Officer? What officer? Obviously Gus wasn't getting his messages from home nor had he talked to Alex. I pulled out my accordion project file and rooted in it for the scrap of paper he'd given me the other day, the one that had his mobile phone number on it. I spread out the various clippings I'd done, surprised at how many pieces of the Yellow Submarine there were. Before I could find the right scrap, though, someone knocked on my cube wall. I looked up to see Roshi Ahmadi, another tester, standing there.

"Time for our meeting," she said. "We're in Lake Calhoun."

Meeting? I looked at the synch cradle, where Barry always sat, waiting to blare out Dire Straits' *Money for Nothing*, my meeting reminder ring tone of choice. Only it wasn't sitting there today. I'd lost track of my days. We always had a meeting of the QA department on Friday at one o'clock. "Damn, where's Barry?" I looked down at my bag, still unpacked from where I'd tossed it that morning.

"John is running the meeting today," Roshi said.

"Nelson's busy."

"That's good," I said, snatching up a notepad and pen. "He's been under a lot of stress lately." I was relieved I wouldn't have to look Nelson in the eyes. I was thinking the guy might be consorting with terrorists, after all. I wasn't sure I could sit in the same room with him and maintain an innocent face.

I looked back at my desk. The Osama Bin Laden Blue Meanie grinned me, evil and malicious. Roshi started edging away after a look at her wristwatch. I grabbed some snip paper and my scissors as I followed her to the conference room.

It was, thankfully, just a standard status meeting. We all reported on our projects, giving a summary of how testing had gone that week and where we stood with deadlines. When my turn came, I gave a non-committal 'wrapped up Nelson's database project and starting the Fairfield contract'. John didn't press me for details and no one else seemed interested, so I didn't have to lie too extensively. After making plans for attendance at Charlie's memorial service the following day, John adjourned the meeting. He gestured to me as I started to leave.

"I read through the report you gave me on the database project. How much more testing do you think it really needs?"

"A week, probably. Although I've been running some test routines on it today."

"Really? I thought you were moving on to the Fairfield thing." He smiled when he said it, so I knew he was just teasing me.

I shrugged. "I thought I saw a connection between Nelson's stuff and Charlie's fragments, the ones he left me in those files."

"A connection?" John leaned back in his conference room chair. His sharp gaze seemed to pin me to the floor. "What kind of connection?"

It suddenly struck me. Was John involved in this? How much did he know? Did he know about Nelson's brother and the terrorist kidnapping? Gus had said initially that he was working with John and with Bob Madison. Gus had called John and I'd talked to him, but...The events of the last few days were all muddled in my head. I decided to play it safe. "I'm not really sure. It's just that some of Charlie's code looked like it might be a good fit as a replacement for some of Nelson's. I thought I'd play with it a bit."

John tapped on the table blotter with a pencil. "You didn't see anything obvious?"

I busied myself with rearranging the snips in my hand so he couldn't see my eyes. My eyes always gave me away when I lied. "Nope. Nothing obvious." *Not a big lie,* I thought. *It wasn't obvious.*

"Move on, Jessie." His voice was low and intense. "Forget about the code."

Unspoken but heard was *if you know what's good for you.* Or was I projecting my worries onto short, pudgy, benign John? I couldn't trust my own judgment any more. "No problem," I said airily. "I'll get started on reviewing the new specs."

"Good. Do that." He smiled but it didn't seem to reach his eyes.

I beat a retreat, not anxious to see more boogie men around me. I went to my cube and dropped into my chair. I swiveled around to stare at my computer screen. As I did, I saw that Osama had moved. He was no longer in the center of my desk but was askew, another snip in the shape of a broccoli-like tree partially on his head. I stared at the vivid blue paper topped by the curvy tree. It reminded me of...someone. Something? Then the implications of his movement struck me. Had someone been in my cube? Or was I once again projecting my worries?

My forgotten half-sandwich called to me. I unwrapped the roast beef on wheat and took a bite, my stomach grumbling at my forgetfulness. I turned to my computer screen and typed in my login to disable the screen saver. The results of my program were displayed in two windows. I stared at the lines of output, trying to make sense of it all. I compared the original data file with the changed data file, the list that came out of the last subroutine.

The names were changed. Not every name—just the odd ones, the ones with apostrophes and hyphens in them.

The foreign names were changed to things like 'Patricia Smith' and 'Samuel Martin'. Somewhere in the program the data that was fed into the program was changed.

But why? Why would someone go to that trouble?

I sat back and took a bite of roast beef. Surely Nelson knew that we didn't just turn programs over to the government and—voila—they got used. After we tested the code and turned it over, government programmers tested it. They'd see this manipulation of data.

Wouldn't they?

I looked at my desk and the pieces of the Yellow Submarine wycinanki. The layers of paper would produce a 3-D effect when I put it all together. Just like Charlie's subroutines had sifted through the layers of Nelson's code. Somehow logic had been introduced that altered the database without producing errors. But even though no errors occurred, government testers would find the changes. Nelson would know that.

I started layering the pieces of the artwork, as always using snip work to kick-start my brain. Nelson had worked in government coding long enough to know his alterations would be found out. Was he counting on that? I shifted Osama to his spot on the white background I was using. Was Nelson counting on the Department of Transportation, or Homeland Security or whoever was using this program, to find out the substitutions he'd made?

It made sense, or at least as much sense as anything did this crazy week. Nelson designed a program to do what he was told to do by the kidnappers who had his brother. But the program wouldn't fool government testers. Maybe he was hoping that producing a program would be enough to save his brother. This all assumed that Nelson was being blackmailed and that his brother was in danger. I was, after all, going on hearsay and speculation about this.

I turned to my computer and opened a new text screen, typing the ideas as they rolled out of my brain and into my fingers:

Nelson designed a program that would substitute ordinary names (like 'John Smith') for the names of foreign nationals. The pertinent parts of his program would not be used unless a data file with a specific marker or designation was used.

I paused, remembering the data file Charlie had given me. I couldn't remember if there'd been a header line in the file that might be a designator. I made a mental note to check it again.

Then the necessary subroutines would be used and the data would be changed. That way, Nelson could ship the code, it could be tested with the standard data that the government used, and no one would find what it did because they didn't have the right kind of data file.

How did Charlie find it?

The program pieces that Charlie gave me were designed to fit into Nelson's code. Charlie must have seen them somehow, somewhere, and started to suspect it. Or else the FBI or Homeland Security or whoever Gus worked for had come in, and asked John or Bob Madison to assign someone to keep an eye on Nelson's work. Charlie had programmed for years before he moved on to become a Marketeer. He'd be a logical choice to evaluate stray bits of code that came his way. If companies could track the keystrokes employees made and the email they sent, they could certainly track one programmer's work.

I looked past my computer screen, out into the atrium. Brian was sitting at his terminal, his back to me. Sunlight glinted on the mirror over his desk. CodeBusters employed some of the most gifted programmers in the Twin Cities, if not the Midwest. I nodded. It would be possible.

Let's say someone was suspicious about Nelson. They'd track his files and his computer usage. It's tricky when we use laptops that plug into the network, but there are troll programs that can sniff through a hard disk even on a laptop that's not always connected to the network.

I finished the last of my sandwich, pushing the remnants away. As I did, my Yellow Submarine pieces shifted. I glared at the CD cover. I still had to do the damn lettering and the more intricate pieces of the design.

I remembered a wycinanki I'd done earlier in the spring for Denise's daughter. I'd agonized over how to snip out the little pieces of a Lord of the Ring movie scene which featured the blonde elf that Lisa so adored. Charlie saw me struggling with it and asked, "Why don't you just copy the hard parts and paste the rest of it on the copy?"

I snatched up the *Yellow Submarine* CD cover. "Charlie, you're a genius," I muttered. I started to leave my cube then saw the file, still displayed on my screen. I clicked 'print'. The nearest printer to me was in the mailroom, which also held a color copier. I could accomplish two missions with one trip.

I'd taken two steps out of my cube when my phone rang. I hesitated then grabbed the receiver. It was Alex Raney. "I thought you were supposed to be off the database thing and working on something else," he said without so much as a '*how did it go with the rude woman who sat on your couch all night?*'

"You got my message? Good. Yeah, I am supposed to be working on the Fairfield project but I had an idea. You remember those files that Charlie left me? I figured out that I could plug them into the other code I was testing and—"

"It won't do any good to tell me about it. You need to talk to the computer forensic tech who's been working on it. I'll get in touch with him and have him call you. I think you'll need to come in and show him what you're talking about."

I thought about the complicated subroutines I'd examined for the past few days. "Yeah, I think I will. Where is he?"

"In Minneapolis, at the downtown department."

I groaned. "I hate driving downtown. Can't he come and see me?"

"No, princess, he can't. Let me call him and see what I can arrange. I'll have somebody come and pick you up."

"I hope it's someone with more personality than the last cop you gave me."

"This isn't a social thing, in case you've forgotten."

"I haven't forgotten. Where's Gus?"

"What?"

"You heard me. Where's Gus? I've tried to call him but I just get his answering machine. Do you have his mobile phone number? I don't think I have it."

"Why do you need to talk to him?"

"None of your business. Just give me his phone number." Then I remembered the times I'd called Alex Raney and Gus had been there, lurking in the background. "Is he there? If he is, put him on, I want to talk to him."

"He's not here. He's...busy."

"Damn it." I was getting tired of all these allusions to Gus's problems. "Is he in trouble? Has he been suspended? He said when he called he'd been reassigned. What does that mean?"

"He called you?" Raney's voice was definitely sharper now. "When?"

"After lunch. Why?"

"That stupid—" I heard him take a long breath, reining in his temper. "He's going to blow this whole operation if he's not careful."

"What? What operation? I thought you said everything was fine and you were just wrapping up the details."

"He can still blow it." Raney's voice was a snarl of rage. "I thought he was smarter than this. I didn't think he'd let his feelings get in the way like this."

"What? What feelings?" I looked at my computer screen. *Your file has printed* appeared in a small banner at the bottom. Shit. I'd forgotten I'd even printed the damn thing. I edged toward the cube door, dragging the phone with me. "Listen, I have to go. What feelings? What are you talking about? Did Gus say something?"

"Don't act dumb. You know how he feels about you."

I stopped in my tracks, the possibility of information overriding my common sense. "No, I don't. How does he feel?" Then I wanted to slap myself on the head. Even if Gus had said something, could I believe Alex Raney?

Raney laughed. "I'm not getting into this. You and Gus will have to hash that out. I'll have that tech call you."

"Tell him to call me in ten minutes. I have to do something."

"Can't you sit still for five minutes while he—"

"No, I can't." The mailroom printer was seldom used but I still didn't want anybody else seeing that printout. "Have him call me. And if you see Gus, have him call me, too." I hung up, snatched up the CD cover and left before the phone could ring again.

I passed the lunchroom and a couple of offices then ducked into the mailroom. The big copier/printer was silent. No printout was on the output tray. I bent over, peeking inside the machine. Nope, no paper. I looked at the LCD readout on front. I'd never used it before to check the printer queue but I knew it could be done. I poked a button experimentally.

Brian came into the room. "Hey, Jessie," he said, going to the mailboxes. "Problems? That printer seems to jam a lot."

"Do you know how it works? I thought you used the one over by your cube." The LCD readout said *status normal*. I glared at it. How could it be normal if my output had vanished? My finger hovered over another button.

"This is the only color one on this floor, I use it now and then. What's wrong?" He came to stand next to me, peering down at the tiny readout.

I glanced at him. As always, he was dressed in the height of absent-minded fashion. His brown V-neck sweater covered a wrinkled blue shirt haphazardly tucked into high-water faded black jeans. His hair, wiry and black, stuck up in small curly clumps and his black-rimmed glasses gave him a raccoonish look.

"Are you printing or copying?" he asked, touching a button on a side panel.

"Both. I printed something and now I want to copy something."

He pressed the small touch screen, rapidly going through a series of menu options. I watched, impressed. "You can access the printer queue from here," he said, looking down at the readout. "It also shows up online if you know the right commands. I check it now and then to make sure the printer isn't busy in case I want to print a big job. It looks like your printer job finished. It should be in the output tray."

I bent over again to check. "Nope. No printout."

Brian opened the front of the machine and peered into the belly. "No jams here. It would say so on the monitor. Maybe somebody picked up your printout. Or—"

He went to the mailboxes. “Here you go.” He pulled something out of my slot and handed it to me. “It must have printed and someone put it in your box.”

I looked down at the paper. My name was in the top corner in bold type, indicating it was my printout. I wondered who'd seen it and if they'd read it. “Thanks, Brian.” I folded the paper and turned to the copy machine.

“So where's that guy?” he asked, digging his hands in his pockets and watching as I positioned the Yellow Submarine CD cover on the copier surface.

“What guy?” My finger hovered over the various selections for enlargement.

“The old guy in the cube next to you.” He bounced up and down on his toes.

“Old guy?” I settled on one-hundred and twenty percent, touched the button and pressed 'Start'.

“You know, the guy with the beard and the glasses.”

My copy slid out of the machine. I examined it. Not big enough. “Gus? I don't know. I think he was called away or something.” I tried one-hundred and forty percent and pressed 'Start'.

“I thought you were dating him.”

I looked around at the odd tone in Brian's voice. He sounded surprised, like I should have an inside track on where Gus was at all times. “Nope. He and I went out for—” I stopped, not wanting to mention my coffee date with Gus in front of a guy with whom I'd had a similar date. “We just talked.” I examined my new copy. This was more like it, but the colors weren't quite as sharp as I wanted. I touched the LCD screen where it said 'Copy machine' and a new menu appeared. I examined the multitude of options.

“Really? I thought you guys were dating or something.”

It was the 'or something' that caught my attention this time. Brian definitely sounded pissed off. I stared at the little menu on the LCD panel, my ears hot with embarrassment. “Not really. Like I said, we just—”

“I seem to remember you saying that it wouldn't be smart to date a co-worker.” He had stopped bouncing up and down. In fact, he was standing close to me. I edged away but there was a wall on the right and not a lot of room to maneuver.

"I believe I did say that." I touched a few spots on the menu pad at random then pressed 'Start'. "And Gus and I aren't dating."

"Oh."

I felt his disbelief like a little cloud, blooming over his head, hovering in my direction.

"Did he get his truck fixed?"

"What?" I edged past him and got my copy out of the bin. The blues were very, very blue. I looked down at the LCD screen, more to avoid Brian's gaze than to adjust the contrast. I touched a few more menu picks at random.

"His truck? I heard him talking about it. He said it broke down at your house."

I tapped 'Start'. "I don't know." I grabbed my latest copy, glanced at it then headed toward the doorway. "This looks just perfect. Thanks for the help, Brian."

He followed me out into the hallway. "Talk to you later, Jessie."

"Sure." I watched him walk away, disappearing around a corner. I waited a second before ducking back into the copy room. I messed around with the copy machine for a few more minutes, finally getting a version that I was happy with. It wasn't until I got back to my desk that I realized what about that conversation had bothered me.

Gus hadn't been in the office since his truck broke down. The night it happened, he spent at my house. The next morning we drove to his apartment and found the abandoned kittens. He was called away and I hadn't seen him since. I'd come to the office yesterday and worked then gone home to find my apartment broken into.

Gus hadn't been here to talk about his truck. So how did Brian know Gus's truck broke down? How did Brian know Gus spent the night at my house? I looked across the atrium. Brian was sitting at his desk again, his back to me. I looked down at the printout lying on my desk. Pieces of the puzzle fell into place, making me dizzy.

Brian could monitor the print queue from his desk. He could go to the printer and pick up anything I printed. His desk was as close, if not closer, to the printer than mine.

I'd printed my survey from Silver Harmony to that printer.

How long would it take to grab my survey, make a copy then put it back in the output tray? Better yet, how long would it take to monitor the queue, make a copy of a document, and print it to the printer near his desk?

For a programmer like Brian? No time at all.

I'd been right when I said Brian wouldn't bother hacking into Silver Harmony's database. He didn't have to. All he had to do was copy my survey answers, turn them in, and Silver Harmony would make the 'match'. He probably set up a fake account and shanghaied my email identity changes, too. Brian was a smart programmer. He'd been a hacker years ago and been given a deal if he helped the police. It happened when he was in high school. John had even joked about it once, saying how lucky it was that it had happened when Brian was a juvenile, otherwise he wouldn't have been able to get Department of Defense clearance. Juvenile offenses were often expunged or given less credence, depending on the crime. It was Brian. I was sure of it. But I didn't have any proof.

I looked at the printout I'd made detailing my suspicions about Charlie and Nelson. I didn't have any proof about that, either. Everything was just guesswork.

My phone rang. I picked it up, my brain still whirling with speculation and unanswered questions. "We'll meet at your house," Alex Raney said. "I've got somebody lined up to follow you home. Once you get there, call me and I'll come over with the computer tech, he's driving here to my office. Give me a call when you're ready to go home for the day. I'll need about ten minutes to get somebody in place."

"Why? I thought you said—"

"Would you just cooperate? We are wrapping this up, but I'd like to get your take on what's in those files. Our tech has come up with some ideas and he'd like to talk them over with you. It's no big deal, but it would be nice to have it spelled out."

"Who killed Charlie?" I demanded.

There was a long pause. "I can't discuss that. What time do you think you'll be leaving?"

I glanced out at the freeway. Light snow was falling,

it was Friday afternoon, and I was tired. "Soon. In fact, now."

"Okay. Wait ten minutes then take off. I'll have someone in an unmarked behind you. Don't drive like a madwoman again like you did the other day."

"What?"

"You heard me—you were speeding. Stay within the posted limits this time. I'll meet you at your place. See you soon."

Relief surged through me. This whole crazy, chaotic week truly was coming to an end. Hopefully I'd see Gus soon, I could turn over my suspicions to Alex Raney, and life would get back to normal.

I shut down my laptop and started packing up to leave. I pulled Barry out of my bag. I hadn't synched it, nor was it charged, but that shouldn't be a problem. I'd have a cop following me home. I tucked Barry and my project portfolio into my briefcase, slung my laptop strap over my shoulder and headed for the stairwell.

My weekend beckoned me.

Chapter Seventeen

I paused near the stairwell door and glanced back into CubeLand. I felt reluctant to leave but I couldn't put my finger on why—my email stalker was sitting in there, a guy probably involved with terrorists was back there someplace, and a V.P. whom I almost suspected was lurking somewhere, too. Why the hell would I want to stay?

I shrugged off the feeling, slung my bags over my shoulder, and jerked open the door. The steps were gritty with sand tracked in, making the footing treacherous. I slowed, not anxious to take a tumble just as relaxation was so close. Now that the solution to Charlie's murder was at hand, I could admit how stressed I'd been. I felt like I'd been on a merry-go-round, spun from one place to another and bobbing up and down to escape the next surprise to come at me.

I smiled at the analogy then amended it. I'd been on a carousel in a fun house—that was it. I never knew what was coming, I'd been spun in circles then tossed up and down, and now here I was, emerging into the light with my sweetie—hopefully—waiting for me. I wondered if I could talk Gus into going to the State Fair with me next summer and take a ride in the Tunnel of Love. Now that might be interesting.

The thought of Gus made me pause on the third floor landing near the badge reader for that floor. Where would we be next summer? Would we be together? New Mexico in the summertime—I shuddered at the thought. I hated anything warmer than eighty degrees and retreated into air conditioning at the first sign of humidity. Could two such opposites truly attract and stay attracted? I'd seen how Gus reacted to the cold and Minnesota was cold half of the year. Could I expect him to stay here with me?

The sound of the door opening above me woke me out of my fog. Man oh man, was I a kumquat or what? I was daydreaming in a drafty stairwell with twenty pounds of office equipment dragging me down. I started downward again as steps echoed above me, rapidly approaching. I had a sudden panicked moment—what if it was Nelson coming after me? I was alone in a stairwell with no one nearby to help if I needed it. This wasn't the smartest place to be if a terrorist wanted to trap me.

I hurried as fast as I dared, passing the second floor landing where I had to make a slight jog down a narrow hallway to get to the last flight of stairs to the ground level. I glanced behind me. The footsteps were scuffling above me on the cement stairs and they sounded closer. I hurried to the last set of steps, almost hurtling in my haste.

The main stairwell didn't go all the way to the basement level, where the underground parking garage was located. In order to reach the garage via the steps, you had to go to the first floor, traverse the lobby then go down another set of steps, these far more ornate than the utilitarian stairwell I'd just raced headlong down. This allowed the general public to use the first floor and the lower level, while keeping the office floors more secure since all the upper floors required the use of security badges via the stairwells for inward access.

I heard footsteps behind me. It was probably my imagination but they sounded BIG. They weren't 'spiky lady boots, tap-tap-tap'. These were 'Army boots, big and heavy, clump-clump-clump.' And they were fast. No way was this some woman in dress shoes, tiptoeing her way down the stairs and trying to avoid a tumble. Not with the speed I was hearing.

I slammed open the heavy gray metal door and emerged into the hall that led to the lobby. The gray and black faux marble tiles glinted in the sunlight that streamed in from the high atrium windows. I squinted in the bright light, briefly disoriented, my heart hammering so hard I was nauseous and sweaty. I made a silent vow to exercise more rigorously. Obviously my jaunts on the treadmill and laps in the swimming pool weren't doing much for my endurance if a dash down the stairs could wind me like that.

I passed by the windows of several offices, seeing people inside behind desks, oblivious to the terrorist threat in their own building. The cavernous lobby was almost empty. Two people sat on the plush seats next to the big windows, bundled up against the cold and staring outside, probably waiting for a ride. I glanced to my right, where the foyer for the bank of elevators led into the small cafeteria. It closed at two in the afternoon so was dark now, but I saw two men standing near the doors, talking. They were silhouetted against the light streaming in through the doors that led to the café. One man was Paul Henderson. The other man had his back to me so I couldn't see who it was.

Paul looked up as my footsteps echoed on the tile floor, his face surprised. I waved but didn't pause, heading for the carpeted stairs that led to the lower level of the parking garage. Outside the front doors I saw bright sunlight, the upper parking lot, and the U.S. flag whipping in the stiff breeze. As I started down, a big sedan pulled up and the two winter-padded people got to their feet, gathering bags and purses.

I looked behind me, curious about who had followed me out of the stairwell. A young-looking man wearing faded jeans, a dark sweater and yes, brown ankle-high lace-up boots, was crossing the tiled portion of the lobby, his dark topcoat open. He was dark-haired with a tanned, craggy face and a slender, athletic build. I didn't recognize him. As I got to the top step of the stairs that led down to the lower lobby, he raised a hand. I hesitated but kept going. Raney said he'd have someone follow me, which I took to mean my escort would wait for me outside. He'd said nothing about anyone inside, following me down the stairwell. And if he'd forgotten to mention it and consequently had scared me like this, I was going to read him the riot act.

I heard voices behind me. I think one was Paul's, raised in a question. I thought I heard my name but couldn't be sure over the echoing noises in the huge lobby as the bundled people opened the doors that led outwards, letting in a *whoosh* of cold air. I sped down the carpeted stairs and made a beeline for the doors to the foyer leading to the parking garage, anxious to get out of the building.

The three-glass-walled foyer offered little protection from the biting cold although it did block the worst of the wind that whistled through the pillars of the garage. Although it was three in the afternoon, the sunlight only penetrated the open sides of the garage. I wondered if my escort would pull up to the door or not. Several cars were idling, their exhaust plumes bright white in the frigid air. One of them was probably the person Alex Raney had assigned to me.

I felt like a target, standing in the cold entryway waiting to see if someone appeared. Raney had said someone would be following me. Did that mean they were here already and waiting out there in their warm car? Perhaps he'd gotten me someone with manners, unlike the lumpish Officer Moran who'd just watched as I hefted my belongings into the building that morning. Maybe I'd actually get some help with my baggage going home.

I jumped when a sharp bang sounded somewhere behind me, echoing in the empty space. I looked back, expecting to see a delivery dolly or maintenance gurney with its contents tipped on the floor, a cursing delivery man nearby. The lower lobby leading to the elevators was empty. I opened the glass doors and peeked inside. I heard shouting above me, from the upper lobby where I'd seen Paul just a few minutes earlier. I wasn't sure what to do—go back and see what was happening? Wait for my supposed escort? Go out to my car?

My laptop case started to slide off my shoulder, overbalancing me. Taking that as a sign from on high to get, I went back into the foyer and pushed open the doors to the garage. A blast of arctic air funneled through and hit me in the face. I fumbled my sunglasses out of my purse, more for wind protection than glare avoidance. I was rendered momentarily blind as I stepped into the darkened garage with my Mickey Mouse shades on.

I lowered my head into the wind, angling toward my car. As I neared Sally the Subaru, I glimpsed a small dark sedan nearby, white exhaust smoke curling around its tailpipe. A woman sat inside. It wasn't Officer Moran but someone more petite, with curly hair, although it was hard to tell behind the dirty windshield. She waved and I waved in return as I dumped my things into Sally's back foot well. Relieved that I didn't have to chase down my escort, I slid into the frigid driver's seat and cranked the engine.

The car started, but with a whiny protest. I considered pulling out Barry to make a note about having the battery checked then I remembered Barry was tucked away, unsynched and presumably uncharged. I settled for jotting myself a note on the pad I kept near the dash and jamming the scrap of paper into my purse. I popped the Grateful Dead's *American Beauty* into the CD player and put the car into gear.

I backed out of the space and my car lurched, angry at being left in the biting cold. I knew it would take a few blocks before the oil actually started to flow and the spark plugs fired without sluggishness. I drove slowly, giving the car and myself a chance to warm up. As I traversed the gray parking garage, I saw the small sedan fall in behind me. Then the blinding sunlight on snow hit me as I drove out of the lower ramp.

I heard sirens in the distance, clear and over-loud in the cold air. The streets were icy in spots where the trees had shaded the road, preventing the sun and the salt tossed down by the road crews from doing any good. My car slipped toward the stop sign at the bottom of the hill leading to the main cross street, skidding into the thankfully empty intersection. I gunned it then glanced in my rear view mirror. The dark sedan was following.

As I approached the freeway I saw a police car careening toward the off ramp, lights flashing and siren wailing. I considered pulling over but it was on the other side of the road and I posed no slow-down threat to them. I passed under the freeway, heading for the county roads that would take me home.

I started tallying what I'd need to work on that night. First of all there was this computer person I had to meet. I bounced on my seat, as much from cold as excitement. I was looking forward to sharing my theory with someone who (a) wasn't a terrorist and (b) would understand what I was talking about. I wanted to get confirmation that my suspicions were right. It had been a complicated bit of programming and I was proud of myself.

Once I got that out of the way, I could deal with the kittens. I had to get them to the Humane Society and into good homes. I doubted my two resident felines would appreciate the addition of five hungry mouths at our dinner table. It was tempting to keep the one kitten who was the Kong-clone, but I wasn't sure I was up to the antics of an energetic youth after years with my sedate elderly beasts. No, the Humane Society was the best bet.

Then there was the all-important question: would I see Gus again and when? He wasn't getting his voice mail at his apartment. I once again remembered the scrap of paper with his phone number on it. I jotted another note to myself, swerving as I scrawled a hasty *Gus: phn no* on a scrap of paper. I jammed it into my bag with the other scrap and made a firm resolution to grill Alex Raney when I saw him in a few minutes

I hummed along with Jerry Garcia and friends as "Ripple " played, tapping on the steering wheel for good measure. That reminded me—I needed to stock up on beer. As I got into town I made a left at the only stop light, squeaking through it on red then scooting down the street to park behind the tiny liquor store next to the delivery truck that was unloading its wares into the building.

It wasn't until I was browsing the meager wine selections that I realized I'd probably left my police escort in the dust, or rather, the snow at the traffic light. The view of the street through the front window of the store was almost obliterated by neon beer lights, signs advertising this week's specials ("Wine In a Box, Always Fresh, ON SALE NOW"), and posters for upcoming high school events such as the big Curling Tournament and the Grand Snowball Battle, to be held in a week. I peered around a life-size cardboard St. Pauli girl, flourishing two big steins of beer that competed with her bosoms for attention, and inspected the roadway outside.

No dark sedan cruising the street. I rooted in my Sak and pulled out Barry, flicking it on. The battery was low but I had enough juice to retrieve my contact list. Nope, I hadn't stored Alex Raney. I'd probably thought, and rightly so, that he would be a temporary contact in my life. I think the last time I'd seen it, his business card was sitting on my desk at home.

I approached Sam, the store manager. “Can I borrow a phone?” I asked, setting down my six-pack of Rolling Rock and the WineInABox I'd grabbed from the display.

“Sure, use the one in the back.” He gestured over one shoulder with his thumb.

I went to the back of the store and ducked into the tiny office next to the restrooms. A phone book sat under the old rotary phone. I found the number for the Chaska Police Department (non-emergency) and asked to be transferred to Alex Raney. It took a long time until someone else finally came on the line.

“He's out of the office,” an unknown male said.

“I know, he's supposed to be meeting me. But I'm going to be delayed.” I considered explaining the policewoman following me but it seemed too complicated to go into with a stranger. “If you have a way to get in touch with him, just tell him Jessie Patrokus called and I'm on my way home. The police person with me got sort of lost, but I'll be there in a few minutes.”

“Jessie Pa—”

I spelled my name. “He knows who I am.” I heard voices in the background, not urgent but several talking at once. Someone said 'task force' very loudly, next to the phone. I wondered what Task Force they were talking about. As far as I knew, nearby Chaska (population seventeen thousand) had no Task Forces on their tiny police force.

“You got lost but you'll meet him soon, right?” The phone must have slipped because the man's voice faded in and out. “Hello? You're lost?”

“No, I didn't get lost, the—” I gave up. “Just tell him I'll be there soon and I'll call when I get there. I think I have his phone number at home. If not, I'll call you and you can get in touch with him, right? You have his cell phone number? Or one of those walkie-talkie things?” I had my doubts about the equipage of the small police department.

“Yeah, we can find him. We're kind of busy here, but thanks for calling.”

I wondered if my message would be relayed or not.

He didn't sound anxious to assist. I replaced the receiver and went back into the store. Sam had my purchases rung up. “Did you hear the news?” he asked as he swiped my credit card.

“What?” I looked out the one clear spot on the window at a police car speeding past, lights flashing. “That's the second squad car I saw today with its lights on.”

“There was a bomb threat called in at Chaska high school.” Sam put down the receipt for me to sign as another police car went past, sirens blaring. “Mavis Farnsworth, over at the Ace Hardware Store, came in and told me about it. Said that somebody had called in saying a kid had a gun and a bomb and was going to shoot the place up.”

“Holy moly.” I tucked the credit card back in my wallet. “I suppose they have to take it seriously after what happened at Red Lake.” The shootings recently on the Indian reservation in northern Minnesota had shaken everyone, especially because it had happened in such an out-of-the-way and insular, rural community.

Sam nodded, his pale blonde hair in the scraggly ponytail snaking over his flannel-shirted shoulder. “I'm glad my kids are graduated,” he said as he sacked my beer. “The world is too weird anymore.”

No shit, I thought as I tucked my purchases into Sally's back seat. Another delivery truck had pulled in, providing a welcome windbreak with big trucks blocking me in on both sides. I hopped into the car and backed out into the little traveled side street. Just a few more blocks, and I'd be home.

As I drove along the snowy streets another squad car passed me, lights on full alert. I pulled to the side, doing my citizenly duty. As I did, I thought I saw the dark sedan at the intersection behind me. Perhaps my escort had caught up to me after all. But as I watched, it made a right-hand turn, going through the residential streets that would lead to the small park whose trail wended its way behind my house. It was probably just some homeowner getting an early start on the weekend, like me.

My street was quiet, all driveways empty and no

children outside. The bitter cold had driven everyone inside or else no one was home yet from work. I pulled into my driveway and pressed my garage door opener, goosing Sally and closing the door behind me. As I unloaded my laptop and briefcase from the back seat, I heard my phone ringing inside. I brought the first load of equipment into the house, dumping it on the boot bench then went back outside for my liquor store purchases as the phone quit ringing. Either the caller had given up or my answering service had kicked in.

Faye came out to greet me, sidling around the corner from the kitchen and regarding me with sleepy curiosity. I heard the kittens, crying from the back of the house in their warm prison. I shed my outerwear and kicked off my boots as my phone rang again.

That reminded me. I pulled Barry out from my Sak and checked the charge. As I suspected, it was so low the 'charge now or lose all data' icon was flashing its ominous little warning. I shut it off as the landline phone rang. I considered making a dash for it but decided whoever was there could leave a message. I gave Faye a good head rub and went into the living room to stare into the woods behind the house. As I expected, nothing was moving. Even the squirrels had taken refuge in their nests, seeking warmth from the appalling cold.

I went down the hall and saw Kong unwinding himself from a tight ball in front of the kitten door where he'd probably been on duty all day. He gave me a reproachful stare but his jaw-cracking yawn told me how vigilant he'd been. I went into the den and saw Alex Raney's business card, tucked into the Disney World desk blotter. I plopped Barry into its charging cradle then pulled out Raney's card. I was just getting ready to call him when I heard the kittens, crying pitifully—and loudly.

"Okay, okay," I muttered. I went back to the kitchen and dished up some canned food, escorted by Faye and Kong. As I juggled the dishes the damn phone rang again, chiming three times then bouncing into my voice mailbox. I diverted Kong and Faye into a corner of the kitchen with their portion of the feast then went into the spare room to deal with the smaller and louder feline tyrants. They tumbled around me in greedy joy, almost tipping over the dishes in their haste to get at the yummy and smelly morsels. I scooped the litter box, filled the water dish and emerged five minutes later with a stinky trashcan.

As I headed for the garage the phone rang again. I picked up on the laundry room extension, peeved at the interruption. "Damn telemarketers," I said to Faye who was watching me from a sunny spot in the living room. "What?" I demanded into the phone.

"Jessie, it's Gus."

He sounded breathless. "Hey, where are you? I left messages for you at your house. Did you get them? I found out—"

"Listen, Jessie. Is the officer Alex assigned to you still with you?"

"No, she left me this morning at the office, why?" I put the nasty trashcan near the garage door and meandered to my thermostat in the living room. It was decidedly chilly.

"This morning? What do you mean? I thought someone was with you all day." Now he sounded worried. Or angry. Or both.

"No, Miss Personality left me at the front door this morning. I'm supposed to call Raney now, he had someone follow me home but I think they got lost or something. I'm going to meet some computer guy here at the house and we're going over the files I put together."

"Damn it! How come you didn't answer your phone—your Blackberry?"

"I didn't have it charged. I could have sworn I'd put it in the cradle this morning but I guess I must have forgotten."

There was a long pause. "Did you talk to Nelson Scott today? Was he in your cube?"

"Huh? What does that—" Then his meaning sank in. "You think Nelson made sure Barry wasn't charged? Oh, no, that's not..." I remembered coming back to my cube and seeing my Osama Blue Meanie in disarray on my desk. Had someone been in there?

I heard what sounded like a car engine, the motor loud in the background behind Gus. "Where are you? Are you at home?"

"I'm in the park near your house. I just got here. Damn that Raney, I told him not to do this unless I was in place. I told him this would backfire. These people are too smart."

I went to the windows and looked out at the woods behind the house. I thought I saw a shadow, probably Broke-Antler Buck, on the far side of the pond. "You're in the park? What are you doing there? You need to get inside, it's below zero and—"

"Listen, Jessie, I don't have time to explain it all. Alex and I talked about doing this but I thought he had decided not to try it."

"Not to try what?" I peered out the windows at the back yard. The crisp air seemed to magnify every black branch silhouetted against the white snow.

"Hold on."

Dead air filled the phone. "Gus?" No answer. I went back into the kitchen and picked up the trashcan, schlepping it out to the garage where it could be stinky without affecting any humans. As I scooted back up the steps into the house, he came back on the line.

"Jessie, it's a trap. I talked to Alex and it's gotten all screwed up. He was supposed to have someone following you but they got diverted when Nelson Scott pulled a gun on Paul Henderson today."

"Nelson did what?" I almost dropped the phone in shock. "Paul? Is he okay? What happened? When? I just saw them, you must be—"

"It's a trap, Jessie. Alex was going to lure out the murderer by having you drive home alone. An officer was supposed to be following you from your office but when the shit hit the fan, he got sidetracked."

"But I just saw Paul. He was in the lobby with..." With who? I strained to remember who the other man had looked like. "Was he with Nelson? Nelson pulled a gun on him? You're kidding."

"I don't have time to give you all the details. Someone was following you then everybody got pulled off because of this bomb threat and Nelson Scott threatening Paul Henderson. Jessie, it's a trap. And you're the bait."

Chapter Eighteen

"What do you mean, bait? You mean like—" Then I stopped. He wasn't talking about ice fishing. This was deadly serious. "Bait? As in, they set a trap and something screwed up and—"

"Jessie, calm down. I can barely understand you. Calm down."

"Calm down? Holy shit, Gus, you're saying I might be in danger, right? You're saying..." I paused in the laundry room, phone pressed to my ear. Faye stared at me, perplexed by this odd human behavior. She was probably girding her feline loins for another onslaught of chaos. This pacing to and fro was alarming, as were the clamoring baby cats, ringing phones and strange men coming and going at all hours. Knowing Faye, she'd pee under the bed just to get even with me.

"Hang on."

I almost howled with rage. What did he mean, 'hang on'? The man was telling me I was in danger then I was supposed to be happy to be put on hold? At least there wasn't any disgusting Muzak, mangling the Beatles' *Eleanor Rigby* or the Rolling Stones' *Satisfaction* as I was forced to listen to a guitarist's version of Hell.

I raced down the hall to the bathroom and peeked through the miniscule crack in the café curtains. There were no ominous cars, snowmobiles or pedestrians lurking outside, waiting to snatch me. Twilight was falling, the shadows from the trees lengthening. The Christmas lights that outlined Tom's front porch had come on and the big inflatable Claus was starting to puff in the Allens' yard up the street, which meant it was four-thirty. Bob Allen always started the Santa so it was inflated when the kids got home from hockey practice. Everything appeared Beaver-Cleaver calm. All that was missing was Jimmy

Stewart running down the street and shouting out his love for Bedford Falls as snow drifted lazily down.

"Jessie?"

"Why are you whispering?"

"I'm on the path leading to the pond, behind your house. I'm following him."

"On the path? You? Gus, you're not cut out for this. It's colder than a rat's ass out there." Then his words penetrated. "Him who him?" I scurried into my den, almost stumbling over Kong, who was ambling back down the hallway to resume his guard post outside the kitten prison door. I heard the small inhabitants, wailing inside, anxious for attention. It looked like the Humane Society would have to wait yet again.

"I followed you from the office. Another car was behind you, a sedan. We lost you somewhere in town."

I crouched low, feeling stupid but not knowing what else to do. "I went to the liquor store." I duck-walked across the room, almost falling over the braided rug in my haste then I huddled below the windowsill. If someone were in the ravine below me, near the pond, they wouldn't see me unless I stood up and peered over my deck. But if someone was in the back yard, they might spot me. I took a chance and stood up, peeking over the sill.

"I drove all around downtown looking for you."

Gus sounded pissed. Oops. Had I known... "I parked in the back lot at the liquor store. Some trucks probably blocked your view. I was there."

"It doesn't matter. I caught sight of the car that was following you. It came to this park. By the time I got here, the car was empty."

I could hear his raspy breath now. Knowing Gus, he was probably out there with that stupid unlined winter coat, those knit gloves that weren't worth shit in the cold, with no hat.

I swept my gaze over the white expanse of my lawn. I could tell the snow was almost hip deep because only the very top of my daylily stalks poked through the whiteness. At the edge of the yard, where the hill dropped down to the pond, I saw the trampled area under the bird feeder where the squirrels, birds, and probably the deer had scraped for food.

No warm-blooded creature was stirring. The white snow, black tree branches and red branches of my dogwood bushes were the only things moving, and they were barely swaying in the breeze. Poor Gus. If he was out there, he was aching with cold. Even a slight breeze like this one would be bone-chilling when the temps hadn't gotten above zero all day.

I snatched my binoculars off their peg, jamming the phone between my shoulder and ear as I focused the lenses. I swung my gaze to the right, beyond my property. The ground sloped down then up again on the other side of the ravine that separated my side of the pond from the houses on the far hill. I could just make out the faint outline of the city trail in the shadows.

“You need to get out of the house, Jessie.” Gus's voice was barely audible. The man wasn't cut out for sub-zero weather. “Get to your neighbor's house. There's safety in numbers.”

I heard a car in the street outside, the tires on the snow sounding as loud as firecrackers in the still, cold air. “Gus, there's a car outside. Hold on, I'll check and see—”

“No, don't. Get down to the basement. Take cover.”

I heard the kittens clamoring for attention, saw Kong strolling past on his way back to the kitchen to check on his food dish (had it miraculously been refilled?) and watched Faye jump onto the couch. I paused then realized Gus was right. My cats would run at the slightest sign of danger. They wouldn't hesitate a minute.

I grabbed my slingshot off the desk where I'd left it the other day, stuffing it into the back pocket of my jeans. “Okay. I'm moving. Where are you?”

“I'm on the trail. I just came over the hill and I'm coming down to the ravine near your house. The guy's ahead of me. I can barely see him.”

If they were where I thought, I should be able to see whoever was out there. I moved to the far side of the window, tucking myself into a corner so I could peer out as far as possible to the spot beyond my house. I gazed out over the deck. I was too low. I stood up on tiptoes cautiously, willing myself to slenderness as I tried to hide behind my sheer curtains. I took a deep breath and held the binoculars steady, trying to make sense of the jumble of images I saw.

A dark shape was moving through the woods behind the house, in the ravine at the bottom of the hill. I wouldn't have seen it but it was crossing a clearing on the side of the pond nearest the house, the two-legged form starkly visible against the white snow. Another movement on the far side of the pond caught my attention and I refocused the binoculars. Broke-Antler Buck was springing away, floundering in the deep drifts until he reached what was obviously a well-used deer trail on the far side of the pond.

Car doors slammed outside. I jumped, almost dropping the binoculars. "Holy shit. Somebody's out there."

"Get to the basement, damn it."

For someone who was whispering, Gus sounded loud—and angry. I started toward the door and the hallway beyond when *I Saw Mommy Kissing Santa Claus* chimed out, scaring me so bad I almost wet my pants. "Barry's ringing," I said into the phone.

"Get to the basement, Jessie."

I peeked out the window again. I could see another two-legged figure now, or what looked like one. It was hard to tell because of the dark shadows, the black branches on the trees, and the flickering light as the sun started to set. I grabbed Barry. "What?" I hissed.

"Where the hell are you?" It was Alex Raney.

"Where the hell are you? Some guard you gave me—where the hell is he? Where's that computer guy? What's going on? Gus said that you laid a trap and it's all goofy and—"

"Gus? Where is he? He just called me. I've been trying to get back in touch with him but his phone is busy. He said he was coming to your house."

"I know his phone is busy. I'm talking to him." I scooted back to the window. I couldn't handle the binoculars, Barry, and the portable phone so I set down the binoculars. I didn't need them, anyway. I definitely saw another figure outside, on the trail and coming down the hill. The first figure had vanished or merged with the deeper shadows at the base of the hill behind my house. "He's outside. I think he's on the trail."

"Damn it. I sent officers to your house, they should be there by now."

At that moment someone pounded on my front door. Faye jumped off the couch, hissing at me, and fled from the room. I knew that cat pee was in my future, either in my laundry basket or under my bed. I heard a mumbling noise from the portable phone I'd pinned against my shoulder as I whispered into Barry.

"Jessie, what's going on?"

"It's Alex Raney, he's on Barry." I hazarded another look out the window. The hill-figure had moved and was coming down the trail, sticking to the snow and the trees, presumably for cover. As I moved to get a better view, I tangled in the curtains, almost pulling them down. I staggered back, dropping both phones.

"Shit." I scrambled for the portable and straightened up as the thumping in front made my door rattle on its hinges. "Someone's at the door."

"Don't answer it, Jessie. Get to the basement."

"But it's Alex Raney, he said—"

"Get to the basement. Do it—now!"

The phone went dead. What did that mean? Couldn't I trust Alex Raney? Why shouldn't I open the door? Speaking of which—I heard squawking from Barry, lying on the rug. Then the shrill 'eep-eep-eep' noise sounded, signaling that Barry was shutting down. I snatched it up but it was too late—the little handheld screen faded from view as the power shut down, conserving the precious memory on my Blackberry.

"Son of a bitch." I plunked it back in the charging cradle, grabbed the portable phone and my binoculars and headed for the basement steps.

Kong sat in the hallway at my front door, glaring at it with implacable fury, all fifteen pounds of thirteen-year-old cat dug in and prepared to defend his home turf. "Oh, for cryin' out loud." I scooped him up and held him against me, dropping the phone and the binoculars in the process. He thrashed as I peeked through the spy hole on my door. Two men stood on the stoop, looking pissed off and cold. They wore heavy parkas with the hoods up and had some kind of insignia on the breast. Gus had said not to open the door, but did he know that Alex Raney had sent people to the house? Kong pushed against my chest, muttering angrily as he sought to get at the intruders.

I put my hand on the doorknob when realization hit me.

Gus was in the woods behind the house.

He was near the pond—the pond that looked frozen and wasn't. He was near the pond whose edges weren't visible because of the heavy snow pack.

I wavered. The whole imagined scene flashed through my mind—badges, dragging men inside, getting to the deck, finding Gus. Or, worse, open the door, confront them, find out they weren't from Alex Raney, and…

No time.

"Holy shit." I raced to the living room, dropping Kong onto the couch along the way. He bounced off and went back to the front door where the pounding started again.

"Open up! Sheriff's Department."

I jerked open the door in the living room that led to the deck. "Go around back," I yelled over my shoulder. "Go around the house—someone's being killed out there." A blast of cold air settled on me. I started out onto the slippery wooden surface then remembered just in time. I slid my socked feet into the clogs I kept at the door.

The pounding was renewed, this time on the laundry room door that led into the open garage. "Miss Patrokus! Alex Raney sent us. We—"

I paused, looking outside. I saw the hill-figure, now not on the hill but much, much closer. In fact, he was so close I could make out his bare head. His gray hair shone in the pale light that filtered through the trees. I saw his goatee and light reflecting off his glasses. Because of my elevation on the hill over the pond, I could easily see the other figure at the bottom of the ravine behind my house, hidden by an outcropping of brush and downed trees.

As I watched, Gus stepped forward. He was holding something—a gun? I couldn't quite tell. I looked at the other figure, fifty yards away and down the hill, almost directly below me.

I could easily see the gun that figure was holding. It was long and propped up on a shoulder. I didn't know much about weapons, but I'd watched enough TV to know what I was seeing. It was a rifle or shotgun or some other weapon that could probably shoot a long distance.

I grabbed a handful of good-sized sharp gravel from the coffee can near the door, jamming it into my jeans pocket. The pounding continued behind me then I heard a door opening. "Miss Patrokus!"

I stepped out onto the deck. My breath steamed out and the snow crunched under my shoes. I slipped, sliding into the deeper snow next to the narrow path I'd cleared to the railing. My ankles burned as snow and ice crept into my low felt clogs. I pulled my slingshot out from my back pocket then I bent down to hide myself, using the icy surface to glide toward the railing. I loaded the slingshot with four or five gray lumps.

"Hey!" My voice echoed through the woods, startling a flock of crows upward from the far side of the pond with angry, strident screams that mimicked me. Gus stopped, turning in surprise. The figure below me didn't move, but remained focused, that long rifle-gun unwavering. I heard voices behind me as I raised the slingshot.

My aim was bad, probably because I was trembling. The rocks thunked into the wood around the crouching figure.

The shot was as loud as the crows had been. I saw a puff of steam or smoke from the gun in the crouching figure's hands. I fumbled in my pocket for another load of rocks as two big men came slipping out onto the deck behind me, Kong chasing them. I would have laughed at the sight if I hadn't been so desperate.

I couldn't see Gus. He'd vanished from sight. I hoped he was hiding. I hoped that shot hadn't—My eyes were watering, either from tears or the cold, I wasn't sure which. I pulled out some pebbles, unable to feel them in my frozen fingers. I managed to load the slingshot again but the sling was stiff and unresponsive in my hands. It was freezing, too. With luck I could get off one more shot, maybe two.

"Miss Patrokus, we're from—"

I glanced at the speaker. He was one of the guys who'd come to the office on the day that Charlie had died. I recognized his blond hair and that impassive, stoic cop-face. I couldn't remember his name, but I'm sure his business card was crumpled up in some jeans pocket somewhere. His face now was red with cold—or anger. "Alex Raney told us to—"

"There's a guy with a gun down there," I said through chattering teeth. I couldn't get a clear target. The shooter was crouched too low, protected by the branches of a downed scrub oak that had tumbled down the hillside. I stepped forward, leaning against the deck railing. "Hey, you! Look at me, you bastard!"

This time the figure looked up over his shoulder at me. I took a deep, steadying breath, the cold piercing my lungs and shocking me into immobility. I took another breath and for an instant, the world was still. I felt no cold, no fear, and no hesitation. My vision focused in on him. I saw the wide, startled eyes. I saw the curly hair.

I saw the woman who'd been on the elevator with Nelson

I saw the woman who'd been in the gym earlier in the afternoon, when Denise and I had worked out. Different hair color and style—a wig? Hair dye? I wasn't sure, but I knew it was the same woman.

Our eyes met. Then she started to turn away.

I released the sling as the man behind me pushed forward, drawing a gun.

We heard the scream as the jagged rocks tore into her face. I could clearly see the blood as it splattered, flinging outward like bright red raindrops on the white snow. She fell back, out of sight into the bushes.

"What the hell?" The man leaned forward. "Who is that?"

"I have no idea but she was shooting at Gus Colcannon." I gripped the wooden railing, peering into the woods, willing Gus to come into sight. "He's out there somewhere. I saw him earlier. I don't know where he is."

The woman below us staggered upward, getting to her feet. The man next to me said over his shoulder, "Suspect getting away. We need people down there."

I looked beyond the woman below me, to the woods surrounding the pond. That's when I saw Gus. "Damn." I whirled, almost falling as I raced back inside the house. Kong took one look at me coming toward him and scrambled out of the way like some cartoon-cat, his nails scrabbling on the wood floors as he bolted down the hall, taking refuge with Faye in their favorite hiding place, under the bed.

I almost knocked over the other officer coming out on the deck. I didn't recognize him but he had the cop look I was coming to recognize after my run-ins with Officer Moran, Alex Raney, and Officer Quinn.

"Where are you—"

I didn't pause. I kicked off my felt clogs, went into the laundry room and jammed my feet into my snow clogs. I snatched up some towels from the stack in the laundry room and flung myself down the steps into the garage. I was around the side of the house and sliding down the hill before the men on the deck above me had even realized I was gone.

I rushed down the slope, careful to keep distance between the woman and me. I wasn't totally stupid—she might still be dangerous, although from the amount of blood I'd seen, I was betting she was hurt. I didn't have time to worry about it. I had to trust that the cops on the deck above me would see what I had seen.

Gus was in the woods. I'd seen him leaning against a tree. He looked limp, dazed, as though only the tree was holding him up. As I got to the top of the hill and headed down the deer trail to the pond, I saw him moving, his steps uncertain.

I didn't have any spare breath to scream. The men on the deck behind me were shouting. The words finally penetrated.

"Down!"

I hit the ground, snow covering me as a booming shot rang out. I dove for an oak tree, putting it between the clump of bushes where I'd last seen the woman shooter and me. I huddled against the frigid bark, clutching the towels to my chest, shivering as snow soaked into my jeans, my shoes, and under the sleeves of my bright red Santa sweater—now liberally covered with camouflaging white snow. I peeked around the side of the tree, looking up at the deck. The men were aiming into the woods, their guns raised.

I took a chance and bolted, jumping down into the next snowdrift, ricocheting off a stump with a painful blow to my hip. I ignored it and kept going, bouncing downward, praying I wouldn't hit a gully or a hidden branch, poking up to stab the unwary.

My Guardian Angel Broke-Antler Buck watched over me. He and his fellows had tramped down a safe path, leading all the way from my bird feeder to the pond. I made a silent promise to buy corn and scatter it for him and his herd as soon as I could. I got to the bottom of the hill and risked a glance back. A man was coming down behind me, his gun raised and pointed to the left, where the woman had hidden. I decided not to worry about it—I had too much else to worry about, like getting frostbite, breaking a leg, or going through thin ice.

I was near where Gus had been. I recognized the grouping of birch trees where I'd last seen him. I ploughed through the snow. "Gus?"

No reply. I crossed the paved trail and moved up the hill on the other side of the ravine, hampered by deep snow and no deer tracks to show me the way. I grabbed a branch to help me but I went down once, slipping on the icy grass under the snow. Had he gone back toward the park? The woods were thick here, but I should be able to see him.

As I looked back down the hill toward the pond, I saw him below me. He was walking unsteadily, following what looked like the paved trail that would go around the pond to the other side.

It wasn't the paved trail, though. This was part of the deer trail. It led to water's edge, where the deer could get to open water to drink. "Gus!"

At that moment, the man who'd followed me into the woods shouted something. Gus turned at the sound. I looked up and saw the man aiming his gun at the woman who'd emerged from cover opposite me. I'd been right—her face was bloody and one eye was puffing shut with a jagged, gory cut above it, streaming red and steaming.

"Jessie?" Gus's voice was weak and disoriented.

"Be careful," I shouted. "The ice isn't safe." I started scrambling down the hill, sliding down on my butt and sledding the last few feet until I landed on the paved trail. I sprang up, the towels still miraculously clutched to my now torn Santa sweater.

I was too late, though.

Gus stepped onto the pond.

What had looked like snow on top of the pond was actually white ice. My brain registered this fact as Gus did a sliding dance, his leather-soled boots gliding on the slick surface.

White ice—ice that was full of oxygen. Anyone who grew up in Minnesota and skated on lakes knew what that meant. White ice was fragile, full of air pockets where the water had frozen and thawed over the course of days. Clear ice would bear the weight of ice fishermen and cars but white ice couldn't support a flock of geese, much less a man.

Gus shuffled forward then turned awkwardly. As I moved toward him, he twisted again. That's when I realized he was trying to find his balance on the ice that shifted under his feet.

With no warning, it gave way and he went down.

Chapter Nineteen

"Shit!" I dropped the towels and headed for the rescue tree, across the paved trail and on the far hillside. I fought my way through deep snow and reached the rope as another shot echoed in the woods.

I ducked but didn't pause. The rope was hard with cold and my fingers were equally stiff, but I managed to pull it off the trunk. As I spun toward the pond I unraveled the rope. I heard shouts behind me but I didn't have the energy to pay attention to anything but the man I saw, floundering in the dead weeds and muck in the shallows of the pond.

At least he was moving. That was a good sign. He hadn't gone into shock yet. The pond was low but it didn't matter. He was already soaked, the icy water weighing down his topcoat, pulling his shoulders and torso back to the bottom of the pool. Even if it were just a foot or two deep, it would be enough to kill him. I slid to the edge of the pond, following the deer tracks and stopping a foot short of where they ended in the deep snow.

I untangled the rope. "Gus!"

I shouted his name two more times before he paused and I knew he'd heard me. "Gus, I'm going to toss you a rope. You'll be okay. It's not deep here. But you have to move. You have to get out. I can't come in." I glanced over my shoulder. Two more men were slipping down the hill, joining the two already at the bottom surrounding the woman with the gun. "I need help!"

They were already moving toward me as fast as they could through the deep snow. I tossed the rope toward Gus. He was lying back, his hands behind him as he tried to prop himself up in the cold water. He struggled to get his legs under his body but his feet slipped and he went down, the fragile ice forming, then cracking around him.

The cold was getting to him. "Damn it, Gus! Grab the rope. If you grab the rope, I can help you upright!"

He managed to push himself forward, flailing out a hand for the rope lying on the ice next to him. His fingers were clumsy, unable to bend. I knew how he felt. My hands were chapped and raw, clutching the rope with small flecks of blood showing where it had rubbed the skin. I didn't care. I couldn't feel it.

"Gus! Grab it!"

Ice coated his hair and goatee, bright red patches of skin standing out in sharp relief on his high cheekbones. He must have been sitting or standing in the shallows now because he had cleared the water from the waist up even though I couldn't see his lower body. He leaned forward and wrapped the rope around one arm. "I can't." His voice wavered. "This is the best I can do."

I pulled slowly on the rope. He leaned forward, tipping dangerously near the water's surface. "Come on—try! Get your feet under you. Take a step. Come on!"

I was pushed aside. "I've got him." Big, gloved hands covered mine on the rope, pulling it out of my grasp.

"Don't jerk it." I tried to let go but my fingers wouldn't move. "Be careful."

"I know." The man pried my fingers off the rope, nudging me to the right.

My hands cramped and I cried out. Someone else put an arm around me as something was flung over my shoulders. "Over here," a male voice said, steering me away from the pond's edge. "You're getting frostbite."

"No." I slipped out of the grasp that held me to watch as the man holding the rope twitched it, gently urging Gus upright. "Damn it—get out of there! It's cold, you idiot! It's dangerous!"

I heard Gus sputtering, either with laughter or swallowed pond water. I prayed it wasn't pond water. God knew what diseases were in there. "No shit, it's cold."

I slipped on the icy ground and went down with a hard thunk. I peered up at the big man towering over me. It was Alex Raney. "You! You son of a bitch, this is all your fault!"

He glared from me to Gus, who was half-crawling, half-staggering out of the pond. "Blame him. He shouldn't have gotten involved."

I tried to push up but my hands sank into the snow. I winced then whapped Raney on the shin for good measure before giving up and settling back on the icy ground. The last thing I heard was Alex Raney shouting, "Hey! She's hurt—there's blood!"

The snow was surprisingly warm.

****

When I woke up, Drew was sitting by my bed. That made so little sense that I went back to sleep. But when I woke up again, he was still there. I peeked at him then closed my eyes before he saw I was awake. I needed a minute to recap everything in my head. Then I opened one gritty eye and peered at him. "Am I in Texas?"

He leapt to his feet and came to my side, sitting gingerly on the edge of the mattress. "Snip, you're back." The relief in his voice was obvious.

"What happened? Am I in the hospital?" I tried to sit up but it was tough. The bed was reclined back and I was weak.

Drew touched some buttons and my upper body creaked upward. Brief nausea flooded me then receded as my head cleared. "Yeah. They brought you to the hospital in Chaska yesterday. I came as soon as I heard." He touched my hand but I didn't feel it. I looked down.

"What happened?" I raised my right arm. It ended in a white mitt-like bandage, making my hand look like the Mummy's. "Ow." My hand started to burn. I hastily laid it back down. My left arm was bare, sticking out of a faded green hospital gown decorated with what looked like ancient flowers—or maybe stars. It was hard to tell.

"Long story or short one?" he asked, smiling at me. Drew always reminded me of the guy who played Chekhov, the navigator from *Star Trek*. I noticed with a pang that now he looked like a graying and worried Chekhov, without the cheeky charm.

"Long." The fact that Gus wasn't by my bed wasn't a good sign. He was either hurt or not around. I wasn't sure if I wanted to know which scenario I was facing. Both were heartbreak.

"That cop, Alex Raney, was working with the FBI. They suspected Nelson Scott, in your office, was being blackmailed into helping a terrorist group."

This was old news. "I know. He wrote them some code that goofed up their No Fly list."

Drew looked confused. "No Fly list? That's not what I heard." He lightly tapped my bandage. "Raney told me it was a list of personnel allowed onto the planes, in between flights."

"What?" I struggled to make sense of what he was saying. I visualized the list of names, the strings of numbers and initials. "How so?"

"I don't know all the details. They wouldn't tell me." He grinned and I saw the impish younger brother who'd tormented me. "I threatened to sue. They pulled the old National Security crap on me."

I snorted. If they wanted to intimidate Drew, they were picking on the wrong lawyer. Both Dad and I had protested the Viet Nam War, our government's involvement in the Gulf War, and countless other idiocies perpetrated by people in Washington. Drew wouldn't be impressed by any National Security argument.

"There's some kind of master security list each airline has that clears people to do maintenance and service work on planes. Nelson Scott was supposed to write a program to manipulate the names and give illegal aliens access to the planes."

I was one step ahead of my brother. If someone without security clearance could get onto the planes, they could plant a bomb, mess with the equipment or do all kinds of damage. What was it Sarah had said as we exercised the other day? *Everybody is supposed to be screened and secure but...*"Did Nelson kill Charlie?"

Drew covered my hand with his. He heard the fright in my voice. "No. The woman assigned to him did that."

"Woman? Oh. The one in the woods? The one who shot at Gus?" I finally sucked up my courage. "Is he okay? Was he shot?" I held my breath, waiting for the answer.

"He's fine. He was hit, but it wasn't bad—just a graze from a ricochet plus shock and mild frostbite. The police called a snowmobile rescue sleigh and got you both out of there. They didn't even keep him overnight." He touched my bandaged hand. "You got it worse than he did. You had frostbite on your fingers plus a bullet grazed your shoulder. You'll be sore for a few weeks."

Drew frowned when he said it and I knew something was being omitted. I decided to pursue that in a minute. For now I wanted to relax, knowing Gus was okay. Then his words soaked in. "Bullet?" I flexed my shoulders and pain lanced through my right one, down my arm and back up my neck, making a headache flare. "Whoa. That really hurts."

He nodded. "You'll be wearing a sling for at least a week or two, until it heals."

"Tell Andrea her Christmas present will be late," I said absently, sifting through what he'd said. "So Nelson put together a program for them and Charlie figured it out? Did Nelson want it to be found? Was that it? Was he—"

"They're still piecing it all together. Here's what I know for fact—on Friday when you left the office, Raney had someone follow you. But when you got to the lobby, Nelson Scott was there with some guy, a Paul somebody."

"Paul Henderson. I saw them."

"Scott was supposed to create a diversion so the woman who was assigned to him by the terrorist group could get at you. So Scott pulled a gun on that Paul guy." I started to speak but Drew barreled ahead. "The FBI agent following you saw the gun and tried to intervene. In the meantime you left. The woman was waiting downstairs to follow you home."

"But Gus followed me, too."

"Raney realized their plans had gone bust. As soon as he knew you were alone, he sent people after you, but with the bomb threat called in at the high school—a fake, by the way—communications got screwed up and it took a while for them to get to your place."

I was miles ahead of him. "My mobile phone wasn't on so no one could call me, I stopped at the liquor store so no one could find me, and if it wasn't for Gus following me, no one would have known what was happening." My tester's brain was slotting fragments of conversation, snippets of ideas, and guesswork into place. I'd been pulled off Nelson's project—to make it look good to the woman who'd been with Nelson. I'd been assigned a guard then the guard was removed—to make it look good. I'd been set up. If it hadn't been for Gus—

I finally asked the question I'd been dreading. "Where's Gus?"

"He's gone."

I looked at the doorway to my room. Alex Raney was coming in, his black jacket and pants reinforcing my idea of him as my own personal little black rain cloud. "You! You almost got me killed, you—you—" I struggled to sit upright but the pain stopped me. "I should sue you. In fact, I think I will." I looked at my brother. "You'll handle it, right? Sue him, the police department and the FBI."

Raney strode in to stand by my bed. Dark circles lined his eyes and his Marine's buzz cut was ragged looking, like he needed a trim. "You can't sue me. It's all got to do with National Security. You can't—"

Both Drew and I blew out a raspberry simultaneously. Raney drew back, surprised.

"That kite don't fly with this family. What do you mean, Gus is gone?" I demanded. "Where is he?"

"He was recalled."

"What's that mean? And if you tell me it has to do with National Security, I'll hit you again. Where is he?"

"That's right, you hit me. I could charge you with assaulting a police officer." Raney glanced at Drew then to me. "Gus was sent back to New Mexico. He's in some trouble."

"Trouble?" This time I did manage to sit up, but the effort almost killed me. I barely noticed the pain, though. My indignation was fueling my energy. "For saving my life?"

"For sleeping with you."

The blunt statement almost made me pause. Almost. "Bullshit."

Raney shook his head. If I weren't so suspicious, I'd have said he was regretful. "Gus almost blew this whole assignment. The FBI doesn't forgive agents who pull stunts like that."

"Why did he get involved in the first place?" Drew asked. His hand was steady on my arm, warning me to stay quiet. For the moment I took his advice.

"What do you mean?"

"Why him? He's based in New Mexico, right? Why

assign him to the case?"

Raney hesitated then said, "He had some programming background and he'd been tracking the group who nabbed Nelson Scott's brother. Plus his stepbrother used to live here. Gus wanted to visit Danny's widow. It seemed to make sense to have him in place here."

I heard the pain in Raney's voice when he mentioned his dead partner's name. "Gus is gone? Reassigned?"

Raney's eyes flickered to Drew then back to me. "Yeah. He's gone."

"Jessie. Trust me on this. It's not how it seems." Drew's quiet voice was soothing but all I could hear was *he's gone*. "I'm sure there's a good explanation. I'm sure you'll hear from him."

"He should have talked to me," I said. "Why didn't he wait so he could talk to me?"

"He wasn't given a choice," Raney said with exasperation. "There's a bit more at stake than your love life. He screwed up big time. He's trying to salvage his career."

I leaned back, barely hearing him. Gus had left. He hadn't cared enough to see me, to say good-bye. I closed my eyes, willing the tears to stay away. "I'm tired. I need to sleep."

"Listen, you don't understand," Raney said. I heard Drew whisper something then Raney said, "Okay. But I'll need to get her statement soon."

"Snip? Why don't you rest now? I'll come back later. Do you want me to bring you anything?"

I shook my head. He couldn't bring me what I wanted.

****

I was released from the hospital that night. Then it took almost five more days to fight through the red tape. Thank God, Drew stayed with me, dealing with the worst of it. I had to give formal statements to different police departments, the FBI, and Homeland Security. Then I had to meet with the forensic computer people, going over the programs Charlie gave me and the programs Nelson coded, showing them what I'd discovered. It was two days before Christmas when I finally drove Drew to the airport to catch his flight home, my shoulder still bandaged but not as painful as it had been.

"I'll see you in five days." He leaned over to kiss me good-bye as I double-parked at the passenger unloading area. "We're all set for our usual spot at Hilton Head." He stared into my eyes, the anxiety in his own dark eyes obvious. "Will you be okay? I hate leaving you alone like this on Christmas."

"I've been alone on Christmas for years," I assured him. "I always celebrate with you guys over New Year's. This year isn't any different."

"Of course it is. This year there's Gus."

I hadn't heard a word from Gus—no card, no call, no sign he'd ever existed. I hadn't gone to the office yet, but I suspected his cube would be cleaned out and there'd be nothing to indicate he'd ever been at CodeBusters. All I had to remember him by was his flannel shirt in a picnic basket and five small kittens who had taken up residence in my house. I didn't have the heart to take them to the Humane Society. Not yet, at least.

"It's okay, Drew. Tell Angela her gift will be late this year." I wiggled my fingers, still stiff from frostbite. "I'll start snipping again tonight."

"Jessie, I wish—"

I shook my head. "It's okay, Drew. Thanks for being here and helping me."

"If I hadn't, Dad would have disowned me." He opened the car door. "Hang in there. Better times are ahead."

I smiled at his optimism. "You bet." I watched him grab his bag out of the back seat then he leaned in one more time.

"Take care, Snip. Rest up for our holiday."

"Will do." I was already looking forward to a long vacation on a beach with a couple of trashy romance novels. Maybe it would distract me from the thoughts I couldn't escape.

Drew disappeared into the crowd and I pointed Sally the Subaru toward the office. I hadn't been back since Nelson had been arrested. I'd dreaded facing everyone and the inevitable questions. We had the next few days off for Christmas, so if I went in today, I probably wouldn't see that many people. I decided to face it.

But when I got to the building, I couldn't. I parked in the lot and stared at the front door, my brain in a jumble. Ten days ago my life changed when Charlie was murdered. Ten short days turned my life upside down.

I thought of poor Nelson. His brother had been executed by his captors weeks ago and Nelson had been duped into helping the terrorists. Now he was sitting in a jail somewhere, waiting to be charged with treason. I'd already told everyone in law enforcement that I would testify on his behalf if it came to trial. I was still convinced he'd deliberately screwed up so we would find out what was happening. It was better than thinking someone I worked with was capable of treason. It made me wonder what I would be capable of in similar circumstances.

I thought of Paul Henderson, who'd been terrorized at gunpoint. Denise had called me when I got out of the hospital to fill me in on company gossip. She said that Paul and Sarah were seen lunching together. Knowing Paul, he was getting mileage out of his brief moment of fame. He'd been unharmed but his two brushes with death—one at the hands of brownies and one at the hands of Nelson—had given him a certain status. I hoped he'd enjoy it.

I thought of Brian, my ex-stalker. I'd had no more emails from him. Presumably he'd given up on me. I remembered Gus's niece. The brief glimpse I'd had of her made me think she'd be a perfect foil for nerdy, intense Brain. They'd be a match made in heaven.

Gus. I leaned my head on the steering wheel. No matter what, it always came back to him. Had I fallen in love with a guy I'd known for just a few days?

Was my heart really breaking?

I wiped away my tears and drove out of the parking lot. I'd face my co-workers when Christmas vacation was over. Maybe by then I'd be able to sit in my cube and remember Gus at his desk without crying all over my keyboard.

I drove home on autopilot, Eric Clapton wailing the blues to me on the CD player. We'd had another small snowstorm that had coated the snow boulders on the sides of the road, giving everything a Currier and Ives look. The stage was set for a perfect Midwest Christmas.

I pulled into the driveway and into the house. Kong greeted me at the door, escorting me to the bench where I kicked off my boots and socks and stuck my feet into my bunny slippers. I wandered into the living room to stare out at the pond. The crime scene tape had been removed and it looked as it always did—serene, lonely, and glittering in the low winter sun.

Something nudged my ankles and I looked down. The two tabby kittens were tumbling around my slippers, nipping at the long pink ears that already looked ragged from kitten attention. At this rate, my bunnies would look more like pigs in a few days. I scooped up the kittens and headed for the kitchen.

As I stood at the counter with cats stropping my legs, someone knocked on my garage door. “Just a minute!” I called out. I waded through the crowd of felines and jerked open the door, expecting to see Tom, my neighbor.

Gus stood on the stoop.

For a minute I thought I was seeing a ghost—a gray-haired, dark-coated ghost. A black and white kitten peeked around my ankles then made a break for it. Gus grabbed him and that shook me out of my paralysis. “What are you doing here?”

He handed me the kitten. “Can I come in?”

I stepped back, setting the kitten on the boot bench. Gus came into the laundry room onto the mat. “I see you didn't find homes for them yet.”

I glanced down at the animals milling around my feet. “I'm driving to Texas next week to meet with my brother and his family for a vacation. I'm taking three of them with me. I guess I'll keep the other two.” I forced myself to look at him. His coat collar was turned up, framing his long, thin face. His hair was shorter than it had been, cropped into shaggy waves on his head. His goatee, too, was shorter, as though it had just been trimmed. “I heard you'd been hurt.”

“Not as bad as you.” He examined my face. “I wanted to see you but I was sort of under house arrest. I told Alex Raney to give you my message.”

“What message?”

He shook his head. "That son of a bitch. He was supposed to tell you I'd be back. Didn't he talk to you? Tell you what was going on?"

"He just said you were in trouble and you had to go back to New Mexico."

"Yeah, I guess you could say I was in trouble." His voice was raspy with irony. "Did you think I'd leave without seeing you, Jessie? I wasn't given that chance."

I flushed and turned away. "I didn't know what to think."

Gus grabbed my sweatshirt and pulled me to a halt. "I had some business to take care of." He tugged on my shirt, reeling me closer to him like a captured fish.

"You could have called."

"I wanted to come here and ask you in person once I got everything settled."

That stopped me. "Ask me what?"

Gus's eyes were bright behind his glasses. "Would you mind commuting to New Mexico?"

"I don't understand."

He sighed, pulling me closer. Inches separated us. "I had a choice. I could retire or I could be fired. I decided to retire. I'm going to do some freelance investigation work but I warn you—" He kissed the tip of my nose. "I won't take any more jobs in Minnesota in the wintertime. I'm strictly a summer kind of guy here."

I stared into his eyes, not sure what I was hearing. "I don't understand."

He enfolded me in a hug. "I love you, Jessie. And if we can work out some kind of arrangement, I'd like to spend one hell of a lot of time with you."

"But—" I leaned against him, inhaling his warm, minty aroma. "What do you mean, you're retired? What are—How—When—?" Ideas, thoughts, imaginings swirled in my brain, making me dizzy. I tried to cling to the one truth I knew—Gus was here, in my arms.

"I screwed up big time, Jessie. Not just with the Bureau but with you, too. I should have been open with you about what was going on. You were almost killed because of that." His arms tightened around me. "I'll never do that again. I'll never hide the truth." He pulled away to look down at me. "I've got a pension, a house in

New Mexico, and a bit of savings. Care to share it with me?"

I gaped at him, so stunned I couldn't talk. Would it work? Could we make something work? Could I take a chance?

I looked into his hazel eyes and made a leap of faith. I nodded.

"I heard we're supposed to get five inches tonight." His breath was soft on my ear.

I shivered and tugged him closer. "I wouldn't mind getting five inches tonight."

He laughed softly. "Would you settle for six?"

"Is that my Christmas present?"

"Among other things." He started to nibble on my ear.

"I guess I'd better get it unwrapped then." I pulled him closer. "The sooner the better."

A word about the author...

I was born in a small town in Iowa, and have traveled extensively in the U.S. and overseas, finally ending up back in the Midwest where I'm married to a glass artist who spends a lot of time in the studio, making amazingly beautiful things. We have assorted animals who live with us and who make regular appearances in my books under various pseudonyms (they know who they are).

In 2003, I read my first romance novel and immediately decided this was the genre for me. But there was a problem: the books I read all featured young heroines, interested in starting a family and having babies. So I started writing romantic suspense (with an occasional side trip into paranormal fantasy) about older women, with some age on' em, who are interested in men and sex and having a good relationship (which may or may not include a marriage).

I hope you enjoy reading about them as much as I enjoy writing about them.

Visit JL at www.jayellwilson.com

www.ingramcontent.com/pod-product-compliance
Lightning Source LLC
LaVergne TN
LVHW050629100826
845148LV00011B/1803

* 9 7 8 1 6 0 1 5 4 0 7 8 2 *